THE EARLY YEARS (1920–26)

The Man in the Shadows: The Complete Black Mask
Cases of Terry Mack *by Carroll John Daly*

Zigzags of Treachery: The Complete Black Mask Cases of the
Continental Op, Volume 1 *by Dashiell Hammett*

THE SHAW YEARS (1926–36)

Blood on the Curb *by Joseph T. Shaw*

Black Harvest: The Complete Black Mask Cases of Jules Tremaine *by Norvell W. Page*

Boomerang Dice: The Complete Black Mask Cases of Johnny Hi Gear *by Stewart Sterling*

The Case-Hardened Samaritan: The Complete Black Mask
Cases of Dal Prentice, Volume 1 *by Roger Torrey*

Dead Evidence: The Complete Black Mask Cases of Harrigan *by Ed Lybeck*

Laughing Death *by Raoul Whitfield*

Luck: The Complete Black Mask Cases of Oscar Sail *by Lester Dent*

Murder Maze: The Complete Black Mask Cases of Jerry
Tracy, Volume 2 *by Theodore A. Tinsley*

The Price of a Dime: The Complete Black Mask Cases of Ben Shaley *by Norbert Davis*

Somewhere in Mexico: The Complete Black Mask Cases
of Jerry Frost, Volume 1 *by Horace McCoy*

South Wind: The Complete Black Mask Cases of
Jerry Tracy, Volume 1 *by Theodore A. Tinsley*

That's Hollywood: The Complete Black Mask Cases of
Bill Lennox, Volume 1 *by W. T. Ballard*

White Talons: The Complete Black Mask Cases of Tex of
the Border Service *by Katherine Brocklebank*

THE LATER YEARS (1936–51)

Dead and Done For: The Complete Black Mask Cases of
Cellini Smith, Volume 1 *by Robert Reeves*

Dog Eat Dog: The Complete Black Mask Cases of Cellini Smith, Volume 2 *by Robert Reeves*

The Hound with the Golden Eye: The Complete Black Mask
Cases of Luther McGavock, Volume 2 *by Merle Constiner*

It Happened at the Lake *by Joseph T. Shaw*

Let the Dead Alone: The Complete Black Mask Cases of
Luther McGavock, Volume 1 *by Merle Constiner*

Murder Costs Money: The Complete Black Mask Cases
of Rex Sackler, Volume 1 *by D. L. Champion*

Murder on the Midway: The Complete Black Mask Cases of
the Human Encyclopedia, Volume 1 *by Frank Gruber*

Murder Pays 7 to 1: The Complete Black Mask Cases of
Rex Sackler, Volume 2 *by D. L. Champion*

ZIGZAGS OF TREACHERY

The Complete

Cases of the Continental Op

1923–24

DASHIELL HAMMETT

introduction by Bob Byrne

cover by Henry C. Murphy

BLACK MASK

2023

Table of Contents

Introduction

BLACK MASK. DASHIELL HAMMETT. Joseph 'Cap' Shaw. Those three names are inextricably linked together as the bedrock of the hardboiled school of mystery fiction. The October 1, 1923, issue of *Black Mask* included "Arson Plus," the first story featuring a nameless detective known as The Continental Op.

Earlier that May, Carroll John Daly's Three Gun Terry Mack had become the first hardboiled dick, and he was followed a month later by Race Williams. The immensely popular Williams was the prototypical gun-slinging Western cowboy who solved every problem with hot lead, but now wearing a suit and transplanted to the urban setting of city streets. Written in heavy-handed, over-the-top prose, Williams relied on guns and massive amounts of testosterone, leaving the city littered with corpses.

As Williams says in the first story, "You can't make a hamburger without grinding up a little meat." And he certainly didn't lose any sleep over it: "But my conscience is clear. I never bumped off a guy what didn't need it." Non-stop violence and a total lack of remorse sums up Race Williams. As does poor grammar.

An employee of The Continental Detective Agency (thus the name), Hammett's The Continental Op functioned as an actual detective who used a mix of brains, determination to complete the job at hand, old fashioned hard work, and a healthy dose of courage. His was a more viable blueprint for an enduring legacy. Hammett started out using the name Peter Collinson ("Peter Collins" was slang for a nobody), but quickly switched to his own name with the Op stories.

So, now we've got *Black Mask,* and Dashiell Hammett writing about The Continental Op. There's a misconception that Cap Shaw made Hammett, and that Shaw turned *Black Mask* into a hardboiled magazine (Shaw himself helped foster the latter misconception, though he also downplayed it as well).

But just as Daly came before Hammett—though the second became the greater—two men edited The Op and steered *Black Mask* into the hardboiled genre before Shaw took the helm. Shaw undeniably turned *Black Mask* into THE definitive hardboiled pulp, but Hammett wrote over half his Op stories before Shaw arrived. Shaw didn't create Hammett the writer—though he did resurrect Hammett the writer. More on that in the next volume.

Nine of the ten stories in this collection came under the oversight of George W. Sutton, who was a writer of automobile and motorboat articles for various publications. Sutton was three months into his editorship when he published "Arson Plus." At that time, *Black Mask* was a mix of Westerns, weird menace, ghost stories, and not-so-hardboiled detective stories. Hammett and Daly truly were the first to walk down those mean streets.

In March of 1924, the Sherlock Holmes story "The Adventure of the Creeping Man," and "Murder on the Links" (the second Hercule Poirot novel), were published. That was the state of the mystery story in England. "Arson Plus" had a rural feel to it, but it was no grotesque mystery, or a golf course murder committed with a paper knife. And it most certainly did not feature a brilliant, eccentric, unconventional private detective solving the case by finding bizarre clues.

This was a reasonably intelligent private eye using logic and shoe leather to figure out who used arson to kill a reclusive man. And this private eye did not blast his way through the story, leaving a trail of corpses, as Race Williams did. In fact, we don't even hear mention of the Op carrying a gun until the fifth story.

The plot in "Arson Plus" could easily have been from a Holmes or Poirot story:

> "But Holmes, Thornburgh's man, Coons, saw him in the window, engulfed in flames." My friend gave me an enigmatic smile. "Did he indeed, Watson?" Holmes could be positively infuriating at times.

But there's none of that here. The Op, aided by a smart but lazy policeman, doggedly works the trail, asking questions and looking for clues. It's not about the specific type of clay on someone's shoe, or the angle of a mirror after a bullet had shattered it—Hammett used his experience as a Pinkerton to write more realistic detective fiction. As Raymond Chandler wrote of Hammett: "He made some of it up; all writers do; but it had a basis in fact; it was made up out of real things."

Someone traveled by train?

> Tracing baggage is no trick at all, if you have the dates and check numbers to start with—as many a bird who is wearing somewhat similar numbers on his chest and back, because he overlooked that detail when making his getaway, can tell you....

A few stories later, the Op relates, "99 percent of detective work is a patient collecting of details—and your details must be got as nearly first-hand as possible, regardless of who else has worked the territory before you." These stories foreshadow the police procedural.

The Oxford English Dictionary describes "fiction" as "Literature in prose form. Describing imaginary events and people." The very first words in Raymond Chandler's *The Simple Art of Murder* are, "Fiction in any form has always intended to be realistic."

In a June 15, 1923, letter to the editor in *Black Mask*, Hammett says that he doubts "…it would be possible to build a character without putting into it at least something of someone the writer has known." Then he says that he had encountered the blackmailing plot (of "The Vicious Circle") as a detective. This was months before he created the Op and wrote "Arson Plus."

So, Hammett was using his real-world Pinkerton experiences for his stories, making them much more realistic than Carroll John Daly's stories. While he wasn't writing dry lessons on detection dressed up as fiction, he still went to great pains to defend the realism.

Hammett included a letter in the same October 15 issue that included "Slippery Fingers." He mentioned that the Berkeley chief of police had made an unrelated statement about fingerprints which essentially made Hammett's story unrealistic. He defended his story, saying that experts would agree it could and had been done, and that "successful experiments were made with it by the experts at the Leavenworth federal prison."

He wasn't done yet. The April 1924 *Black Mask* issue included an article from a Mr. Reeves, which stated three infallible "facts" about fingerprints and does not appear to have been supportive of Hammett's story. In the June 1925 issue, Hammett wrote a letter, almost one-third as long as the entire "Slippery Fingers" story, in response to Reeves' article. Hammett doesn't rant, but he's clearly rankled. He discusses each of the three facts in depth, and goes on to talk about scientific and circumstantial evidence. This is his second *Black Mask* response defending his use of fingerprints in the story.

Hammett didn't turn his Pinkerton cases into boring detective stories. Or, as Chandler wrote, "He made the detective story fun to write, not an exhausting concatenation of insignificant clues." (And his prose wasn't as snobbish as Chandler's would be, as evidenced by that quote.)

Realism (both professionally and philosophically) were the bedrock of Hammett's mystery fiction. And at least early on, he was going to great lengths to defend that realism.

"Crooked Souls" and "Slippery Fingers" (apparently two-word titles were all the rage) followed "Arson Plus" two weeks later, and Hammett's presence in *Black Mask* was firmly established.

Hammett also wrote a letter to the editor which went with "Crooked Souls." The story was about the kidnapping of a grown daughter, and that same month Hercule Poirot would solve the kidnapping of a young son. But that's the only thing in common between "The Adventure of Johnnie Waverly" and Hammett's story.

They are good examples of the contrast between the "country manor sensibilities" of Britain's Golden Age of Detection Fiction, and the urban street style of the newly developing American hardboiled school.

The bad guy gets the drop on the Op in the final scene of "It," and as the Op puts up his hands, he explains, "I didn't have a pistol with me, not being in the habit of carrying one except when I thought I was going to need it...."

You could easily find at least one quote in every single Race Williams story that is the polar opposite of this.

In the fifth story, "Bodies Piled Up," we finally see the Op carrying a gun. Two very bad guys are shooting it out in an Italian restaurant. The customers have all fled, and the Op has hidden behind a wall. "I had my gun out, but I was playing a waiting game... I kept away from the bullets that were flying around as best I could and waited."

Williams would never take cover and let the bad guys shoot it out. He seemed to exist to commit violence and mayhem.

Race Williams and the Op were contemporaries. There is no denying that *Black Mask* readers were titillated by the violence and fast-paced action of Daly's stories. It was said that Daly's name on the cover was good for a fifteen (I've also seen twenty) percent bump in sales for that issue. And it's the same type of two-fisted violence that would make Mickey Spillane the genre's best-selling author ever (with a healthy serving of sex added in). There's no denying it played a huge part in *Black Mask's* increasing popularity.

In one story, the Op says that if he were a movie actor or the like, he would have jumped out of a window, caught the neighboring roof, and made an acrobatic escape. But he didn't do any of that because dangling in space didn't appeal to him. He immediately follows with "Then I did another not-at-all heroic thing." Rather than stalking his dangerous captors (he is unarmed, himself) in a dark house, he turns on the lights,

lights a cigarette, and waits for them on the bed.

The hardboiled school was literally being birthed, and two very different babies were being born. In 1930, Daly was handily chosen as *Black Mask* readers' favorite author. Erle Stanley Gardner was second, with Hammett third. Daly's stories were more popular in the short run, but Hammett has long been considered the far better writer.

"Bodies Piled Up" has one of my favorite openings for a hardboiled PI story, and the gun play at the end was a step towards more action in Hammett's stories. The next story (the sixth), "The Tenth Clue," was as long as the previous two stories combined. Story eight, "Zigzags of Treachery," would be even longer, and Hammett was moving towards novella, and then novel-length storytelling.

Unlike his more famous counterpart, Sam Spade, the Op works hand-in-hand with the police in many of his cases. He might as well be a de facto member of the force in these first few stories. He is all but partnered up with Sacramento deputy McCump in the first story. He frequently works with San Francisco detective-sergeant O'Gar, with whom he had "hit it off excellently." In "The Tenth Clue," O'Gar asks someone a question that puzzles the Op, and the latter asks him to loosen up and fill him in. O'Gar obediently does so. There's none of the friction we often see in many private detective stories, as with Spade and Lieutenant Dundee.

Hammett did not recycle his short stories to turn them into novels, as Raymond Chandler would later do (to great success). But it seems pretty obvious that he revisited "Night Shots" (story seven) when he cranked out his third and final Sam Spade short story, "They Can Only Hang You Once."

In "Zigzags of Treachery," Hammett uses the Op to give the four rules of successful tailing. And we also see a more hardboiled Op. While undercover, he provokes his mark, who angrily pulls a gun on him. The Op is not passive this time:

> Firing from my pocket, I shot it out of his hand. "Now behave!" I ordered.

The Op then goes on to logically explain that while it looks impressive, it's not really such a big deal to make that shot, and why. As Hammett instructs the reader on both shadowing and shooting, the realism and his experience are always in play. He included a letter in the same issue as this story, talking more about shadowing and his experiences with it as a Pinkerton.

In these early stories, Hammett's belief in civic corruption, and the cynicism that would become hallmarks of his hardboiled stories, aren't nearly as present as they would be later. But there was an ongoing umbrella of realism over the Op from the very start.

We also see that the Op can be cold-blooded in "Zigzags of Treachery." He lightly explains it away, but it's a first look at this type of hard-bitten morality—something that Race Williams would have dismissed with a comment like "They make their own beds. I just tuck them in at night. Permanently!"

"One Hour" sees a return to the shorter story. San Francisco attorney Vance Richmond, the client in "Zigzags of Treachery," brings another case. The Op pulls a gun on a suspect but finds himself quite outnumbered in a fierce mêlée. Hammett puts us inside the Op's head as he desperately struggles to survive, using both his fists and his wits. And even a cuspidor! It's a tense action scene in a fast-paced story that entirely takes place in only one hour.

"One Hour" appeared in the April 1, 1924, issue, which was the first for new editor Philip Cody. But given the timing, it's reasonable to assume that it was written for and accepted by Sutton.

Cody took over from Sutton, and immediately changed the tone of *Black Mask*. It would more resemble the magazine of the Cap Shaw Era, with a leaner, harder style. Hammett's own writing had steered in that direction, and there was more of an edge to his work for Cody. We'll talk about Cody's impact on *Black Mask,* Hammett, and the hardboiled school, in the next volume. A mention here of Harry North, who was assistant editor to both Sutton and Cody, and stayed on with Shaw. He played an important role in the development of the hardboiled genre, and I'll try to talk a little more about him in the future.

Hammett is widely regarded as the greatest hardboiled writer of them all (yes, I know there's a Chandler camp—just go with me here). He didn't start out as the best, right from story one. While these early stories weren't always overly exciting, they were realistic.

Hammett, who had attended Munson's Business College (that always makes me think of Tim Robbins' 'Muncie College of Business Administration' in the terrific *The Hudsucker Proxy*), was learning the craft of writing fiction and incorporating his experience as a Pinkerton detective. It was that combination which shaped the newborn hardboiled school. *Black Mask* was full of melodramas, and Carroll John Daly had started writing his outlandishly violent detective stories. Hammett was grounding the genre while he learned more about plotting and characterization by rapidly pushing out stories.

And we see the growth—the low-key, laconic pace and lack of danger in "Arson Plus" is a mere memory by the action-oriented "Bodies Piled Up." And as we arrive at "The House in Turk Street," Hammett is about to master the intriguing hard-boiled PI story.

His style had been developing with nine Op stories in only seven months. And he had been gradually ratcheting up the gunplay and the violence under Sutton. From the very first story with Cody at the helm, you could drop the "gradually."

For me, it's in "The House in Turk Street" (which was adapted for the 2002 Samuel L. Jackson movie, *No Good Deed*) where we really see the classic Hammett for the first time. The characters, the pace, the tension, the plot elements: he was moving from learning to improving to the verge of mastering.

The young punk, Hook, presages *The Maltese Falcon's* Wilmer (though he's no gunsel); Elivra gives us a future glimpse of Brigid O'Shaughnessy; and the short, fat, British, Tai Choon Tau brings to mind Casper Gutman: albeit, a Chinese version. It's bonds instead of a bird, but there's even a Mexican standoff with a line similar to Joel Cairo's "But we certainly have you." It's a compact, exciting story that takes place in less than a day, in one house. I think it would make a good stage play.

Elvira is Hammett's first femme fatale. Edna ("Zigzags of Treachery") is a seasoned grifter, but she's just a supporting player. Elvira carves her presence as the kind of hard, seductive, wily female that leaves a trail of despair and disaster throughout the genre, playing on men's affections for her own gain.

Hammett did not start out submitting perfect stories. Three

of the first four begin with the kind of heavy-handed info dumps that are common to new—or not good—writers. Lots of exposition that buries the reader with all the relevant information to get the story going. The short story requires a deft hand to avoid this—check out Lawrence Block and Ed McBain to see two masters at it. And you have time to go in the kitchen and make a sandwich while the crook gives a long-winded, convoluted explanation of EVERYTHING near the end of "Zigzags of Treachery."

But Hammett was honing his craft, and these early stories were different from anything else being written. Daly was also doing the hardboiled private eye, but Hammett was doing it cleaner, leaner, and tighter. With realism and characterization; not simple shoot-'em-up action.

George Sutton preferred Hammett's realistic, well-written private eye stories to the ultra-violent, simplistic action yarns of Carroll John Daly. Philip Cody urged Hammett to pack in more action, and the stories would improve. But Cody would publish him less frequently; deny his request for a raise (even though Erle Stanley Gardner offered to take a pay cut to help fund Hammett): and would be the reason that Hammett quit *Black Mask*. Fortunately, Cap Shaw would coax Hammett back and build *Black Mask* around the author.

We've seen so many hardboiled PI stories and movies over the past hundred years: We need to remember that Hammett was a literary pioneer. Nobody had done with the mystery story what he was doing in each issue of *Black Mask*. Carroll John Daly was also covering new ground, but not nearly as well.

Hammett's first ten Continental Op stories don't constitute his greatest hits. But something special was happening, story by story. By the time he completed his first two stories for Phil Cody, Hammett had laid the groundwork for a genre that still influences the mystery field a century later.

—Bob Byrne

Arson Plus

This is a detective story you'll have a hard time solving before the end. Form your ideas of the outcome as you go along and then see how near you guessed it.

JIM TARR PICKED up the cigar I rolled across his desk, looked at the band, bit off an end, and reached for a match.

"Fifteen cents straight," he said. "You must want me to break a *couple* of laws for you this time."

I had been doing business with this fat sheriff of Sacramento County for four or five years—ever since I came to the Continental Detective Agency's San Francisco office—and I had never known him to miss an opening for a sour crack; but it didn't mean anything.

"Wrong both times," I told him. "I get two of them for a quarter; and I'm here to do you a favor instead of asking for one. The company that insured Thornburgh's house thinks somebody touched it off."

"That's right enough, according to the fire department. They tell me the lower part of the house was soaked with gasoline, but God knows how they could tell—there wasn't a stick left standing. I've got McClump working on it, but he hasn't found anything to get excited about yet."

"What's the layout? All I know is that there was a fire."

Tarr leaned back in his chair, turned his red face to the ceiling, and bellowed:

"Hey, Mac!"

The pearl push-buttons on his desk are ornaments as far as he is concerned. Deputy sheriffs McHale, McClump and Macklin came to the door together—MacNab apparently wasn't within hearing.

"What's the idea?" the sheriff demanded of McClump. "Are you carrying a bodyguard around with you?"

The two other deputies, thus informed as to who "Mac" referred to this time, went back to their cribbage game.

"We got a city slicker here to catch our firebug for us," Tarr told his deputy. "But we got to tell him what it's all about first."

McClump and I had worked together on an express robbery, several months before. He's a rangy, towheaded youngster of twenty-five or six, with all the nerve in the world—and most of the laziness.

"Ain't the Lord good to us?"

He had himself draped across a chair by now—always his first objective when he comes into a room.

"Well, here's how she stands: This fellow Thornburgh's house was a couple miles out of town, on the old county road—an old frame house. About midnight, night before last, Jeff Pringle—the nearest neighbor, a half-mile or so to the east—saw a glare in the sky from over that way, and phoned in the alarm; but by the time the fire wagons got there, there wasn't enough of the house left to bother about. Pringle was the first of the neighbors to get to the house, and the roof had already fell in then.

"Nobody saw anything suspicious—no strangers hanging around or nothing. Thornburgh's help just managed to save themselves, and that was all. They don't know much about what happened—too scared, I reckon. But they did see Thornburgh at his window just before the fire got him. A fellow here in town—name of Handerson—saw that part of it too. He was driving home from Wayton, and got to the house just before the roof caved in.

"The fire department people say they found signs of gasoline.

The Coonses, Thornburgh's help, say they didn't have no gas on the place. So there you are."

"Thornburgh have any relatives?"

"Yeah. A niece in San Francisco—a Mrs. Evelyn Trowbridge. She was up yesterday, but there wasn't nothing she could do, and she couldn't tell us nothing much, so she went back home."

"Where are the servants now?"

"Here in town. Staying at a hotel on I Street. I told 'em to stick around for a few days."

"Thornburgh own the house?"

"Uh-huh. Bought it from Newning & Weed a couple months ago."

"You got anything to do this morning?"

"Nothing but this."

"Good! Let's get out and dig around."

We found the Coonses in their room at the hotel on I Street. Mr. Coons was a small-boned, plump man with the smooth, meaningless face, and the suavity of the typical male house-servant.

His wife was a tall, stringy woman, perhaps five years older than her husband—say, forty—with a mouth and chin that seemed shaped for gossiping. But he did all the talking, while she nodded her agreement to every second or third word.

"We went to work for Mr. Thornburgh on the fifteenth of June, I think," he said, in reply to my first question. "We came to Sacramento, around the first of the month, and put in applications at the Allis Employment Bureau. A couple of weeks later they sent us out to see Mr. Thornburgh, and he took us on."

"Where were you before you came here?"

"In Seattle, sir, with a Mrs. Comerford; but the climate there didn't agree with my wife—she has bronchial trouble—so we decided to come to California. We most likely would have stayed in Seattle, though, if Mrs. Comerford hadn't given up her house."

"What do you know about Thornburgh?"

"Very little, sir. He wasn't a talkative gentleman. He hadn't any business that I know of. I think he was a retired seafaring man. He never said he was, but he had that manner and look. He never went out or had anybody in to see him, except his niece once, and he didn't write or get any mail. He had a room next to his bedroom fixed up as a sort of workshop. He spent most of his time in there. I always thought he was working on some kind of invention, but he kept the door locked, and wouldn't let us go near it."

"Haven't you any idea at all what it was?"

"No, sir. We never heard any hammering or noises from it, and never smelt anything either. And none of his clothes were ever the least bit soiled, even when they were ready to go out to the laundry. They would have been if he had been working on anything like machinery."

"Was he an old man?"

"He couldn't have been over fifty, sir. He was very erect, and his hair and beard were thick, with no grey hairs."

"Ever have any trouble with him?"

"Oh, no, sir! He was, if I may say it, a very peculiar gentleman in a way; and he didn't care about anything except having his meals fixed right, having his clothes taken care of—he was very particular about them—and not being disturbed. Except early in the morning and at night, we'd hardly see him all day."

"Now about the fire. Tell us the whole thing—everything you remember."

"Well, sir, I and my wife had gone to bed about ten o'clock, our regular time, and had gone to sleep. Our room was on the second floor, in the rear. Some time later—I never did exactly know what time it was—I woke up, coughing. The room was all full of smoke, and my wife was sort of strangling. I jumped up, and dragged her down the back stairs and out the back door, not thinking of anything but getting her out of there.

"When I had her safe in the yard, I thought of Mr. Thornburgh, and tried to get back in the house; but the whole first floor was just flames. I ran around front then, to see if he had got out, but didn't see anything of him. The whole yard was as light as day by then. Then I heard him scream—a horrible scream, sir—I can hear it yet! And I looked up at his window— that was the front second-story room—and saw him there, trying to get out the window. But all the woodwork was burning, and he screamed again and fell back, and right after that the roof over his room fell in.

"There wasn't a ladder or anything that I could have put up to the window for him—there wasn't anything I could have done.

"In the meantime, a gentleman had left his automobile in the road, and come up to where I was standing; but there wasn't anything we could do—the house was burning everywhere and falling in here and there. So we went back to where I had left my wife, and carried her farther away from the fire, and brought her to—she had fainted. And that's all I know about it, sir."

"Hear any noises earlier that night? Or see anybody hanging around?"

"No, sir."

"Have any gasoline around the place?"

"No, sir. Mr. Thornburgh didn't have a car."

"No gasoline for cleaning?"

"No, sir, none at all, unless Mr. Thornburgh had it in his workshop. When his clothes needed cleaning, I took them to town, and all his laundry was taken by the grocer's man, when he brought our provisions."

"Don't know anything that might have some bearing on the fire?"

"No, sir. I was surprised when I heard that somebody had set the house afire. I could hardly believe it. I don't know why anybody should want to do that."

"What do you think of them?" I asked McClump, as we left the hotel.

"They might pad the bills, or even go South with some of the silver, but they don't figure as killers in my mind."

That was my opinion, too; but they were the only persons known to have been there when the fire started except the man who had died. We went around to the Allis Employment Bureau and talked to the manager.

He told us that the Coonses had come into his office on June second, looking for work; and had given Mrs. Edward Comerford, 45 Woodmansee Terrace, Seattle, Washington, as reference. In reply to a letter—he always checked up the references of servants—Mrs. Comerford had written that the Coonses had been in her employ for a number of years, and had been "extremely satisfactory in every respect." On June thirteenth, Thornburgh had telephoned the bureau, asking that a man and his wife be sent out to keep house for him; and Allis had sent two couples that he had listed. Neither had been employed by Thornburgh, though Allis considered them more desirable than the Coonses, who were finally hired by Thornburgh.

All that would certainly seem to indicate that the Coonses hadn't deliberately maneuvered themselves into the place, unless they were the luckiest people in the world—and a detective can't afford to believe in luck or coincidence, unless he has unquestionable proof of it.

At the office of the real estate agents, through whom Thornburgh had bought the house—Newning & Weed—we were told that Thornburgh had come in on the eleventh of June, and had said that he had been told that the house was for sale, had looked it over, and wanted to know the price. The deal had been closed the next morning, and he had paid for the house with a check for $4,500 on the Seamen's Bank of San Francisco. The house was already furnished.

After luncheon, McClump and I called on Howard Handerson—the man who had seen the fire while driving home from Wayton. He had an office in the Empire Building, with his name and the title "Northern California Agent, Instant-Sheen Cleanser Company," on the door. He was a big, careless-looking man of forty-five or so, with the professionally jovial smile that belongs to the salesman.

He had been in Wayton on business the day of the fire, he said, and had stayed there until rather late, going to dinner and afterward playing pool with a grocer named Hammersmith—one of his customers. He had left Wayton in his machine, at about ten-thirty, and set out for Sacramento. At Tavender he had stopped at the garage for oil and gas and to have one of his tires blown up.

Just as he was about to leave the garage, the garage-man had called his attention to a red glare in the sky, and had told him that it was probably from a fire somewhere along the old county road that paralleled the State road into Sacramento; so Handerson had taken the county road, and had arrived at the burning house just in time to see Thornburgh try to fight his way through the flames that enveloped him.

It was too late to make any attempt to put out the fire, and the man upstairs was beyond saving by then—undoubtedly dead even before the roof collapsed; so Handerson had helped Coons revive his wife, and stayed there watching the fire until it had burned itself out. He had seen no one on that county road while driving to the fire.

"What do you know about Handerson?" I asked McClump, when we were on the street.

"Came here, from somewhere in the East, I think, early in the summer to open that Cleanser agency. Lives at the Garden Hotel. Where do we go next?"

"We get a machine, and take a look at what's left of the Thornburgh house."

AN ENTERPRISING INCENDIARY couldn't have found a lovelier spot in which to turn himself loose, if he looked the whole county over. Tree-topped hills hid it from the rest of the world, on three sides; while away from the fourth, an uninhabited plain rolled down to the river. The county road that passed the front gate was shunned by automobiles, so McClump said, in favor of the State Highway to the north.

Where the house had been, was now a mound of blackened ruins. We poked around in the ashes for a few minutes—not that we expected to find anything, but because it's the nature of man to poke around in ruins.

A garage in the rear, whose interior gave no evidence of recent occupation, had a badly scorched roof and front, but was otherwise undamaged. A shed behind it, sheltering an ax, a shovel, and various odds and ends of gardening tools, had escaped the fire altogether. The lawn in front of the house, and the garden behind the shed—about an acre in all—had been pretty thoroughly cut and trampled by wagon wheels, and the feet of the firemen and the spectators.

Having ruined our shoe-shines, McClump and I got back in our machine and swung off in a circle around the place, calling at all the houses within a mile radius, and getting little besides jolts for our trouble.

The nearest house was that of Pringle, the man who had turned in the alarm; but he not only knew nothing about the dead man, but said he had never seen him. In fact, only one of the neighbors had ever seen him: a Mrs. Jabine, who lived about a mile to the south.

She had taken care of the key to the house while it was vacant; and a day or two before he bought it, Thornburgh had come to her house, inquiring about the vacant one. She had gone over there with him and showed him through it, and he had told her that he intended buying it, if the price, of which neither of them knew anything, wasn't too high.

He had been alone, except for the chauffeur of the hired car in which he had come from Sacramento, and, save that he had no family, he had told her nothing about himself.

Hearing that he had moved in, she went over to call on him several days later—"just a neighborly visit"—but had been told by

Mrs. Coons that he was not at home. Most of the neighbors had talked to the Coonses, and had got the impression that Thornburgh did not care for visitors, so they had let him alone. The Coonses were described as "pleasant enough to talk to when you meet them," but reflecting their employer's desire not to make friends.

McClump summarized what the afternoon had taught us as we pointed our machine toward Tavender: "Any of these folks could have touched off the place, but we got nothing to show that any of 'em even knew Thornburgh, let alone had a bone to pick with him."

Tavender turned out to be a crossroads settlement of a general store and post office, a garage, a church, and six dwellings, about two miles from Thornburgh's place. McClump knew the storekeeper and postmaster, a scrawny little man named Philo, who stuttered moistly.

"I n-n-never s-saw Th-thornburgh," he said, "and I n-n-never had any m-mail for him. C-coons"—it sounded like one of these things butterflies come out of—"used to c-come in once a week t-to order groceries—they d-didn't have a phone. He used to walk in, and I'd s-send the stuff over in my c-c-car. Th-then I'd s-see him once in a while, waiting f-for the stage to S-s-sacramento."

"Who drove the stuff out to Thornburgh's?"

"M-m-my b-boy. Want to t-talk to him?"

The boy was a juvenile edition of the old man, but without the stutter. He had never seen Thornburgh on any of his visits, but his business had taken him only as far as the kitchen. He hadn't noticed anything peculiar about the place.

"Who's the night man at the garage?" I asked him, after we had listened to the little he had to tell.

"Billy Luce. I think you can catch him there now. I saw him go in a few minutes ago."

We crossed the road and found Luce.

"Night before last—the night of the fire down the road—was there a man here talking to you when you first saw it?"

He turned his eyes upward in that vacant stare which people use to aid their memory.

"Yes, I remember now! He was going to town, and I told him that if he took the county road instead of the State Road he'd see the fire on his way in."

"What kind of looking man was he?"

"Middle-aged—a big man, but sort of slouchy. I think he had on a brown suit, baggy and wrinkled."

"Medium complexion?"

"Yes."

"Smile when he talked?"

"Yes, a pleasant sort of fellow."

"Curly brown hair?"

"Have a heart!" Luce laughed. "I didn't put him under a magnifying glass."

From Tavender, we drove over to Wayton. Luce's description had fit Handerson all right; but while we were at it, we thought we might as well check up to make sure that he had been coming from Wayton.

We spent exactly twenty-five minutes in Wayton; ten of them finding Hammersmith, the grocer with whom Handerson had said he dined and played pool; five minutes finding the proprietor of the pool-room; and ten verifying Handerson's story.

"What do you think of it now, Mac?" I asked, as we rolled back toward Sacramento.

Mac's too lazy to express an opinion, or even form one, unless he's driven to it; but that doesn't mean they aren't worth listening to, if you can get them.

"There ain't a hell of a lot to think," he said cheerfully. "Handerson is out of it, if he ever was in it. There's nothing to show that anybody but the Coonses and Thornburgh were there when the fire started—but there may have been a regiment there. Them Coonses ain't too honest looking, maybe, but they ain't killers, or I miss my guess. But the fact remains that they're the only bet we got so far. Maybe we ought to try to get a line on them."

"All right," I agreed. "I'll get a wire off to our Seattle office asking them to interview Mrs. Comerford, and see what she can tell about them as soon as we get back in town. Then I'm going to catch a train for San Francisco, and see Thornburgh's niece in the morning."

NEXT MORNING, AT the address McClump had given me—a rather elaborate apartment building on California Street—I had to wait three-quarters of an hour for Mrs. Evelyn Trowbridge to dress. If I had been younger, or a social caller, I suppose I'd have felt amply rewarded when she finally came in—a tall, slender woman of less than thirty; in some sort of clinging black affair; with a lot of black hair over a very white face, strikingly set off by a small red mouth and big hazel eyes that looked black until you got close to them.

But I was a busy, middle-aged detective, who was fuming over having his time wasted; and I was a lot more interested in finding the bird who struck the match than I was in feminine beauty. However, I smothered my grouch, apologized for disturbing her at such an early hour, and got down to business.

"I want you to tell me all you know about your uncle—his family, friends, enemies, business connections, everything."

I had scribbled on the back of the card I had sent into her what my business was.

"He hadn't any family," she said; "unless I might be it. He was my mother's brother, and I am the only one of that family now living."

"Where was he born?"

"Here in San Francisco. I don't know the date, but he was about fifty years old, I think—three years older than my mother."

"What was his business?"

"He went to sea when he was a boy, and, so far as I know, always followed it until a few months ago."

"Captain?"

"I don't know. Sometimes I wouldn't see or hear from him for several years, and he never talked about what he was doing; though he would mention some of the places he had visited—Rio de Janeiro, Madagascar, Tobago, Christiania. Then, about three months ago—some time in May—he came here and told me that he was through with wandering; that he was going to take a house in some quiet place where he could work undisturbed on an invention in which he was interested.

"He lived at the Francisco Hotel while he was in San Francisco. After a couple of weeks, he suddenly disappeared. And then, about a month ago, I received a telegram from him, asking me to come to see him at his house near Sacramento. I went up the very next day, and I thought that he was acting very queerly—he seemed very excited over something. He gave me a will that he had just drawn up and some life insurance policies in which I was beneficiary.

"Immediately after that he insisted that I return home, and hinted rather plainly that he did not wish me to either visit him again or write until I heard from him. I thought all that rather peculiar, as he had always seemed fond of me. I never saw him again."

"What was this invention he was working on?"

"I really don't know. I asked him once, but he became so excited—even suspicious—that I changed the subject, and never mentioned it again."

"Are you sure that he really did follow the sea all those years?"

"No, I am not. I just took it for granted; but he may have been doing something altogether different."

"Was he ever married?"

"Not that I know of."

"Know any of his friends or enemies?"

"No, none."

"Remember anybody's name that he ever mentioned?"

"No."

"I don't want you to think this next question insulting, though I admit it is. But it has to be asked. Where were you the night of the fire?"

"At home; I had some friends here to dinner, and they stayed until about midnight. Mr. and Mrs. Walker Kellogg, Mrs. John Dupree, and a Mr. Killmer, who is a lawyer. I can give you their addresses, or you can get them from the phone book, if you want to question them."

From Mrs. Trowbridge's apartment I went to the Francisco Hotel. Thornburgh had been registered there from May tenth to June thirteenth, and hadn't attracted much attention. He had been a tall, broad-shouldered, erect man of about fifty, with rather long brown hair brushed straight back; a short, pointed brown beard, and healthy, ruddy complexion—grave, quiet, punctilious in dress and manner; his hours had been regular and he had had no visitors that any of the hotel employees remembered.

At the Seamen's Bank—upon which Thornburgh's check, in payment of the house, had been drawn—I was told that he had opened an account there on May fifteenth, having been introduced by W.W. Jeffers & Sons, local stock brokers. A balance of a little more than four hundred dollars remained to his credit. The canceled checks on hand were all to the order of various life insurance companies; and for amounts that, if they represented premiums, testified to rather large policies. I jotted down the names of the life insurance companies, and then went to the offices of W.W. Jeffers & Sons.

Thornburgh had come in, I was told, on the tenth of May with $4,000 worth of Liberty bonds that he wanted sold. During one of his conversations with Jeffers, he had asked the broker to recommend a bank, and Jeffers had given him a letter of introduction to the Seamen's Bank.

That was all Jeffers knew about him. He gave me the numbers of the bonds, but tracing Liberty bonds isn't the easiest thing in the world.

The reply to my Seattle telegram was waiting for me at the Agency when I arrived.

MRS. EDWARD COMERFORD RENTED APARTMENT
AT ADDRESS YOU GIVE ON MAY TWENTY-FIVE GAVE

IT UP JUNE SIX TRUNKS TO SAN FRANCISCO SAME
DAY CHECK NUMBERS GN FOUR FIVE TWO FIVE
EIGHT SEVEN AND EIGHT AND NINE

Tracing baggage is no trick at all, if you have the dates and check numbers to start with—as many a bird who is wearing somewhat similar numbers on his chest and back, because he overlooked that detail when making his getaway, can tell you—and twenty-five minutes in a baggage-room at the Ferry and half an hour in the office of a transfer company gave me my answer.

The trunks had been delivered to Mrs. Evelyn Trowbridge's apartment!

I got Jim Tarr on the phone and told him about it.

"Good shooting!" he said, forgetting for once to indulge his wit. "We'll grab the Coonses here and Mrs. Trowbridge there, and that's the end of another mystery."

"Wait a minute!" I cautioned him. "It's not all straightened out yet! There's still a few kinks in the plot."

"It's straight enough for me. I'm satisfied."

"You're the boss, but I think you're being a little hasty. I'm going up and talk with the niece again. Give me a little time before you phone the police here to make the pinch. I'll hold her until they get there."

Evelyn Trowbridge let me in this time, instead of the maid who had opened the door for me in the morning, and she led me to the same room in which we had had our first talk. I let her pick out a seat, and then I selected one that was closer to either door than hers was.

On the way up I had planned a lot of innocent-sounding

questions that would get her all snarled up; but after taking a good look at this woman sitting in front of me, leaning comfortably back in her chair, coolly waiting for me to speak my piece, I discarded the trick stuff and came out cold-turkey.

"Ever use the name Mrs. Edward Comerford?"

"Oh, yes." As casual as a nod on the street.

"When?"

"Often. You see, I happen to have been married not so long ago to Mr. Edward Comerford. So it's not really strange that I should have used the name."

"Use it in Seattle recently?"

"I would suggest," she said sweetly, "that if you are leading up to the references I gave Coons and his wife, you might save time by coming right to it?"

"That's fair enough," I said. "Let's do that."

There wasn't a half-tone, a shading, in voice, manner, or expression to indicate that she was talking about anything half so serious or important to her as a possibility of being charged with murder. She might have been talking about the weather, or a book that hadn't interested her particularly.

"During the time that Mr. Comerford and I were married, we lived in Seattle, where he still lives. After the divorce, I left Seattle and resumed my maiden name. And the Coonses were in our employ, as you might learn if you care to look it up. You'll find my husband—or former husband—at the Chelsea apartments, I think.

"Last summer, or late spring, I decided to return to Seattle. The truth of it is—I suppose all my personal affairs will be aired anyhow—that I thought perhaps Edward and I might patch up our differences; so I went back and took an apartment on Woodmansee Terrace. As I was known in Seattle as Mrs. Edward Comerford, and as I thought my using his name might influence him a little, perhaps, I used it while I was there.

"Also I telephoned the Coonses to make tentative arrangements in case Edward and I should open our house again; but Coons told me that they were going to California, and so I gladly gave them an excellent recommendation when, some days later, I received a letter of inquiry from an employment bureau in Sacramento. After I had been in Seattle for about two weeks, I changed my mind about the reconciliation— Edward's interest, I learned, was all centered elsewhere; so I returned to San Francisco."

"Very nice! But—"

"If you will permit me to finish," she interrupted. "When I went to see my uncle in response to his telegram, I was surprised to find the Coonses in his house. Knowing my uncle's peculiarities, and finding them now increased, and remembering his extreme secretiveness about his mysterious invention, I cautioned the Coonses not to tell him that they had been in my employ.

"He certainly would have discharged them, and just as certainly would have quarreled with me—he would have thought that I was having him spied upon. Then, when Coons telephoned me after the fire, I knew that to admit that the Coonses had been formerly in my employ, would, in view of the fact that I was my uncle's heir, cast suspicion on all three of us. So we foolishly agreed to say nothing about it and carry on the deception."

That didn't sound all wrong, but it didn't sound all right. I wished Tarr had taken it easier and let us get a better line on these people, before having them thrown in the coop.

"The coincidence of the Coonses stumbling into my uncle's house is, I fancy, too much for your detecting instincts," she went on, as I didn't say anything. "Am I to consider myself under arrest?"

I'm beginning to like this girl; she's a nice, cool piece of work.

"Not yet," I told her. "But I'm afraid it's going to happen pretty soon."

She smiled a little mocking smile at that, and another when the doorbell rang.

It was O'Hara from police headquarters. We turned the apartment upside down and inside out, but didn't find anything of importance except the will she had told me about, dated July eighth, and her uncle's life insurance policies. They were all dated between May fifteenth and June tenth, and added up to a little more than $200,000.

I spent an hour grilling the maid after O'Hara had taken Evelyn Trowbridge away, but she didn't know any more than I did. However, between her, the janitor, the manager of the apartments, and the names Mrs. Trowbridge had given me, I learned that she had really been entertaining friends on the night of the fire—until after eleven o'clock, anyway—and that was late enough.

Half an hour later I was riding the Short Line back to Sacramento. I was getting to be one of the line's best customers, and my anatomy was on bouncing terms with every bump in the road; and the bumps, as "Rubberhead" Davis used to say about the flies and mosquitoes in Alberta in summer, "is freely plentiful."

Between bumps I tried to fit the pieces of this Thornburgh

puzzle together. The niece and the Coonses fit in somewhere, but not just where we had them. We had been working on the job sort of lop-sided, but it was the best we could do with it. In the beginning we had turned to the Coonses and Evelyn Trowbridge because there was no other direction to go; and now we had something on them—but a good lawyer could make hash of our case against them.

The Coonses were in the county jail when I got to Sacramento. After some questioning they had admitted their connection with the niece, and had come through with stories that matched hers in every detail.

Tarr, McClump, and I sat around the sheriff's desk and argued.

"Those yarns are pipe-dreams," the sheriff said. "We got all three of 'em cold, and there's nothing else to it. They're as good as convicted of murder!"

McClump grinned derisively at his superior, and then turned to me.

"Go on! You tell him about the holes in his little case. He ain't your boss, and can't take it out on you later for being smarter than he is!"

Tarr glared from one of us to the other.

"Spill it, you wise guys!" he ordered.

"Our dope is," I told him, figuring that McClump's view of it was the same as mine, "that there's nothing to show that even Thornburgh knew he was going to buy that house before the tenth of June, and that the Coonses were in town looking for work on the second. And besides, it was only by luck that they got the jobs. The employment office sent two couples out there ahead of them."

"We'll take a chance on letting the jury figure that out."

"Yes? You'll also take a chance on them figuring out that Thornburgh, who seems to have been a nut all right, might have touched off the place himself! We've got something on these people, Jim, but not enough to go into court with them! How are you going to prove that when the Coonses were planted in Thornburgh's house—if you can even prove they were—they and the Trowbridge woman knew he was going to load up with insurance policies?"

The sheriff spat disgustedly.

"You guys are the limit! You run around in circles, digging up the dope on these people until you get enough to hang 'em, and then you run around hunting for outs! What the hell's the matter with you now?"

I answered him from half-way to the door—the pieces were beginning to fit together under my skull.

"Going to run some more circles! Come on, Mac!"

McClump and I held a conference on the fly, and then I got a machine from the nearest garage and headed for Tavender. We made time going out, and got there before the general store had closed for the night. The stuttering Philo separated himself from the two men with whom he had been talking Hiram Johnson, and followed me to the rear of the store.

"Do you keep an itemized list of the laundry you handle?"

"N-n-no; just the amounts."

"Let's look at Thornburgh's."

He produced a begrimed and rumpled account book and we picked out the weekly items I wanted: $2.60, $3.10, $2.25, and so on.

"Got the last batch of laundry here?"

"Y-yes," he said. "It j-just c-c-came out from the city t-today."

I tore open the bundle—some sheets, pillow-cases, table-cloths, towels, napkins; some feminine clothing; some shirts, collars, underwear, sox that were unmistakably Coons's. I thanked Philo while running back to my machine.

Back in Sacramento again, McClump was waiting for me at the garage where I had hired the car.

"Registered at the hotel on June fifteenth, rented the office on the sixteenth. I think he's in the hotel now," he greeted me.

We hurried around the block to the Garden Hotel.

"Mr. Handerson went out a minute or two ago," the night clerk told us. "He seemed to be in a hurry."

"Know where he keeps his car?"

"In the hotel garage around the corner."

We were within two pavements of the garage, when Handerson's automobile shot out and turned up the street.

"Oh, Mr. Handerson!" I cried, trying to keep my voice level and smooth.

He stepped on the gas and streaked away from us.

"Want him?" McClump asked; and, at my nod, stopped a passing roadster by the simple expedient of stepping in front of it.

We climbed aboard, McClump flashed his star at the bewildered driver, and pointed out Handerson's dwindling tail-light. After he had persuaded himself that he wasn't being boarded by a couple of bandits, the commandeered driver did his best, and we picked up Handerson's tail-light after two or three turnings, and closed in on him—though his machine was going at a good clip.

By the time we reached the outskirts of the city, we had

crawled up to within safe shooting distance, and I sent a bullet over the fleeing man's head. Thus encouraged, he managed to get a little more speed out of his car; but we were definitely overhauling him now.

Just at the wrong minute Handerson decided to look over his shoulder at us—an unevenness in the road twisted his wheels—his machine swayed—skidded—went over on its side. Almost immediately, from the heart of the tangle, came a flash and a bullet moaned past my ear. Another. And then, while I was still hunting for something to shoot at in the pile of junk we were drawing down upon, McClump's ancient and battered revolver roared in my other ear.

Handerson was dead when we got to him—McClump's bullet had taken him over one eye.

McClump spoke to me over the body.

"I ain't an inquisitive sort of fellow, but I hope you don't mind telling me why I shot this lad."

"Because he was Thornburgh."

He didn't say anything for about five minutes. Then: "I reckon that's right. How'd you guess it?"

We were sitting beside the wreckage now, waiting for the police that we had sent our commandeered chauffeur to phone for.

"He had to be," I said, "when you think it all over. Funny we didn't hit on it before! All that stuff we were told about Thornburgh had a fishy sound. Whiskers and an unknown profession, immaculate and working on a mysterious invention, very secretive and born in San Francisco—where the fire wiped out all the old records—just the sort of fake that could be cooked up easily.

"Then nobody but the Coonses, Evelyn Trowbridge and Handerson ever saw him except between the tenth of May and the middle of June, when he bought the house. The Coonses and the Trowbridge woman were tied up together in this affair somehow, we knew—so that left only Handerson to consider. You had told me he came to Sacramento sometime early this summer—and the dates you got tonight show that he didn't come until after Thornburgh had bought his house. All right! Now compare Handerson with the descriptions we got of Thornburgh.

"Both are about the same size and age, and with the same color hair. The differences are all things that can be manufac-tured—clothes, a little sunburn, and a month's growth of beard, along with a little acting, would do the trick. Tonight I went out to Tavender and took a look at the last batch of laundry, and there wasn't any that didn't fit the Coonses—and none of the bills all the way back were large enough for Thornburgh to have been as careful about his clothes as we were told he was."

"It must be great to be a detective!" McClump grinned as the police ambulance came up and began disgorging policemen. "I reckon somebody must have tipped Handerson off that I was asking about him this evening." And then, regretfully: "So we ain't going to hang them folks for murder after all."

"No, but we oughtn't have any trouble convicting them of arson plus conspiracy to defraud, and anything else that the Prosecuting Attorney can think up."

Crooked Souls

We've all seen the modern girl. She's a rare bird and here she is in all her glory—if that's what it is. A good detective yarn, this, with lots of action and some real people. Go to it.

HARVEY GATEWOOD HAD issued orders that I was to be admitted as soon as I arrived, so it only took me a little less than fifteen minutes to thread my way past the door-keepers, office boys, and secretaries who filled up most of the space between the Gatewood Lumber Corporation's front door and the president's private office. His office was large, all mahogany and bronze and green plush, with a mahogany desk as big as a bed in the center of the floor.

Gatewood, leaning across the desk, began to bark at me as soon as the obsequious clerk who had bowed me in bowed himself out.

"My daughter was kidnapped last night! I want the… that did it if it takes every cent I got!"

"Tell me about it," I suggested, drawing up the chair that he hadn't thought to offer me.

But he wanted results, it seemed, and not questions, and so I wasted nearly an hour getting information that he could have given me in fifteen minutes.

He's a big bruiser of a man, something over two hundred pounds of hard red flesh, and a czar from the top of his bullet head to the toes of his shoes that would have been at least number twelves if they hadn't been made to measure.

He had made his several millions by sandbagging everybody that stood in his way, and the rage that he's burning up with now doesn't make him any easier to deal with.

His wicked jaw is sticking out like a knob of granite and his eyes are filmed with blood—he's in a lovely frame of mind. For a while it looks as if the Continental Detective Agency is going to lose a client; because I've made up my mind that he's going to tell me all I want to know, or I'm going to chuck up the job. But finally I got the story out of him.

His daughter Audrey had left their house on Clay street at about seven o'clock the preceding evening, telling her maid that she was going for a walk. She had not returned that night—though Gatewood had not known that until after he had read the letter that came this morning.

The letter had been from someone who said that she had been kidnapped. It demanded fifty thousand dollars for her release; and instructed Gatewood to get the money ready in hundred dollar bills, so that there might be no delay when he is told in what manner it is to be paid over to his daughter's captors. As proof that the demand was not a hoax, a lock of the girl's hair, a ring she always wore, and a brief note from her, asking her father to comply with the demands, had been enclosed.

Gatewood had received the letter at his office, and had telephoned to his house immediately. He had been told that the girl's bed had not been slept in the previous night, and that none of the servants had seen her since she started out for her walk. He had then notified the police, turning the letter over to them; and, a few minutes later, he had decided to employ private detectives also.

"Now," he burst out, after I had wormed these things out of him, and he had told me that he knew nothing of his daughter's associates or habits, "go ahead and do something! I'm not paying you to sit around and talk about it!"

"What are you going to do?" I asked.

"Me? I'm going to put those… behind the bars if it takes every cent I've got in the world!"

"Sure! But first you can get that fifty thousand ready, so you can give it to them when they ask for it."

He clicked his jaw shut and thrust his face into mine.

"I've never been clubbed into doing anything in my life! And I'm too old to start now!" he said. "I'm going to call these people's bluff!"

"That's going to make it lovely for your daughter. But, aside from what it'll do to her, it's the wrong play. Fifty thousand isn't a whole lot to you, and paying it over will give us two chances that we haven't got now. One when the payment is made—a chance to either nab whoever comes for it or get a line on them. And the other when your daughter is returned. No matter how careful they are it's a cinch that she'll be able to tell us something that will help us grab them."

He shook his head angrily, and I was tired of arguing with him. So I left him, hoping that he'd see the wisdom of the course I had advised before too late.

At the Gatewood residence I found butlers, second men, chauffeurs, cooks, maids, upstairs girls, downstairs girls, and a raft of miscellaneous flunkies—he had enough servants to run a hotel.

What they told me amounted to this: The girl had not received a phone call, note by messenger, or telegram—the time-honored devices for luring a victim out to a murder or abduction—before she left the house. She had told her maid that she would be back within an hour or two; but the maid had not been alarmed when her mistress failed to return all that night.

Audrey was the only child, and since her mother's death she had come and gone to suit herself. She and her father didn't hit it off very well together—their natures were too much alike, I gathered—and he never knew where she was; and there was nothing unusual about her remaining away all night, as she seldom bothered to leave word when she was going to stay overnight with friends.

She was nineteen years old, but looked several years older; about five feet five inches tall, and slender. She had blue eyes, brown hair,—very thick and long,—was pale and very nervous. Her photographs, of which I took a handful, showed that her eyes were large, her nose small and regular, and her chin obstinately pointed.

She was not beautiful, but in the one photograph where a smile had wiped off the sullenness of her mouth, she was at least pretty.

When she left the house she had worn a light tweed skirt and jacket with a London tailor's labels in them, a buff silk shirtwaist with stripes a shade darker, brown wool stockings, low-heeled brown oxfords, and an untrimmed grey felt hat.

I went up to her rooms—she had three on the third floor—and looked through all her stuff. I found nearly a bushel of photographs of men, boys, and girls; and a great stack of letters of varying degrees of intimacy, signed with a wide assortment of names and nicknames. I made notes of all the addresses I found.

Nothing there seemed to have any bearing on her abduction, but there was a chance that one of the names and addresses might be of someone who had served as a decoy. Also, some of her friends might be able to tell us something of value.

I dropped in at the Agency and distributed the names and

addresses among the three operatives who were idle, sending them out to see what they could dig up.

Then I reached the police detectives who were working on the case—O'Gar and Thode—by telephone, and went down to the Hall of Justice to meet them. Lusk, a post office inspector, was also there. We turned the job around and around, looking at it from every angle, but not getting very far. We were all agreed, however, that we couldn't take a chance on any publicity, or work in the open, until the girl was safe.

They had had a worse time with Gatewood than I—he had wanted to put the whole thing in the newspapers, with the offer of a reward, photographs and all. Of course, Gatewood was right in claiming that this was the most effective way of catching the kidnappers—but it would have been tough on his daughter if her captors happened to be persons of sufficiently hardened character. And kidnappers as a rule aren't lambs.

I looked at the letter they had sent. It was printed with pencil on ruled paper of the kind that is sold in pads by every stationery dealer in the world. The envelope was just as common, also addressed in pencil, and post-marked "San Francisco, September 20, 9 P.M." That was the night she had been seized.

The letter reads:

SIR:

WE HAVE YOUR CHARMING DAUGHTER AND PLACE A VALUE OF $50,000 UPON HER. YOU WILL GET THE MONEY READY IN $100 BILLS AT ONCE SO THERE WILL BE NO DELAY WHEN WE TELL YOU HOW IT IS TO BE PAID OVER TO US.

WE BEG TO ASSURE YOU THAT THINGS WILL GO BADLY

WITH YOUR DAUGHTER SHOULD YOU NOT DO AS YOU
ARE TOLD, OR SHOULD YOU BRING THE POLICE INTO
THIS MATTER, OR SHOULD YOU DO ANYTHING FOOLISH.
$50,000 IS ONLY A SMALL FRACTION OF WHAT YOU
STOLE WHILE WE WERE LIVING IN MUD AND BLOOD IN
FRANCE FOR YOU, AND WE MEAN TO GET THAT MUCH
OR…!

THREE.

A peculiar note in several ways. They are usually written with a great pretense of partial illiterateness. Almost always there's an attempt to lead suspicion astray. Perhaps the ex-service stuff was there for that purpose… or perhaps not.

Then there was a postscript:

WE KNOW A CHINAMAN WHO WILL BUY HER EVEN
AFTER WE ARE THROUGH WITH HER—IN CASE YOU
WON'T LISTEN TO REASON.

The letter from the girl was written jerkily on the same kind of paper, apparently with the same pencil.

Daddy—
  Please do as they ask! I am so afraid—

Audrey

A door at the other end of the room opened, and a head came through.

"O'Gar! Thode! Gatewood just called up. Get up to his office right away!"

The four of us tumbled out of the Hall of Justice and into a machine.

Gatewood was pacing his office like a maniac when we pushed aside enough hirelings to get to him. His face was hot with blood and his eyes had an insane glare in them.

"She just phoned me!" he cried thickly, when he saw us.

It took a minute or two to get him calm enough to tell us about it.

"She called me on the phone. Said, 'Oh, daddy! Do something! I can't stand this—they're killing me!' I asked her if she knew where she was, and she said, 'No, but I can see Twin Peaks from here. There's three men and a woman, and—' And then I heard a man curse, and a sound as if he had struck her, and the phone went dead. I tried to get central to give me the number, but she couldn't! It's a damned outrage the way the telephone system is run. We pay enough for service, God knows, and we…."

O'Gar scratched his head and turned away from Gatewood.

"In sight of Twin Peaks! There are hundreds of houses that are!"

Gatewood meanwhile had finished denouncing the telephone company and was pounding on his desk with a paperweight to attract our attention.

"Have you people done anything at all?" he demanded.

I answered him with another question: "Have you got the money ready?"

"No," he said, "I won't be held up by anybody!"

But he said it mechanically, without his usual conviction—the talk with his daughter had shaken him out of some of his stubbornness. He was thinking of her safety a little now instead of altogether of his own fighting spirit.

We went at him hammer and tongs for a few minutes, and after a while he sent a clerk out for the money.

We split up the field then. Thode was to take some men from headquarters and see what he could find in the Twin Peaks end of town; but we weren't very optimistic over the prospects there—the territory was too large.

Lusk and O'Gar were to carefully mark the bills that the clerk brought from the bank, and then stick as close to Gatewood as they could without attracting attention. I was to go out to Gatewood's house and stay there.

The abductors had plainly instructed Gatewood to get the money ready immediately so that they could arrange to get it on short notice—not giving him time to communicate with anyone or make any plans.

Gatewood was to get hold of the newspapers, give them the whole story, with the $10,000 reward he was offering for the abductors' capture, to be published as soon as the girl was safe—so that we would get the help of publicity at the earliest moment possible without jeopardizing the girl.

The police in all the neighboring towns had already been notified—that had been done before the girl's phone message had assured us that she was held in San Francisco.

Nothing happened at the Gatewood residence all that evening. Harvey Gatewood came home early; and after dinner he paced his library floor and drank whiskey until bedtime, demanding every few minutes that we, the detectives in the case, do something besides sit around like a lot of damned mummies. O'Gar, Lusk and Thode were out in the street, keeping an eye on the house and neighborhood.

At midnight Harvey Gatewood went to bed. I declined a bed

in favor of the library couch, which I dragged over beside the telephone, an extension of which was in Gatewood's bedroom.

At two-thirty the bell rang. I listened in while Gatewood talked from his bed.

A man's voice, crisp and curt: "Gatewood?"

"Yes."

"Got the dough?"

"Yes."

Gatewood's voice was thick and blurred—I could imagine the boiling that was going on inside him.

"Good!" came the brisk voice. "Put a piece of paper around it, and leave the house with it, right away! Walk down Clay street, keeping on the same side as your house. Don't walk too fast and keep walking. If everything's all right, and there's no elbows tagging along, somebody'll come up to you between your house and the water-front. They'll have a handkerchief up to their face for a second, and then they'll let it fall to the ground.

"When you see that, you'll lay the money on the pavement, turn around and walk back to your house. If the money isn't marked, and you don't try any fancy tricks, you'll get your daughter back in an hour or two. If you try to pull anything—remember what we wrote you about the Chink! Got it straight?"

Gatewood sputtered something that was meant for an affirmative, and the telephone clicked silent.

I didn't waste any of my precious time tracing the call—it would be from a public telephone, I knew—but yelled up the stairs to Gatewood:

"You do as you were told, and don't try any foolishness!"

Then I ran out into the early morning air to find the police detectives and the post office inspector.

They had been joined by two plainclothes men, and had two automobiles waiting. I told them what the situation was, and we laid hurried plans.

O'Gar was to drive in one of the machines down Sacramento street, and Thode, in the other, down Washington street. These streets parallel Clay, one on each side. They were to drive slowly, keeping pace with Gatewood, and stopping at each cross street to see that he passed.

When he failed to cross within a reasonable time they were to turn up to Clay street—and their actions from then on would have to be guided by chance and their own wits.

Lusk was to wander along a block or two ahead of Gatewood, on the opposite side of the street, pretending to be mildly intoxicated, and keeping his eyes and ears open.

I was to shadow Gatewood down the street, with one of the plainclothes men behind me. The other plainclothes man was to turn in a call at headquarters for every available man to be sent to Clay street. They would arrive too late, of course, and as likely as not it would take them some time to find us; but we had no way of knowing what was going to turn up before the night was over.

Our plan was sketchy enough, but it was the best we could do—we were afraid to grab whoever got the money from Gatewood. The girl's talk with her father that afternoon had sounded too much as if her captors were desperate for us to take any chances on going after them rough-shod until she was out of their hands.

We had hardly finished our plans when Gatewood, wearing

a heavy overcoat, left his house and turned down the street.

Farther down, Lusk, weaving along, talking to himself, was almost invisible in the shadows. There was no one else in sight. That meant that I had to give Gatewood at least two blocks' lead, so that the man who came for the money wouldn't tumble to me. One of the plainclothes men was half a block behind me, on the other side of the street.

Two blocks down we walked, and then a little chunky man in a derby hat came into sight. He passed Gatewood, passed me, went on.

Three blocks more.

A touring-car, large, black, powerfully engined, and with lowered curtains, came from the rear, passed us, went on. Possibly a scout! I scrawled its license number down on my pad without taking my hand out of my overcoat pocket.

Another three blocks.

A policeman passed, strolling along in ignorance of the game being played under his nose; and then a taxicab with a single male passenger. I wrote down its license number.

Four blocks with no one in sight ahead of me but Gatewood—I couldn't see Lusk any more.

Just ahead of Gatewood a man stepped out of a black doorway—turned around—called up to a window for someone to come down and open the door for him.

We went on.

Coming from nowhere, a woman stood on the sidewalk fifty feet ahead of Gatewood, a handkerchief to her face. It fluttered to the pavement.

Gatewood stopped, standing stiff-legged. I could see his right hand come up, lifting the side of the overcoat in which it was pocketed—and I knew the hand was gripped around a pistol.

For perhaps half a minute he stood like a statue. Then his left hand came out of his pocket, and the bundle of money fell to the sidewalk in front of him, where it made a bright blur in the darkness. Gatewood turned abruptly, and began to retrace his steps homeward.

The woman had recovered her handkerchief. Now she ran to the bundle, picked it up, and scuttled to the black mouth of an alley, a few feet distant—a rather tall woman, bent, and in dark clothes from head to feet.

In the black mouth of the alley she vanished.

I had been compelled to slow up while Gatewood and the woman stood facing each other, and I was more than a block away now. As soon as the woman disappeared I took a chance, and started pounding my rubber soles against the pavement.

The alley was empty when I reached it.

It ran all the way through to the next street, but I knew that the woman couldn't have reached the other end before I got to this one. I carry a lot of weight these days, but I can still step a block or two in good time. Along both sides of the alley were the rears of apartment buildings, each with its back door looking blankly, secretively at me.

The plainclothes man who had been trailing behind me came up, then O'Gar and Thode in their machines, and soon, Lusk. O'Gar and Thode rode off immediately to wind through the neighboring streets, hunting for the woman. Lusk and the plainclothes man each planted himself on a corner from which two of the streets enclosing the block could be watched.

I went through the alley, hunting vainly for an unlocked

door, an open window, a fire-escape that would show recent use—any of the signs that a hurried departure from the alley might leave.

Nothing!

O'Gar came back shortly with some reïnforcements from headquarters that he had picked up, and Gatewood.

Gatewood was burning.

"Bungled the damn thing again! I won't pay your agency a nickel, and I'll see that some of these so-called detectives get put back in a uniform and set to walking beats!"

"What'd the woman look like?" I asked him.

"I don't know! I thought you were hanging around to take care of her! She was old and bent, kind of, I guess, but I couldn't see her face for her veil. I don't know! What the hell were you men doing? It's a damned outrage the way…."

I finally got him quieted down and took him home, leaving the city men to keep the neighborhood under surveillance. There was fourteen or fifteen of them on the job now, and every shadow held at least one.

The girl would naturally head for home as soon as she was released and I wanted to be there to pump her. There was an excellent chance of catching her abductors before they got very far if she could tell us anything at all about them.

Home, Gatewood went up against the whiskey bottle again, while I kept one ear cocked at the telephone and the other at the front door. O'Gar or Thode phoned every half hour or so to ask if we'd heard from the girl. They had still found nothing.

At nine o'clock they, with Lusk, arrived at the house. The woman in black had turned out to be a man, and had gotten away.

In the rear of one of the apartment buildings that touched the alley—just a foot or so within the back-door—they found a woman's skirt, long coat, hat and veil—all black. Investigating the occupants of the house, they had learned that an apartment had been rented to a young man named Leighton three days before.

Leighton was not at home when they went up to his apartment. His rooms held a lot of cold cigarette butts, and an empty bottle, and nothing else that had not been there when he rented it.

The inference was clear: he had rented the apartment so that he might have access to the building. Wearing woman's clothes over his own, he had gone out of the back door—leaving it unlatched behind him—to meet Gatewood.

Then he had run back into the building, discarded his disguise, and hurried through the building, out the front door, and away before we had our feeble net around the block; perhaps dodging into dark doorways here and there to avoid O'Gar and Thode in their automobiles.

Leighton, it seemed, was a man of about thirty, slender, about five feet eight or nine inches tall, with dark hair and eyes; rather good-looking, and well-dressed, on the two occasions when people living in the building had seen him, in a brown suit and a light brown felt hat.

There was no possibility, according to the opinions of both of the detectives and the post office inspector, that the girl might have been held, even temporarily, in Leighton's apartment.

Ten o'clock came, and no word from the girl.

Gatewood had lost his domineering bull-headedness by now and was breaking up. The suspense was getting him, and the liquor he had put away wasn't helping him. I didn't like him either personally or by reputation, but at that I felt sorry for him this morning.

I talked to the agency over the phone and got the reports of the operatives who had been looking up Audrey's friends. The last person to see her had been an Agnes Dangerfield, who had seen her walking down Market street near Sixth, alone, on the night of her abduction—some time between 8:15 and 8:45. Audrey had been too far away for the Dangerfield girl to speak to her.

For the rest, the boys had learned nothing except that Audrey was a wild, spoiled youngster who hadn't shown any great care in selecting her friends—just the sort of girl who could easily fall into the hands of a mob of highbinders!

Noon struck. No sign of the girl. We told the newspapers to turn loose the story, with the added developments of the past few hours.

Gatewood was broken; he sat with his head in his hands, looking at nothing. Just before I left to follow a hunch I had, he looked up at me, and I'd never have recognized him if I hadn't seen the change take place.

"What do you think is keeping her away?" he asked.

I didn't have the heart to tell him what I was beginning to suspect, now that the money had been paid and she had failed to show up. So I stalled with some vague assurances, and left.

I caught a street-car and dropped off down in the shopping district. I visited the five largest department stores, going to all the women's wear departments from shoes to hats, and trying to learn if a man—perhaps one answering Leighton's description—had been buying clothes that would fit Audrey Gatewood within the past couple days.

Failing to get any results, I turned the rest of the local stores over to one of the boys from the agency, and went across the bay to canvass the Oakland stores.

At the first one I got action. A man who might easily have been Leighton had been in the day before, buying clothes that could easily fit Audrey. He had bought lots of them, everything from lingerie to a cloak, and—my luck was hitting on all its cylinders—had had his purchases delivered to T. Offord, at an address on Fourteenth street.

At the Fourteenth street address, an apartment house, I found Mr. and Mrs. Theodore Offord's names under the vestibule telephone for apartment 202.

I had just found them when the front door opened and a stout, middle-aged woman in a gingham house-dress came out. She looked at me a bit curiously, so I asked:

"Do you know where I can find the manager?"

"I'm the manager," she said.

I handed her a card and stepped indoors with her.

"I'm from the bonding department of the North American Casualty Company"—a repetition of the lie that was printed on the card I had given her—"and a bond for Mr. Offord has been applied for. Is he all right so far as you know?" With the slightly apologetic air of one going through with a necessary but not too important formality.

She frowned.

"A bond? That's funny! He is going away tomorrow."

"Well, I can't say what the bond is for," I said lightly. "We investigators just get the names and addresses. It may be for his present employer, or perhaps the man he is going to work for wherever he's going has applied for it. Or some firms have us look up prospective employees before they hire them, just to be safe."

"Mr. Offord, so far as I know, is a very nice young man," she said, "but he has been here only a week."

"Not staying long, then?"

"No. They came here from Denver, intending to stay, but the low altitude doesn't agree with Mrs. Offord, so they are going back."

"Are you sure they came from Denver?"

"Well," she said, "they told me they did."

"How many of them are there?"

"Only the two of them; they're young people."

"Well, how do they impress you?" I asked, trying to get the impression that I thought her a woman of shrewd judgment over.

"They seem to be a very nice young couple. You'd hardly know they were in their apartment most of the time, they are so quiet. I am sorry they can't stay."

"Do they go out much?"

"I really don't know. They have their keys, and unless I should happen to pass them going in or out I'd never see them."

"Then, as a matter of fact, you couldn't say whether they stayed away all night some nights or not. Could you?"

She eyed me doubtfully—I was stepping way over my pretext now, but I didn't think it mattered—and shook her head.

"No, I couldn't say."

"They have many visitors?"

"I don't know. Mr. Offord is not—"

She broke off as a man came in quietly from the street, brushed past me, and started to mount the steps to the second floor.

"Oh, dear!" she whispered. "I hope he didn't hear me talking about him. That's Mr. Offord."

A slender man in brown, with a light brown hat—Leighton perhaps.

I hadn't seen anything of him except his back, nor he anything except mine. I watched him as he climbed the stairs. If he had heard the manager mention his name he would use the turn at the head of the stairs to sneak a look at me.

He did. I kept my face stolid, but I knew him. He was "Penny" Quayle, a con man who had been active in the East four or five years before. His face was as expressionless as mine. But he knew me.

A door on the second floor shut. I left the manager and started for the stairs.

"I think I'll go up and talk to him," I told her.

Coming silently to the door of apartment 202, I listened. Not a sound. This was no time for hesitation. I pressed the bell-button.

As close together as the tapping of three keys under the fingers of an expert typist, but a thousand times more vicious, came three pistol shots. And waist-high in the door of apartment 202 were three bullet holes.

The three bullets would have been in my fat carcass if I hadn't learned years ago to stand to one side of strange doors when making uninvited calls.

Inside the apartment sounded a man's voice, sharp, commanding.

"Cut it, kid! For God's sake, not that!"

A woman's voice, shrill, bitter, spiteful screaming blasphemies.

Two more bullets came through the door.

"Stop! No! No!" The man's voice had a note of fear in it now.

The woman's voice, cursing hotly. A scuffle. A shot that didn't hit the door.

I hurled my foot against the door, near the knob, and the lock broke away.

On the floor of the room, a man—Quayle—and a woman were tussling. He was bending over her, holding her wrists, trying to keep her down. A smoking automatic pistol was in one of her hands. I got to it in a jump and tore it loose.

"That's enough!" I called to them when I was planted. "Get up and receive company."

Quayle released his antagonist's wrists, whereupon she struck at his eyes with curved, sharp-nailed fingers, tearing his cheek open. He scrambled away from her on hands and knees, and both of them got to their feet.

He sat down on a chair immediately, panting and wiping his bleeding cheek with a handkerchief.

She stood, hands on hips, in the center of the room, glaring at me.

"I suppose," she spat, "you think you've raised hell!"

I laughed—I could afford to.

"If your father is in his right mind," I told her, "he'll do it with a razor strop when he gets you home again. A fine joke you picked out to play on him!"

"If *you'd* been tied to him as long as I have, and had been bullied and held down as much, I guess *you'd* do most anything to get enough money so that you could go away and live your own life."

I didn't say anything to that. Remembering some of the business methods Harvey Gatewood had used—particularly some of his war contracts that the Department of Justice was still investigating—I suppose the worst that could be said about Audrey was that she was her father's own daughter.

"How'd you rap to it?" Quayle asked me, politely.

"Several ways," I said. "First, I'm a little doubtful about grown persons being kidnapped in cities. Maybe it really happens sometimes, but at least nine-tenths of the cases you hear about are fakes. Second, one of Audrey's friends saw her on Market street between 8:15 and 8:45 the night she disappeared; and your letter to Gatewood was post-marked 9 P.M. Pretty fast work. You should have waited a while before mailing it, even if it had to miss the first morning delivery. I suppose she dropped it in the post office on her way over here?"

Quayle nodded.

"Then third," I went on, "there was that phone call of hers. She knew it took anywhere from ten to fifteen minutes to get her father on the wire at the office. If time had been as valuable as it would have been if she had gotten to a phone while imprisoned, she'd have told her story to the first person she got hold of—the phone girl, most likely. So that made it look as if, besides wanting to throw out that Twin Peaks line, she wanted to stir the old man out of his bull-headedness.

"When she failed to show up after the money was paid I figured it was a sure bet that she had kidnapped herself. I knew that if she came back home after faking this thing we'd find it out before we'd talked to her very long—and I figured she knew that too, and would stay away.

"The rest was easy, as I got some good breaks. We knew a man was working with her after we found the woman's clothes you left behind, and I took a chance on there being no one else in it. Then I figured she'd need clothes—she couldn't have taken any from home without tipping her mitt—and there was an even chance that she hadn't laid in a stock beforehand. She's got too many girl friends of the sort that do a lot of shopping to make it safe for her to risk showing herself in stores. Maybe, then, the man would buy what she needed for her. And it turned out that he did, and that he was too lazy to carry away his purchases, or perhaps there was too many of them, and so he had them sent out. That's the story."

Quayle nodded again.

"I was damned careless," he said, and then, jerking a contemptuous thumb toward the girl. "But what can you expect? She's had a skin full of hop ever since we started. Took all my time and attention keeping her from running wild and gumming the works. Just now was a sample—I told her you were coming up and she goes crazy and tries to add your corpse to the wreck!"

The Gatewood reunion took place in the office of the captain of inspectors, on the second floor of the Oakland City Hall, and it was a merry little party. For an hour it was a toss-up whether Harvey Gatewood would die of apoplexy, strangle his daughter, or send her off to the state reformatory until she was of age. But Audrey licked him. Besides being a chip off the old block, she was young enough to be careless of consequences, while her father, for all his bullheadedness, had had some caution hammered into him.

The card she beat him with was a threat of spilling everything she knew about him to the newspapers, and at least one of the San Francisco papers had been trying to get his scalp for years. I don't know what she had on him, and I don't think he was any too sure himself; but, with his war contracts even then being investigated by the Department of Justice, he couldn't afford to take a chance. There was no doubt at all that she would have done as she threatened.

And so, together, they left for home, sweating hate for each other at every pore.

We took Quayle upstairs and put him in a cell, but he was too experienced to let that worry him. He knew that if the girl was to be spared, he himself couldn't very easily be convicted of anything.

Slippery Fingers

*You'll have the time of your life trying to solve
this crime before you get to the end of the story.
You'll think some of the characters don't act
logically, but when you figure it out afterward
you'll decide they were all pretty wise.*

"YOU ARE ALREADY familiar, of course, with the particulars of my father's—ah—death?"

"The papers are full of it, and have been for three days," I said, "and I've read them; but I'll have to have the whole story first-hand."

"There isn't very much to tell."

This Frederick Grover was a short, slender man of something under thirty years, and dressed like a picture out of *Vanity Fair*. His almost girlish features and voice did nothing to make him more impressive, but I began to forget these things after a few minutes. He wasn't a sap. I knew that downtown, where he was rapidly building up a large and lively business in stocks and bonds without calling for too much help from his father's millions, he was considered a shrewd article; and I wasn't surprised later when Benny Forman, who ought to know, told me that Frederick Grover was the best poker player west of Chicago. He was a cool, well-balanced, quick-thinking little man.

"Father has lived here alone with the servants since mother's death, two years ago," he went on. "I am married, you know, and live in town. Last Saturday evening he dismissed Barton— Barton was his butler-valet, and had been with father for quite a few years—at a little after nine, saying that he did not want to be disturbed during the evening.

"Father was here in the library at the time, looking through some papers. The servants' rooms are in the rear, and none of the servants seem to have heard anything during the night.

"At seven-thirty the following morning—Sunday—Barton found father lying on the floor, just to the right of where you are sitting, dead, stabbed in the throat with the brass paper-knife that was always kept on the table here. The front door was ajar.

"The police found bloody finger-prints on the knife, the table, and the front door; but so far they have not found the man who left the prints, which is why I am employing your agency. The physician who came with the police placed the time of father's death at between eleven o'clock and midnight.

"Later, on Monday, we learned that father had drawn $10,000 in hundred-dollar bills from the bank Saturday morning. No trace of the money has been found. My finger-prints, as well as the servants', were compared with the ones found by the police, but there was no similarity. I think that is all."

"Do you know of any enemies your father had?"

He shook his head.

"I know of none, though he may have had them. You see, I really didn't know my father very well. He was a very reticent man and, until his retirement, about five years ago, he spent most of his time in South America, where most of his mining interests were. He may have had dozens of enemies, though Barton—who probably knew more about him than anyone— seems to know of no one who hated father enough to kill him."

"How about relatives?"

"I was his heir and only child, if that is what you are getting at. So far as I know he had no other living relatives."

"I'll talk to the servants," I said.

The maid and the cook could tell me nothing, and I learned very little more from Barton. He had been with Henry Grover since 1912, had been with him in Yunnan, Peru, Mexico, and Central America, but apparently he knew little or nothing of his master's business or acquaintances.

He said that Grover had not seemed excited or worried on the night of the murder, and that nearly every night Grover dismissed him at about the same time, with orders that he be not disturbed; so no importance was to be attached to that part of it. He knew of no one with whom Grover had communicated during the day, and he had not seen the money Grover had drawn from the bank.

I made a quick inspection of the house and grounds, not expecting to find anything; and I didn't. Half the jobs that come to a private detective are like this one: three or four days—and often as many weeks—have passed since the crime was committed. The police work on the job until they are stumped; then the injured party calls in a private sleuth, dumps him down on a trail that is old and cold and badly trampled, and expects—Oh, well! I picked out this way of making a living, so....

I looked through Grover's papers—he had a safe and a desk full of them—but didn't find anything to get excited about. They were mostly columns of figures.

"I'm going to send an accountant out here to go over your father's books," I told Frederick Grover. "Give him everything he asks for, and fix it up with the bank so they'll help him."

I caught a street-car and went back to town, called at Ned Root's office, and headed him out toward Grover's. Ned is a human adding machine with educated eyes, ears, and nose. He can spot a kink in a set of books farther than I can see the covers.

"Keep digging until you find something, Ned, and you can charge Grover whatever you like. Give me something to work on—quick!"

The murder had all the earmarks of one that had grown out of blackmail, though there was—there always is—a chance that it might have been something else. But it didn't look like the work of an enemy or a burglar: either of them would have packed his weapon with him, would not have trusted to finding it on the grounds. Of course, if Frederick Grover, or one of the servants, had killed Henry Grover... but the finger-prints said "No."

Just to play safe, I put in a few hours getting a line on Frederick. He had been at a ball on the night of the murder; he had never, so far as I could learn, quarreled with his father; his father was liberal with him, giving him everything he wanted; and Frederick was taking in more money in his brokerage office than he was spending. No motive for a murder appeared on the surface there.

At the city detective bureau I hunted up the police sleuths who had been assigned to the murder; Marty O'Hara and George Dean. It didn't take them long to tell me what they knew about it. Whoever had made the bloody finger-prints was not known to the police here: they had not found the prints in their files. The classifications had been broadcast to every large city in the country, but with no results so far.

A house four blocks from Grover's had been robbed on the night of the murder, and there was a slim chance that the same man *might* have been responsible for both jobs. But the burglary had occurred after one o'clock in the morning, which made the connection look not so good. A burglar who had killed a man, and perhaps picked up $10,000 in the bargain, wouldn't be likely to turn his hand to another job right away.

I looked at the paper-knife with which Grover had been killed, and at the photographs of the bloody prints, but they couldn't help me much just now. There seemed to be nothing to do but get out and dig around until I turned up something somewhere.

Then the door opened, and Joseph Clane was ushered into the room where O'Hara, Dean and I were talking.

Clane was a hard-bitten citizen, for all his prosperous look; fifty or fifty-five, I'd say, with eyes, mouth and jaw that held plenty of humor but none of what is sometimes called the milk of human kindness.

He was a big man, beefy, and all dressed up in a tight-fitting checkered suit, fawn-colored hat, patent-leather shoes with buff uppers, and the rest of the things that go with that sort of combination. He had a harsh voice that was as empty of expression as his hard red face, and he held his body stiffly, as if he was afraid the buttons on his too-tight clothes were about to pop off. Even his arms hung woodenly at his sides, with thick fingers that were lifelessly motionless.

He came right to the point. He had been a friend of the murdered man's, and thought that perhaps what he could tell us would be of value.

He had met Henry Grover—he called him "Henny"—in 1894, in Ontario, where Grover was working a claim: the gold mine that had started the murdered man along the road to wealth. Clane had been employed by Grover as foreman, and the two men had become close friends. A man named Denis Waldeman had a claim adjoining Grover's and a dispute had arisen over their boundaries. The dispute ran on for some time—the men coming to blows once or twice—but finally Grover seems to have triumphed, for Waldeman suddenly left the country.

Clane's idea was that if we could find Waldeman we might find Grover's murderer, for considerable money had been involved in the dispute, and Waldeman was "a mean cuss, for a fact," and not likely to have forgotten his defeat.

Clane and Grover had kept in touch with each other, corresponding or meeting at irregular intervals, but the murdered man had never said or written anything that would throw a light on his death. Clane, too, had given up mining, and now had a small string of race-horses which occupied all his time.

He was in the city for a rest between racing-meets, had arrived two days before the murder, but had been too busy with his own affairs—he had discharged his trainer and was trying to find another—to call upon his friend. Clane was staying at the Marquis hotel, and would be in the city for a week or ten days longer.

"How come you've waited three days before coming to tell us all this?" Dean asked him.

"I wasn't noways sure I had ought to do it. I wasn't never sure in my mind but what maybe Henny done for that fellow Waldeman—he disappeared sudden-like. And I didn't want to do nothing to dirty Henny's name. But finally I decided to do the right thing. And then there's another thing: you found some finger-prints in Henny's house, didn't you? The newspapers said so."

"We did."

"Well, I want you to take mine and match them up. I was

out with a girl the night of the murder"—he leered suddenly, boastingly—"all night! And she's a good girl, got a husband and a lot of folks; and it wouldn't be right to drag her into this to prove that I wasn't in Henny's house when he was killed, in case you'd maybe think I killed him. So I thought I better come down here, tell you all about it, and get you to take my finger-prints, and have it all over with."

We went up to the identification bureau and had Clane's prints taken. They were not at all like the murderer's.

After we pumped Clane dry I went out and sent a telegram to our Toronto office, asking them to get a line on the Waldeman angle. Then I hunted up a couple of boys who eat, sleep, and breathe horse racing. They told me that Clane was well known in racing circles as the owner of a small string of near-horses that ran as irregularly as the stewards would permit.

At the Marquis hotel I got hold of the house detective, who is a helpful chap so long as his hand is kept greased. He verified my information about Clane's status in the sporting world, and told me that Clane had stayed at the hotel for several days at a time, off and on, within the past couple years.

He tried to trace Clane's telephone calls for me but—as usual when you want them—the records were jumbled. I arranged to have the girls on the switchboard listen in on any talking he did during the next few days.

Ned Root was waiting for me when I got down to the office the next morning. He had worked on Grover's accounts all night, and had found enough to give me a start. Within the past year—that was as far back as Ned had gone—Grover had drawn out of his bank-accounts nearly fifty thousand dollars that couldn't be accounted for; nearly fifty thousand exclusive of the ten thousand he had drawn the day of the murder. Ned gave me the amounts and the dates:

    May 6, 1922, $15,000
    June 10, 5,000
    August 1, 5,000
    October 10, 10,000
    January 3, 1923, 12,500

Forty-seven thousand, five hundred dollars! Somebody was getting fat off him!

The local managers of the telegraph companies raised the usual howl about respecting their patrons' privacy, but I got an order from the Prosecuting Attorney and put a clerk at work on the files of each office.

Then I went back to the Marquis hotel and looked at the old registers. Clane had been there from May 4th to 7th, and from October 8th to 15th last year. That checked off two of the dates upon which Grover had made his withdrawals.

I had to wait until nearly six o'clock for my information from the telegraph companies, but it was worth waiting for. On the third of last January Henry Grover had telegraphed $12,500 to Joseph Clane in San Diego. The clerks hadn't found anything on the other dates I had given them, but I wasn't at all dissatisfied. I had Joseph Clane fixed as the man who had been getting fat off Grover.

I sent Dick Foley—he is the Agency's shadow-ace—and Bob Teal—a youngster who will be a world-beater some day—over to Clane's hotel.

"Plant yourselves in the lobby," I told them. "I'll be over in a few minutes to talk to Clane, and I'll try to bring him down in the lobby where you can get a good look at him. Then I want him shadowed until he shows up at police headquarters tomorrow. I want to know where he goes and who he talks to. And if he spends much time talking to any one person, or their conversation seems very important, I want one of you boys to trail the other man, to see who he is and what he does. If Clane tries to blow town, grab him and have him thrown in the can, but I don't think he will."

I gave Dick and Bob time enough to get themselves placed, and then went to the hotel. Clane was out, so I waited. He came in a little after eleven and I went up to his room with him. I didn't hem-and-haw, but came out cold-turkey:

"All the signs point to Grover's having been blackmailed. Do you know anything about it?"

"No," he said.

"Grover drew a lot of money out of his banks at different times. You got some of it, I know, and I suppose you got most of it. What about it?"

He didn't pretend to be insulted, or even surprised by my talk. He smiled a little grimly, maybe, but as if he thought it the most natural thing in the world—and it was, at that—for me to suspect him.

"I told you that me and Henny were pretty chummy, didn't I? Well, you ought to know that all us fellows that fool with the bang-tails have our streaks of bad luck. Whenever I'd get up against it I'd hit Henny up for a stake; like at Tiajuana last winter where I got into a flock of bad breaks. Henny lent me twelve or fifteen thousand and I got back on my feet again. I've done that often. He ought to have some of my letters and wires in his stuff. If you look through his things you'll find them."

I didn't pretend that I believed him.

"Suppose you drop into police headquarters at nine in the morning and we'll go over everything with the city dicks," I told him.

And then, to make my play stronger:

"I wouldn't make it much later than nine—they might be out looking for you."

"Uh-huh," was all the answer I got.

I went back to the Agency and planted myself within reach of a telephone, waiting for word from Dick and Bob. I thought I was sitting pretty. Clane had been blackmailing Grover—I didn't have a single doubt of that—and I didn't think he had been very far away when Grover was killed. That woman alibi of his sounded all wrong!

But the bloody finger-prints were not Clane's—unless the police identification bureau had pulled an awful boner—and the man who had left the prints was the bird I was setting my cap for. Clane had let three days pass between the murder and his appearance at headquarters. The natural explanation for that would be that his partner, the actual murderer, had needed nearly that much time to put himself in the clear.

My present game was simple: I had stirred Clane up with the knowledge that he was still suspected, hoping that he would have to repeat whatever precautions were necessary to protect his accomplice in the first place.

He had taken three days then. I was giving him about nine hours now: time enough to do something, but not too much time, hoping that he would have to hurry things along and that in his haste he would give Dick and Bob a chance to turn up his partner: the owner of the fingers that had smeared blood on the knife, the table, and the door.

At a quarter to one in the morning Dick telephoned that Clane had left the hotel a few minutes behind me, had gone to an apartment house on Polk Street, and was still there.

I went up to Polk Street and joined Dick and Bob. They told me that Clane had gone in apartment number 27, and that the directory in the vestibule showed this apartment was occupied by George Farr. I stuck around with the boys until about two o'clock, when I went home for some sleep.

At seven I was with them again, and was told that our man had not appeared yet. It was a little after eight when he came out and turned down Geary Street, with the boys trailing him, while I went into the apartment house for a talk with the manager. She told me that Farr had been living there for four or five months, lived alone, and was a photographer by trade, with a studio on Market Street.

I went up and rang his bell. He was a husky of thirty or thirty-two with bleary eyes that looked as if they hadn't had much sleep that night. I didn't waste any time with him.

"I'm from the Continental Detective Agency and I am interested in Joseph Clane. What do you know about him?"

He was wide awake now.

"Nothing."

"Nothing at all?"

"No," sullenly.

"Do you know him?"

"No."

What can you do with a bird like that?

"Farr," I said, "I want you to go down to headquarters with me."

He moved like a streak and his sullen manner had me a little off my guard; but I turned my head in time to take the punch above my ear instead of on the chin. At that, it carried me off my feet and I wouldn't have bet a nickel that my skull wasn't dented; but luck was with me and I fell across the doorway, holding the door open, and managed to scramble up, stumble through some rooms, and catch one of his feet as it was going through the bathroom window to join its mate on the fire-escape. I got a split lip and a kicked shoulder in the scuffle, but he behaved after a while.

I didn't stop to look at his stuff—that could be done more regularly later—but put him in a taxicab and took him to the Hall of Justice. I was afraid that if I waited too long Clane would take a run-out on me.

Clane's mouth fell open when he saw Farr, but neither of them said anything.

I was feeling pretty chirp in spite of my bruises.

"Let's get this bird's finger-prints and get it over with," I said to O'Hara.

Dean was not in.

"And keep an eye on Clane. I think maybe he'll have another story to tell us in a few minutes."

We got in the elevator and took our men up to the identification bureau, where we put Farr's fingers on the pad. Phels—he is the department's expert—took one look at the results and turned to me.

"Well, what of it?"

"What of what?" I asked.

"This isn't the man who killed Henry Grover!"

Clane laughed, Farr laughed, O'Hara laughed, and Phels laughed. I didn't! I stood there and pretended to be thinking, trying to get myself in hand.

"Are you sure you haven't made a mistake?" I blurted, my face a nice, rosy red.

You can tell how badly upset I was by that: it's plain suicide to say a thing like that to a finger-print expert!

Phels didn't answer; just looked me up and down.

Clane laughed again, like a crow cawing, and turned his ugly face to me.

"Do you want to take my prints again, Mr. Slick Private Detective?"

"Yeah," I said, "just that!"

I had to say something.

Clane held his hands out to Phels, who ignored them, speaking to me with heavy sarcasm.

"Better take them yourself this time, so you'll be sure it's been done right."

I was mad clean through—of course it was my own fault—but I was pig-headed enough to go through with anything, particularly anything that would hurt somebody's feelings; so I said:

"That's not a bad idea!"

I walked over and took hold of one of Clane's hands. I'd never taken a finger-print before, but I had seen it done often enough to throw a bluff. I started to ink Clane's fingers and found that I was holding them wrong—my own fingers were in the way.

Then I came back to earth. The balls of Clane's fingers were too smooth—or rather, too slick—without the slight clinging feeling that belongs to flesh. I turned his hand over so fast that I nearly upset him and looked at the fingers. I don't know what I had expected to find but I didn't find anything—not anything that I could name.

"Phels," I called, "look here!"

He forgot his injured feelings and bent to look at Clane's hand.

"I'll be—" he began, and then the two of us were busy for a few minutes taking Clane down and sitting on him, while O'Hara quieted Farr, who had also gone suddenly into action.

When things were peaceful again Phels examined Clane's hands carefully, scratching the fingers with a finger-nail.

He jumped up, leaving me to hold Clane, and paying no attention to my, "What is it?" got a cloth and some liquid, and washed the fingers thoroughly. We took his prints again. They matched the bloody ones taken from Grover's house!

Then we all sat down and had a nice talk.

"I told you about the trouble Henny had with that fellow Waldeman," Clane began, after he and Farr had decided to come clean: there was nothing else they could do. "And how he won out in the argument because Waldeman disappeared. Well, Henny done for him—shot him one night and buried him—and I saw it. Grover was one bad actor in them days, a tough hombre to tangle with, so I didn't try to make nothing out of what I knew.

"But after he got older and richer he got soft—a lot of men go like that—and must have begun worrying over it; because when I ran into him in New York accidentally about four years ago it didn't take me long to learn that he was pretty well tamed, and he told me that he hadn't been able to forget the look on Waldeman's face when he drilled him.

"So I took a chance and braced Henny for a couple thousand. I got them easy, and after that, whenever I was flat I either went to him or sent him word, and he always came across. But I was careful not to crowd him too far. I knew what a terror he was in the old days, and I didn't want to push him into busting loose again.

"But that's what I did in the end. I 'phoned him Friday that I needed money and he said he'd call me up and let me know where to meet him the next night. He called up around half past nine Saturday night and told me to come out to the house. So I went out there and he was waiting for me on the porch and took me upstairs and gave me the ten thousand. I told him this was the last time I'd ever bother him—I always told him that—it had a good effect on him.

"Naturally I wanted to get away as soon as I had the money but he must have felt sort of talkative for a change, because he kept me there for half an hour or so, gassing about men we used to know up in the province.

"After awhile I began to get nervous. He was getting a look in his eyes like he used to have when he was young. And then all of a sudden he flared up and tied into me. He had me by the throat and was bending me back across the table when my hand touched that brass knife. It was either me or him—so I let him have it where it would do the most good.

"I beat it then and went back to the hotel. The newspapers were full of it next day, and had a whole lot of stuff about bloody finger-prints. That gave me a jolt! I didn't know nothing about finger-prints, and here I'd left them all over the dump.

"And then I got to worrying over the whole thing, and it

seemed like Henny must have my name written down some-wheres among his papers, and maybe had saved some of my letters or telegrams—though *they* were wrote in careful enough language. Anyway I figured the police would want to be asking me some questions sooner or later; and there I'd be with fingers that fit the bloody prints, and nothing for what Farr calls a alibi.

"That's when I thought of Farr. I had his address and I knew he had been a finger-print sharp in the East, so I decided to take a chance on him. I went to him and told him the whole story and between us we figured out what to do.

"He said he'd dope my fingers, and I was to come here and tell the story we'd fixed up, and have my finger-prints taken, and then I'd be safe no matter what leaked out about me and Henny. So he smeared up the fingers and told me to be care-ful not to shake hands with anybody or touch anything, and I came down here and everything went like three of a kind.

"Then that little fat guy"—meaning me—"came around to the hotel last night and as good as told me that he thought I had done for Henny and that I better come down here this morning. I beat it for Farr's right away to see whether I ought to run for it or sit tight, and Farr said, 'Sit tight!' So I stayed there all night and he fixed up my hands this morning. That's my yarn!"

Phels turned to Farr.

"I've seen faked prints before, but never any this good. How'd you do it?"

These scientific birds are funny. Here was Farr looking a nice, long stretch in the face as "accessory after the fact," and yet he brightened up under the admiration in Phel's tone and answered with a voice that was chock-full of pride.

"It's simple! I got hold of a man whose prints I knew weren't in any police gallery—I didn't want any slip up there—and took his prints and put them on a copper plate, using the ordinary photo-engraving process, but etching it pretty deep. Then I coated Clane's fingers with gelatin—just enough to cover all his markings—and pressed them against the plates. That way I got everything, even to the pores, and…."

When I left the bureau ten minutes later Farr and Phels were still sitting knee to knee, jabbering away at each other as only a couple of birds who are cuckoo on the same subject can.

It

Calling a detective to solve a crime that turns out to be something quite different from the first diagnosis makes a very unusual story of this. You'll be surprised!

"NOW LISTEN, MR. ZUMWALT, you're holding out on me; and it won't do! If I'm going to work on this for you I've got to have the whole story."

He looked thoughtfully at me for a moment through screwed-up blue eyes. Then he got up and went to the door of the outer office, opening it. Past him I could see the book-keeper and the stenographer sitting at their desks. Zumwalt closed the door and returned to his desk, leaning across it to speak in a husky undertone.

"You are right, I suppose. But what I am going to tell you must be held in the strictest confidence."

I nodded, and he went on:

"About two months ago one of our clients, Stanley Gorham, turned $100,000 worth of Liberty bonds over to us. He had to go to the Orient on business, and he had an idea that the bonds might go to par during his absence; so he left them with us to be sold if they did. Yesterday I had occasion to go to the safe deposit box where the bonds had been put—in the Golden Gate Trust Company's vault—and they were gone!"

"Anybody except you and your partner have access to the box?"

"No."

"When did you see the bonds last?"

"They were in the box the Saturday before Dan left. And one of the men on duty in the vault told me that Dan was there the following Monday."

"All right! Now let me see if I've got it all straight. Your partner, Daniel Rathbone, was supposed to leave for New York on the twenty-seventh of last month, Monday, to meet an R.W. DePuy. But Rathbone came into the office that day with his baggage and said that important personal affairs made it necessary for him to postpone his departure, that he had to be in San Francisco the following morning. But he didn't tell you what that personal business was.

"You and he had some words over the delay, as you thought it important that he keep the New York engagement on time. You weren't on the best of terms at the time, having quarreled a couple of days before that over a shady deal Rathbone had put over. And so you—"

"Don't misunderstand me," Zumwalt interrupted. "Dan had done nothing dishonest. It was simply that he had engineered several transactions that—well, I thought he had sacrificed ethics to profits."

"I see. Anyhow, starting with your argument over his not leaving for New York that day, you and he wound up by dragging in all of your differences, and practically decided to dissolve partnership as soon as it could be done. The argument was concluded in your house out on Fourteenth Avenue; and, as it was rather late by then and he had checked out of his hotel before he had changed his mind about going to New York, he stayed there with you that night."

"That's right," Zumwalt explained. "I have been living at a hotel since Mrs. Zumwalt has been away, but Dan and I went out to the house because it gave us the utmost privacy for our talk; and when we finished it was so late that we remained there."

"Then the next morning you and Rathbone came down to the office and—"

"No," he corrected me. "That is, we didn't come down here together. I came here while Dan went to transact whatever it was that had held him in town. He came into the office a little after noon, and said he was going East on the evening train. He sent Quimby, the bookkeeper, down to get his reservations and to check his baggage, which he had left in the office here overnight. Then Dan and I went to lunch together, came back to the office for a few minutes—he had some mail to sign—and then he left."

"I see. After that, you didn't hear from or of him until about ten days later, when DePuy wired to find out why Rathbone hadn't been to see him?"

"That's right! As soon as I got DePuy's wire I sent one to Dan's brother in Chicago, thinking perhaps Dan had stopped over with him, but Tom wired back that he hadn't seen his brother. Since then I've had two more wires from DePuy. I was sore with Dan for keeping DePuy waiting, but still I didn't worry a lot.

"Dan isn't a very reliable person, and if he suddenly took a notion to stop off somewhere between here and New York for a few days he'd do it. But yesterday, when I found that the bonds were gone from the safe deposit box and learned that Dan had been to the box the day before he left, I decided that I'd have to do something. But I don't want the police brought into it if it can be avoided.

"I feel sure that if I can find Dan and talk to him we can straighten the mess out somehow without scandal. We had our differences, but Dan's too decent a man, and I like him too well, for all his occasional wildness, to want to see him in jail. So I want him found with as much speed and as little noise as possible."

"Has he got a car?"

"Not now. He had one but he sold it five or six months ago."

"Where'd he bank? I mean his personal account?"

"At the Golden Gate Trust Company."

"Got any photos of him?"

"Yes."

He brought out two from a desk drawer—one full-face, and the other a three-quarter view. They showed a man in the middle of his life, with shrewd eyes set close together in a hatchet face, under dark, thin hair. But the face was rather pleasant for all its craftiness.

"How about his relatives, friends, and so on—particularly his feminine friends?"

"His only relative is the brother in Chicago. As to his friends: he probably has as many as any man in San Francisco. He was a wonderful mixer.

"Recently he has been on very good terms with a Mrs. Earnshaw, the wife of a real estate agent. She lives on Pacific Street, I think. I don't know just how intimate they were, but he used to call her up on the phone frequently, and she called him here nearly every day. Then there is a girl named Eva Duthie, a cabaret entertainer, who lives in the 1100 block of Bush Street. There were probably others, too, but I know of only those two."

"Have you looked through his stuff, here?"

"Yes, but perhaps you'd like to look for yourself."

He led me into Rathbone's private office: a small box of a room, just large enough for a desk, a filing cabinet, and two chairs, with doors leading into the corridor, the outer office, and Zumwalt's.

"While I'm looking around you might get me a list of the serial numbers of the missing bonds," I said. "They probably won't help us right away, but we can get the Treasury Department to let us know when the coupons come in, and from where."

I didn't expect to find anything in Rathbone's office and I didn't.

Before I left I questioned the stenographer and the bookkeeper. They already knew that Rathbone was missing, but they didn't know that the bonds were gone too.

The girl, Mildred Narbett was her name, said that Rathbone had dictated a couple of letters to her on the twenty-eighth—the day he left for New York—both of which had to do with the partner's business—and told her to send Quimby to check his baggage and make his reservations. When she returned from lunch she had typed the two letters and taken them in for him to sign, catching him just as he was about to leave.

John Quimby, the bookkeeper, described the baggage he had checked: two large pigskin bags and a cordovan Gladstone bag. Having a bookkeeper's mind, he had remembered the number of the berth he had secured for Rathbone on the evening train—lower 4, car 8. Quimby had returned with the checks and tickets while the partners were out at luncheon, and had put them on Rathbone's desk.

At Rathbone's hotel I was told that he had left on the morning of the twenty-seventh, giving up his room, but leaving his two trunks there, as he intended living there after his return from New York, in three or four weeks. The hotel people could tell me little worth listening to, except that he had left in a taxicab.

At the taxi stand outside I found the chauffeur who had carried Rathbone.

"Rathbone? Sure, I know him!" he told me around a limp cigarette. "Yeah, I guess it was about that date that I took him down to the Golden Gate Trust Company. He had a coupla big yellow bags and a little brown one. He busted into the bank, carrying the little one, and right out again, looking like somebody had kicked him on his corns. Had me take him to the Phelps Building"—the offices of Rathbone & Zumwalt were in that building—"and didn't give me a jit over my fare!"

At the Golden Gate Trust Company I had to plead and talk a lot, but they finally gave me what I wanted—Rathbone had drawn out his account, a little less than $5,000, on the twenty-fifth of the month, the Saturday before he left town.

From the trust company I went down to the Ferry Building baggage-rooms and cigared myself into a look at the records for the twenty-eighth. Only one lot of three bags had been checked to New York that day.

I telegraphed the numbers and Rathbone's description to the Agency's New York office, instructing them to find the bags and, through them, find him.

Up in the Pullman Company's offices I was told that car "8" was a through car, and that they could let me know within a couple hours whether Rathbone had occupied his berth all the way to New York.

On my way up to the 1100 block of Bush Street I left one of Rathbone's photographs with a photographer, with a rush order for a dozen copies.

I found Eva Duthie's apartment after about five minutes of searching vestibule directories, and got her out of bed. She was an undersized blonde girl of somewhere between nineteen and twenty-nine, depending upon whether you judged by her eyes or by the rest of her face.

"I haven't seen or heard from Mr. Rathbone for nearly a month," she said. "I called him up at his hotel the other night—had a party I wanted to ring him in on—but they told me that he was out of town and wouldn't be back for a week or two."

Then, in answer to another question:

"Yes, we were pretty good friends, but not especially thick. You know what I mean: we had a lot of fun together but neither of us meant anything to the other outside of that. Dan is a good sport—and so am I."

Mrs. Earnshaw wasn't so frank. But she had a husband, and that makes a difference. She was a tall, slender woman, as dark as a gypsy, with a haughty air and a nervous trick of chewing her lower lip.

We sat in a stiffly furnished room and she stalled me for about fifteen minutes, until I came out flat-footed with her.

"It's like this, Mrs. Earnshaw," I told her. "Mr. Rathbone has disappeared, and we are going to find him. You're not helping me and you're not helping yourself. I came here to get what you know about him.

"I could have gone around asking a lot of questions among your friends; and if you don't tell me what I want to know that's what I'll have to do. And, while I'll be as careful as possible, still there's bound to be some curiosity aroused, some wild guesses, and some talk. I'm giving you a chance to avoid all that. It's up to you."

"You are assuming," she said coldly, "that I have something to hide."

"I'm not assuming anything. I'm hunting for information about Daniel Rathbone."

She bit her lip on that for a while, and then the story came out bit by bit, with a lot in it that wasn't any too true, but straight enough in the long run. Stripped of the stuff that wouldn't hold water, it went like this:

She and Rathbone had planned to run away together. She had left San Francisco on the twenty-sixth, going directly to New Orleans. He was to leave the next day, apparently for New York, but he was to change trains somewhere in the Middle West and meet her in New Orleans. From there they were to go by boat to Central America.

She pretended ignorance of his designs upon the bonds. Maybe she hadn't known. Anyhow, she had carried out her part of the plan, but Rathbone had failed to show up in New Orleans. She hadn't shown much care in covering her trail and private detectives employed by her husband had soon found her. Her husband had arrived in New Orleans and, apparently not knowing that there was another man in the deal, had persuaded her to return home.

She wasn't a woman to take kindly to the jilting Rathbone had handed her, so she hadn't tried to get in touch with him, or to learn what had kept him from joining her.

Her story rang true enough, but just to play safe, I put out a few feelers in the neighborhood, and what I learned seemed to verify what she had told me. I gathered that a few of the neighbors had made guesses that weren't a million miles away from the facts.

I got the Pullman Company on the telephone and was told that lower 4, car 8, leaving for New York on the twenty-eighth, hadn't been occupied at all.

Zumwalt was dressing for dinner when I went up to his room at the hotel where he was staying.

I told him all that I had learned that day, and what I thought of it.

"Everything makes sense up until Rathbone left the Golden Gate Trust Company vault on the twenty-seventh, and after that nothing does! He had planned to grab the bonds and elope with this Mrs. Earnshaw, and he had already drawn out of the bank all his own money. That's all orderly. But why should he have gone back to the office? Why should he have stayed in town that night? What was the important business that held him? Why should he have ditched Mrs. Earnshaw? Why didn't he use his reservations at least part of the way across the country, as he had planned? False trail, maybe, but a rotten one! There's nothing to do, Mr. Zumwalt, but to call in the police and the newspapers, and see what publicity and a nation-wide search will do for us."

"But that means jail for Dan, with no chance to quietly straighten the matter up!" he protested.

"It does! But it can't be helped. And remember, you've got to protect yourself. You're his partner, and, while not criminally responsible, you are financially responsible for his actions. You've got to put yourself in the clear!"

He nodded reluctant agreement and I grabbed the telephone.

For two hours I was busy giving all the dope we had to the police, and as much as we wanted published to the newspapers, who luckily had photographs of Rathbone, taken a year before when he had been named as co-respondent in a divorce suit.

I sent off three telegrams. One to New York, asking that Rathbone's baggage be opened as soon as the necessary authority could be secured. (If he hadn't gone to New York the baggage should be waiting at the station.) One to Chicago, asking that Rathbone's brother be interviewed and then shadowed for a few days. And one to New Orleans, to have the city searched for him. Then I headed for home and bed.

News was scarce, and the papers the next day had Rathbone spread out all over the front pages, with photographs and descriptions and wild guesses and wilder clues that had materialized somehow within the short space between the time the newspapers got the story and the time they went to press.

I spent the morning preparing circulars and plans for having the country covered; and arranging to have steamship records searched.

Just before noon a telegram came from New York, itemizing the things found in Rathbone's baggage. The contents of the two large bags didn't mean anything. They might have been packed for use or for a stall. But the things in the Gladstone bag, which had been found unlocked, were puzzling.

Here's the list:

Two suits silk pajamas, 4 silk shirts, 8 linen collars, 4 suits underwear, 6 neckties, 6 pairs sox, 18 handkerchiefs, 1 pair military brushes, 1 comb, 1 safety razor, 1 tube shaving cream, 1 shaving brush, 1 tooth brush, 1 tube tooth paste, 1 can talcum powder, 1 bottle hair tonic, 1 cigar case holding 12 cigars, 1 .32 Colt's revolver, 1 map of Honduras, 1 Spanish English dictionary, 2 books postage stamps, 1 pint Scotch whiskey, and 1 manicure set.

Zumwalt, his bookkeeper, and his stenographer were watching two men from headquarters search Rathbone's office when I arrived there. After I showed them the telegram the detectives went back to their examination.

"What's the significance of that list?" Zumwalt asked.

"It shows that there's no sense to this thing the way it now stands," I said. "That Gladstone bag was packed to be carried. Checking it was all wrong—it wasn't even locked. And nobody ever checks Gladstone bags filled with toilet articles—so checking it for a stall would have been the bunk! Maybe he checked it as an afterthought—to get rid of it when he found he wasn't going to need it. But what could have made it unnecessary to him? Don't forget that it's apparently the same bag that he carried into the Golden Gate Trust Company vault when he went for the bonds. Damned if I can dope it!"

"Here's something else for you to dope," one of the city detectives said, getting up from his examination of the desk and holding out a sheet of paper. "I found it behind one of the drawers, where it had slipped down."

It was a letter, written with blue ink in a firm, angular and unmistakably feminine hand on heavy white note paper.

Dear Dannyboy:

If it isn't too late I've changed my mind about going. If you can wait another day, until Tuesday, I'll go. Call me up as soon as you get this, and if you still want me I'll pick you up in the roadster at the Shattuck Avenue station Tuesday afternoon.

More than ever yours,

"Boots."

It was dated the twenty-sixth—the Sunday before Rathbone had disappeared.

"That's the thing that made him lay over another day, and made him change his plans," one of the police detectives said. "I guess we better run over to Berkeley and see what we can find at the Shattuck Avenue station."

"Mr. Zumwalt," I said, when he and I were alone in his office, "how about this stenog of yours?"

He bounced up from his chair and his face turned red.

"What about her?"

"Is she— How friendly was she with Rathbone?"

"Miss Narbett," he said heavily, deliberately, as if to be sure that I caught every syllable, "is to be married to me as soon as my wife gets her divorce. That is why I canceled the order to sell my house. Now would you mind telling me just why you asked?"

"Just a random guess!" I lied, trying to soothe him. "I don't want to overlook any bets. But now that's out of the way."

"It is," he was still talking deliberately, "and it seems to me that most of your guesses have been random ones. If you will have your office send me a bill for your services to date, I think I can dispense with your help."

"Just as you say. But you'll have to pay for a full day today; so, if you don't mind, I'll keep on working at it until night."

"Very well! But I am busy, and you needn't bother about coming in with any reports."

"All right," I said, and bowed myself out of the office, but not out of the job.

That letter from "Boots" had not been in the desk when I searched it. I had taken every drawer out and even tilted the desk to look under it. The letter was a plant!

And then again: maybe Zumwalt had given me the air because he was dissatisfied with the work I had done and peeved at my question about the girl—and maybe not.

Suppose (I thought, walking up Market Street, bumping shoulders and stepping on people's feet) the two partners were in this thing together. One of them would have to be the goat, and that part had fallen to Rathbone. Zumwalt's manner and actions since his partner's disappearance fit that theory well enough.

Employing a private detective before calling in the police was a good play. In the first place it gave him the appearance of innocence. Then the private sleuth would tell him everything he learned, every step he took, giving Zumwalt an opportunity to correct any mistakes or oversights in the partners' plans before the police came into it; and if the private detective got on dangerous ground he could be called off.

And suppose Rathbone was found in some city where he was unknown—and that would be where he'd go. Zumwalt would volunteer to go forward to identify him. He would look at him and say, "No, that's not him," Rathbone would be turned loose, and that would be the end of that trail.

This theory left the sudden change in Rathbone's plans unaccounted for; but it made his return to the office on the afternoon of the twenty-seventh more plausible. He had come back to confer with his partner over that unknown necessity for the change, and they had decided to leave Mrs. Earnshaw out of it. Then they had gone out to Zumwalt's house. For what? And why had Zumwalt decided not to sell the house? And why had he taken the trouble to give me an explanation? Could they have cached the bonds there?

A look at the house wouldn't be a bad idea!

I telephoned Bennett, at the Oakland Police Department.

"Do me a favor, Frank? Call Zumwalt on the phone. Tell him you've picked up a man who answers Rathbone's description to a T; and ask him to come over and take a look at him. When he gets there stall him as long as you can—pretending that the man is being fingerprinted and measured, or something like that—and then tell him that you've found that the man isn't Rathbone, and that you are sorry to have brought him over there, and so on. If you only hold him for half or three-quarters of an hour it'll be enough—it'll take him more than half an hour traveling each way. Thanks!"

I stopped in at the office, stuck a flashlight in my pocket, and headed for Fourteenth Avenue.

Zumwalt's house was a two-story, semi-detached one; and the lock on the front door held me up about four minutes. A burglar would have gone through it without checking his stride. This breaking into the house wasn't exactly according to the rules, but on the other hand, I was legally Zumwalt's agent until I discontinued work that night—so this crashing in couldn't be considered illegal.

I started at the top floor and worked down. Bureaus, dressers, tables, desks, chairs, walls, woodwork, pictures, carpets, plumbing—I looked at everything that was thick enough to hold paper. I didn't take things apart, but it's surprising how speedily and how thoroughly you can go through a house when you're in training.

I found nothing in the house itself, so I went down into the cellar.

It was a large cellar and divided in two. The front part was paved with cement, and held a full coal-bin, some furniture, some canned goods, and a lot of odds and ends of house-keeping accessories. The rear division, behind a plaster partition where the steps ran down from the kitchen, was without windows, and illuminated only by one swinging electric light, which I turned on.

A pile of lumber filled half the space; on the other side barrels and boxes were piled up to the ceiling; two sacks of cement lay beside them, and in another corner was a tangle of broken furniture. The floor was of hard dirt.

I turned to the lumber pile first. I wasn't in love with the job ahead of me—moving the pile away and then back again. But I needn't have worried.

A board rattled behind me, and I wheeled to see Zumwalt rising from behind a barrel and scowling at me over a black automatic pistol.

"Put your hands up," he said.

I put them up. I didn't have a pistol with me, not being in the habit of carrying one except when I thought I was going to need it; but it would have been all the same if I had had a pocket full of them. I don't mind taking chances, but there's no chance when you're looking into the muzzle of a gun that a determined man is holding on you.

So I put my hands up. And one of them brushed against the swinging light globe. I drove my knuckles into it. As the cellar went black I threw myself backward and to one side. Zumwalt's gun streaked fire.

Nothing happened for a while. I found that I had fallen across the doorway that gave to the stairs and the front cellar. I figured that I couldn't move without making a noise that would draw lead, so I lay still.

Then began a game that made up in tenseness what it lacked in action.

The part of the cellar where we were was about twenty by twenty feet and blacker than a new shoe. There were two doors. One, on the opposite side, opened into the yard and was, I supposed, locked. I was lying on my back across the other, waiting for a pair of legs to grab. Zumwalt, with a gun out of which only one bullet had been spent, was somewhere in the blackness, and aware, from his silence, that I was still alive.

I figured I had the edge on him. I was closest to the only practicable exit; he didn't know that I was unarmed; he didn't know whether I had help close by or not; time was valuable to him, but not necessarily so to me. So I waited.

Time passed. How much I don't know. Maybe half an hour.

The floor was damp and hard and thoroughly uncomfortable. The electric light had cut my hand when I broke it, and I couldn't determine how badly I was bleeding. I thought of Tad's "blind man in a dark room hunting for a black hat that wasn't there," and knew how he felt.

A box or barrel fell over with a crash—knocked over by Zumwalt, no doubt, moving out from the hiding-place wherein he had awaited my arrival.

Silence for a while. And then I could hear him moving cautiously off to one side.

Without warning two streaks from his pistol sent bullets into the partition somewhere above my feet. I wasn't the only one who was feeling the strain.

Silence again, and I found that I was wet and dripping with perspiration.

Then I could hear his breathing, but couldn't determine

whether he was nearer or was breathing more heavily.

A soft, sliding, dragging across the dirt floor! I pictured him crawling awkwardly on his knees and one hand, the other hand holding the pistol out ahead of him—the pistol that would spit fire as soon as its muzzle touched something soft. And I became uneasily aware of my bulk. I am thick through the waist; and there in the dark it seemed to me that my paunch must extend almost to the ceiling—a target that no bullet could miss.

I stretched my hands out toward him and held them there. If they touched him first I'd have a chance.

He was panting harshly now; and I was breathing through a mouth that was stretched as wide as it would go, so that there would be no rasping of the large quantities of air I was taking in and letting out.

Abruptly he came.

Hair brushed the fingers of my left hand. I closed them about it, pulling the head I couldn't see viciously toward me, driving my right fist beneath it. You may know that I put everything I had in that smack when I tell you that not until later, when I found that one of my cheeks was scorched, did I know that his gun had gone off.

He wiggled, and I hit him again.

Then I was sitting astride him, my flashlight hunting for his pistol. I found it, and yanked him to his feet.

As soon as his head cleared I herded him into the front cellar and got a globe to replace the one I had smashed.

"Now dig it up," I ordered.

That was a safe way of putting it. I wasn't sure what I wanted or where it would be, except that his selecting this part of the cellar to wait for me in made it look as if this was the right place.

"You'll do your own digging!" he growled.

"Maybe," I said, "but I'm going to do it now, and I haven't time to tie you up. So if I've got to do the digging, I'm going to crown you first, so you'll sleep peacefully until it's all over."

All smeared with blood and dirt and sweat, I must have looked capable of anything, for when I took a step toward him he gave in.

From behind the lumber pile he brought a spade, moved some of the barrels to one side, and started turning up the dirt.

When a hand—a man's hand—dead-yellow where the damp dirt didn't stick to it—came into sight I stopped him.

I had found "it," and I had no stomach for looking at "it" after three weeks of lying in the wet ground.

NOTE: IN COURT, Lester Zumwalt's plea was that he had killed his partner in self-defense. Zumwalt testified that he had taken the Gorham bonds in a futile attempt to recover losses in the stock market; and that when Rathbone—who had intended taking them and going to Central America with Mrs. Earnshaw—had visited the safe deposit box and found them gone, he had returned to the office and charged Zumwalt with the theft.

Zumwalt at that time had not suspected his partner's own dishonest plans, and had promised to restore the bonds. They had gone to Zumwalt's house to discuss the matter; and, Rathbone, dissatisfied with his partner's plan of restitution, had attacked Zumwalt, and had been killed in the ensuing struggle.

Then Zumwalt had told Mildred Narbett, his stenographer,

the whole story and had persuaded her to help him. Between them they had made it appear that Rathbone had been in the office for a while the next day—the twenty-eighth—and had left for New York.

However, the jury seemed to think that Zumwalt had lured his partner out to the Fourteenth Avenue house for the purpose of killing him; so Zumwalt was found guilty of murder in the first degree.

The first jury before which Mildred Narbett was tried disagreed. The second jury acquitted her, holding that there was nothing to show that she had taken part in either the theft of the bonds or the murder, or that she had any knowledge of either crime until afterward; and that her later complicity was, in view of her love for Zumwalt, not altogether blameworthy.

Bodies Piled Up

One of our best detectives is this nameless sleuth of Mr. Hammett's. He's deductive, practical, and maybe a little unromantic. Probably that's why he runs into such wild adventures and takes such horrible chances. In this story he walks into a whirlwind of death. Go to it.

THE MONTGOMERY HOTEL'S regular detective had taken his last week's rake-off from the hotel bootlegger in merchandise instead of cash, had drunk it down, had fallen asleep in the lobby, and had been fired. I happened to be the only idle operative in the Continental Detective Agency's San Francisco branch at the time, and thus it came about that I had three days of hotel-coppering while a man was being found to take the job permanently.

The Montgomery is a quiet hotel of the better sort, and so I had a very restful time of it—until the third and last day.

Then things changed.

I came down into the lobby that afternoon to find Stacey, the assistant manager on duty at the time, hunting for me.

"One of the maids just phoned that there's something wrong up in 906," he said.

We went up to that room together. The door was open. In the center of the floor stood a maid, staring goggle-eyed at the closed door of the clothespress. From under it, extending perhaps a foot across the floor toward us, was a snake-shaped ribbon of blood.

I stepped past the maid and tried the door. It was unlocked. I opened it. Slowly, rigidly, a man pitched out into my arms—pitched out backward—and there was a six-inch slit down the back of his coat, and the coat was wet and sticky.

That wasn't altogether a surprise: the blood on the floor had prepared me for something of the sort. But when another followed him—facing me, this one, with a dark, distorted face—I dropped the one I had caught and jumped back.

And as I jumped a third man came tumbling out after the others.

From behind me came a scream and a thud as the maid fainted. I wasn't feeling any too steady myself. I'm no sensitive plant, and I've looked at a lot of unlovely sights in my time, but for weeks afterward I could see those three dead men coming out of that clothespress to pile up at my feet: coming out slowly—almost deliberately—in a ghastly game of "follow your leader."

Seeing them, you couldn't doubt that they were really dead. Every detail of their falling, every detail of the heap in which they now lay, had a horrible certainty of lifelessness in it.

I turned to Stacey, who, deathly white himself, was keeping on his feet only by clinging to the foot of the brass bed.

"Get the woman out! Get doctors—police!"

I pulled the three dead bodies apart, laying them out in a grim row, faces up. Then I made a hasty examination of the room.

A soft hat, which fitted one of the dead men, lay in the center of the unruffled bed. The room key was in the door, on the inside. There was no blood in the room except what had leaked out of the clothespress, and the room showed no signs of having been the scene of a struggle.

The door to the bathroom was open. In the bottom of the bath tub was a shattered gin bottle, which, from the strength of the odor and the dampness of the tub, had been nearly full when broken. In one corner of the bathroom I found a small whisky glass, and another under the tub. Both were dry, clean, and odorless.

The inside of the clothespress door was stained with blood from the height of my shoulder to the floor, and two hats lay in the puddle of blood on the closet floor. Each of the hats fitted one of the dead men.

That was all. Three dead men, a broken gin bottle, blood.

Stacey returned presently with a doctor, and while the doctor was examining the dead men, the police detectives arrived.

The doctor's work was soon done.

"This man," he said, pointing to one of them, "was struck on the back of the head with a small blunt instrument, and then strangled. This one," pointing to another, "was simply strangled. And the third was stabbed in the back with a blade perhaps five inches long. They have been dead for about two hours—since noon or a little after."

The assistant manager identified two of the bodies. The man who had been stabbed—the first to fall out of the clothes-press—had arrived at the hotel three days before, registering as Tudor Ingraham of Washington, D.C., and had occupied room 915, three doors away.

The last man to fall out—the one who had been simply choked—was the occupant of this room. His name was Vincent Develyn. He was an insurance broker and had made the hotel his home since his wife's death, some four years before.

The third man had been seen in Develyn's company frequently, and one of the clerks remembered that they had come into the hotel together at about five minutes after twelve this day. Cards and letters in his pockets told us that he was Homer Ansley, a member of the law firm of Lankershim and Ansley, whose offices were in the Miles Building—next door to Develyn's office, in fact.

Develyn's pockets held between $150 and $200; Ansley's wallet contained more than $100; Ingraham's pockets yielded nearly $300, and in a money belt around his waist we found $2200 and two medium-sized unset diamonds. All three had watches—Develyn's was a valuable one—in their pockets, and Ingraham wore two rings, both of which were expensive ones. Ingraham's room key was in his pocket.

Beyond this money—whose presence would seem to indicate that robbery hadn't been the motive behind the three killings—we found nothing on any of their persons to throw the slightest light on the crime. Nor did the most thorough examination of both Ingraham's and Develyn's rooms teach us anything.

In Ingraham's room we found a dozen or more packs of carefully marked cards, some crooked dice, and an immense amount of data on racehorses. Also we found that he had a wife who lived on East Delavan Avenue in Buffalo, and a brother on Crutcher Street in Dallas; as well as a list of names and addresses that we carried off to investigate later. But nothing in either room pointed, even indirectly, at murder.

Phels, the police department Bertillon man, found a number of fingerprints in Develyn's room, but we couldn't tell whether they would be of any value or not until he had worked them up. Though Develyn and Ansley had apparently been strangled by hands, Phels was unable to get prints from either their necks or their collars.

The maid who had discovered the blood said that she had straightened up Develyn's room between ten and eleven that morning, but had not put fresh towels in the bathroom. It was for this purpose that she had gone to the room in the afternoon. She had found the door unlocked, with the key on the inside, and, as soon as she entered, had seen the blood and telephoned Stacey. She had seen no one in the corridor nearby as she entered the room.

She had straightened up Ingraham's room, she said, at a few minutes after one. She had gone there earlier—between 10:20 and 10:45—for that purpose, but Ingraham had not then left it.

The elevator man who had carried Ansley and Develyn up from the lobby at a few minutes after twelve remembered that they had been laughingly discussing their golf scores of the previous day during the ride. No one had seen anything suspicious in the hotel around the time at which the doctor had placed the murders. But that was to be expected.

The murderer could have left the room, closing the door behind him, and walked away secure in the knowledge that at noon a man in the corridors of the Montgomery would attract little attention. If he was staying at the hotel he would simply have gone to his room; if not, he would have either walked all the way down to the street, or down a floor or two and then caught an elevator.

None of the hotel employees had ever seen Ingraham and Develyn together. There was nothing to show that they had even the slightest acquaintance. Ingraham habitually stayed in his room until noon, and did not return to it until very late at night. Nothing was known of his affairs.

At the Miles Building we—that is, Marty O'Hara and George Dean of the police department homicide detail, and I—questioned Ansley's partner and Develyn's employees. Both Develyn and Ansley, it seemed, were ordinary men who led ordinary lives: lives that held neither dark spots nor queer kinks. Ansley was married and had two children; he lived on Lake Street. Both men had a sprinkling of relatives and friends scattered here and there through the country; and, so far as we could learn, their affairs were in perfect order.

They had left their offices this day to go to luncheon together, intending to visit Develyn's room first for a drink apiece from a bottle of gin someone coming from Australia had smuggled in to him.

"Well," O'Hara said, when we were on the street again, "this much is clear. If they went up to Develyn's room for a drink, it's a cinch that they were killed almost as soon as they got in the room. Those whisky glasses you found were dry and clean. Whoever turned the trick must have been waiting for them. I wonder about this fellow Ingraham."

"I'm wondering, too," I said. "Figuring it out from the positions I found them in when I opened the closet door, Ingraham sizes up as the key to the whole thing. Develyn was back against the wall, with Ansley in front of him, both facing the door. Ingraham was facing them, with his back to the door. The clothespress was just large enough for them to be packed in it— too small for any of them to slip down while the door was closed.

"Then there was no blood in the room except what had come from the clothespress. Ingraham, with that gaping slit in his back, couldn't have been stabbed until he was inside the closet, or he'd have bled elsewhere. He was standing close to the other men when he was knifed, and whoever knifed him closed the door quickly afterward.

"Now, why should he have been standing in such a position? Do you dope it out that he and another killed the two friends, and that while he was stowing their bodies in the closet his accomplice finished him off?"

"Maybe," Dean said.

AND THAT "MAYBE" was still as far as we had gone three days later.

We had sent and received bales of telegrams, having relatives and acquaintances of the dead men interviewed; and we had found nothing that seemed to have any bearing upon their deaths. Nor had we found the slightest connecting link between Ingraham and the other two. We had traced those other two back step by step almost to their cradles. We had accounted for every minute of their time since Ingraham had arrived in San Francisco—thoroughly enough to convince us that neither of them had met Ingraham.

Ingraham, we had learned, was a book-maker and all around crooked gambler. His wife and he had separated, but were on good terms. Some fifteen years before, he had been convicted of "assault with intent to kill" in Newark, N.J., and had served two years in the state prison. But the man he had assaulted— one John Pellow—had died of pneumonia in Omaha in 1914.

Ingraham had come to San Francisco for the purpose of opening a gambling club, and all our investigations had tended to show that his activities while in the city had been toward that end alone.

The fingerprints Phels had secured had all turned out to belong to Stacey, the maid, the police detectives, or myself. In short, we had found nothing!

So much for our attempts to learn the motive behind the three murders.

We now dropped that angle and settled down to the detail-studying, patience-taxing grind of picking up the murderer's trail. From any crime to its author there is a trail. It may be—as in this case—obscure; but, since matter cannot move without disturbing other matter along its path, there always is—there must be—a trail of some sort. And finding and following such trails is what a detective is paid to do.

In the case of a murder it is possible sometimes to take a short-cut to the end of the trail, by first finding the motive. A knowledge of the motive often reduces the field of possibilities; sometimes points directly to the guilty one. It is on this account that murderers are, as a rule, more easily apprehended than any other class of criminals.

But a knowledge of the motive isn't indispensable—quite a few murder mysteries are solved without its help. And in a fair proportion—say, ten to twenty per cent—of cases where men are convicted justly of murder, the motive isn't clearly shown even at the last, and sometimes is hardly guessed at.

So far, all we knew about the motive in the particular case we were dealing with was that it hadn't been robbery; unless something we didn't know about had been stolen—something of sufficient value to make the murderer scorn the money in his victims' pockets.

We hadn't altogether neglected the search for the murderer's trail, of course, but—being human—we had devoted most of our attention to trying to find a short-cut. Now we set out to find our man, or men, regardless of what had urged him or them to commit the crimes.

Of the people who had been registered at the hotel on the day of the killing there were nine men of whose innocence we hadn't found a reasonable amount of proof. Four of these were still at the hotel, and only one of that four interested us very strongly. That one—a big rawboned man of forty-five or fifty, who had registered as J.J. Cooper of Anaconda, Montana—

wasn't, we had definitely established, really a mining man, as he pretended to be. And our telegraphic communications with Anaconda failed to show that he was known there. Therefore we were having him shadowed—with few results.

Five men of the nine had departed since the murders; three of them leaving forwarding addresses with the mail clerk. Gilbert Jacquemart had occupied room 946 and had ordered his mail forwarded to him at a Los Angeles hotel. W.F. Salway, who had occupied room 1022, had given instructions that his mail be readdressed to a number on Clark Street in Chicago. Ross Orrett, room 609, had asked to have his mail sent to him care of General Delivery at the local post office.

Jacquemart had arrived at the hotel two days before, and had left on the afternoon of the murders. Salway had arrived the day before the murders and had left the day after them. Orrett had arrived on the day of the murders and had left the following day.

Sending telegrams to have the first two found and investigated, I went after Orrett myself. A musical comedy named "What For?" as being widely advertised just then with gaily printed plum-colored hand-bills. I got one of them and, at a stationery store, an envelope to match, and mailed it to Orrett at the Montgomery Hotel. There are concerns that make a practice of securing the names of arrivals at the principal hotels and mailing them advertisements. I trusted that Orrett, knowing this, wouldn't be suspicious when my gaudy envelope, forwarded from the hotel, reached him through the General Delivery window.

Dick Foley—the Agency's shadow specialist—planted himself in the post office, to loiter around with an eye on the

"O" window until he saw my plum-colored envelope passed out, and then to shadow the receiver.

I spent the next day trying to solve the mysterious J.J. Cooper's game, but he was still a puzzle when I knocked off that night.

At a little before five the following morning Dick Foley dropped into my room on his way home to wake me up and tell me what he had done for himself.

"This Orrett baby is our meat!" he said. "Picked him up when he got his mail yesterday afternoon. Got another letter besides yours. Got an apartment on Van Ness Avenue. Took it the day after the killing, under the name of B.T. Quinn. Packing a gun under his left arm—there's that sort of a bulge there. Just went home to bed. Been visiting all the dives in North Beach. Who do you think he's hunting for?

"Who?"

"Guy Cudner."

That was news! This Guy Cudner, alias "The Darkman," was the most dangerous bird on the Coast, if not in the country. He had only been nailed once, but if he had been convicted of all the crimes that everybody knew he had committed he'd have needed half a dozen lives to crowd his sentences into, besides another half-dozen to carry to the gallows. However, he had decidedly the right sort of backing—enough to buy him everything he needed in the way of witnesses, alibis, even juries, and—so the talk went—an occasional judge.

I don't know what went wrong with his support that one time he was convicted up North and sent over for a one-to-fourteen-year hitch; but it adjusted itself promptly, for the ink was hardly dry on the press notices of his conviction before he was loose again on parole.

"Is Cudner in town?"

"Don't know," Dick said, "but this Orrett, or Quinn, or whatever his name is, is surely hunting for him. In Rick's place, at 'Wop' Healey's and at Pigatti's. 'Porky' Grout tipped me off. Says Orrett doesn't know Cudner by sight, but is trying to find him. Porky didn't know what he wants with him."

This Porky Grout was a dirty little rat who would sell out his family—if he ever had one—for the price of a flop. But with these lads who play both sides of the game it's always a question of which side they're playing when you think they're playing yours.

"Think Porky was coming clean?" I asked.

"Chances are—but you can't gamble on him."

"Is Orrett acquainted here?"

"Doesn't seem to be. Knows where he wants to go but has to ask how to get there. Hasn't spoken to anybody that seemed to know him."

"What's he like?"

"Not the kind of egg you'd want to tangle with offhand, if you ask me. He and Cudner would make a good pair. They don't look alike. This egg is tall and slim, but he's built right—those fast, smooth muscles. Face is sharp without being thin, if you get me. I mean all the lines in it are straight. No curves. Chin, nose, mouth, eyes—all straight, sharp lines and angles. Looks like the kind of egg we know Cudner is. Make a good pair. Dresses well and doesn't look like a rowdy—but harder than hell! A big game hunter! Our meat, I bet you!"

"It doesn't look bad," I agreed. "He came to the hotel the morning of the day the men were killed, and checked out the next morning. He packs a rod, and changed his name after he left. And now he's paired off with The Darkman. It doesn't look bad at all!"

"I'm telling you," Dick said, "this fellow looks like three killings wouldn't disturb his rest any. I wonder where Cudner fits in."

"I can't guess. But, if he and Orrett haven't connected yet, then Cudner wasn't in on the murders; but he may give us the answer."

Then I jumped out of bed.

"I'm going to gamble on Porky's dope being on the level! How would you describe Cudner?"

"You know him better than I do."

"Yes, but how would you describe him to me if I didn't know him?"

"A little fat guy with a red forked scar on his left cheek. What's the idea?"

"It's a good one," I admitted. "That scar makes all the difference in the world. If he didn't have it and you were to describe him you'd go into all the details of his appearance. But he has it, so you simply say, 'A little fat guy with a red forked scar on his left cheek.' It's a ten to one that that's just how he has been described to Orrett. I don't look like Cudner, but I'm his size and build, and with a scar on my face Orrett will fall for me."

"What then?"

"There's no telling; but I ought to be able to learn a lot if I can get Orrett talking to me as Cudner. It's worth a try anyway."

"You can't get away with it—not in San Francisco. Cudner is too well known."

"What difference does that make, Dick? Orrett is the only one I want to fool. If he takes me for Cudner, well and good.

If he doesn't, still well and good. I won't force myself on him."

"How are you going to fake the scar?"

"Easy! We have pictures of Cudner, showing the scar, in the criminal gallery. I'll get some collodion—it's sold in drug stores under several trade names for putting on cuts and scratches—color it, and imitate Cudner's scar on my cheek. It dries with a shiny surface and, put on thick, will stand out just enough to look like an old scar."

IT WAS A little after eleven the following night when Dick telephoned me that Orrett was in Pigatti's place, on Pacific Street, and apparently settled there for some little while. My scar already painted on, I jumped into a taxi and within a few minutes was talking to Dick, around the corner from Pigatti's.

"He's sitting at the last table back on the left side. And he was alone when I came out. You can't miss him. He's the only egg in the joint with a clean collar."

"You better stick outside—half a block or so away—with the taxi," I told Dick. "Maybe brother Orrett and I will leave together and I'd just as leave have you standing by in case things break wrong."

Pigatti's place is a long, narrow, low-ceilinged cellar, always dim with smoke. Down the middle runs a narrow strip of bare floor for dancing. The rest of the floor is covered with closely packed tables, whose cloths are always soiled; and the management hasn't yet verified the rumor that the country has gone dry.

Most of the tables were occupied when I came in, and half a dozen couples were dancing. Few of the faces to be seen were strangers to the morning "line up" at police headquarters.

Peering through the smoke, I saw Orrett at once, seated alone in a far corner, looking at the dancers with the set blank face of one who masks an all-seeing watchfulness. I walked down the other side of the room and crossed the strip of dance-floor directly under a light, so that the scar might be clearly visible to him. Then I selected a vacant table not far from his, and sat down facing him.

Ten minutes passed while he pretended an interest in the dancers and I affected a thoughtful stare at the dirty cloth on my table; but neither of us missed so much as a flicker of the other's lids.

His eyes—grey eyes that were pale without being shallow, with black needle-point pupils—met mine after a while in a cold, steady, inscrutable stare; and, very slowly, he got to his feet. One hand—his right—in a side pocket of his dark coat, he walked straight across to my table and sat down opposite me.

"Cudner?"

"Looking for me, I hear," I replied, trying to match the icy smoothness of his voice, as I was matching the steadiness of his gaze.

He had sat down with his left side turned slightly toward me, which put his right arm in not too cramped a position for straight shooting from the pocket that still held his hand.

"You were looking for me, too."

I didn't know what the correct answer to that would be, so I just grinned. But the grin didn't come from my heart. I had, I realized, made a mistake—one that might cost me something before we were done. This bird wasn't hunting for Cudner as a friend, as I had carelessly assumed, but was on the war path.

I saw those three dead men falling out of the closet in room 906!

My gun was inside the waist-band of my trousers, where I could get it quickly, but his was in his hand. So I was careful to keep my own hands motionless on the edge of the table, while I widened my grin.

His eyes were changing now, and the more I looked at them the less I liked them. The grey in them had darkened and grown duller, and the pupils were larger, and white crescents were showing beneath the gray. Twice before I had looked into eyes such as these—and I hadn't forgotten what they meant—the eyes of the congenital killer!

"Suppose you speak your piece," I suggested after a while.

But he wasn't to be beguiled into conversation. He shook his head a mere fraction of an inch and the corners of his compressed mouth dropped down a trifle. The white crescents of eyeballs were growing broader, pushing the grey circles up under the upper lids.

It was coming! And there was no use waiting for it!

I drove a foot at his shins under the table, and at the same time pushed the table into his lap and threw myself across it. The bullet from his gun went off to one side. Another bullet— not from his gun—thudded into the table that was upended between us.

I had him by the shoulders when the second shot from behind took him in the left arm, just below my hand. I let go then and fell away, rolling over against the wall and twisting around to face the direction from which the bullets were coming.

I twisted around just in time to see—jerking out of sight behind a corner of the passage that gave to a small dining room—Guy Cudner's scarred face. And as it disappeared a bullet from Orrett's gun splattered the plaster from the wall where it had been.

I grinned at the thought of what must be going on in Orrett's head as he lay sprawled out on the floor confronted by two Cudners. But he took a shot at me just then and I stopped grinning. Luckily, he had to twist around to fire at me, putting his weight on his wounded arm, and the pain made him wince, spoiling his aim.

Before he had adjusted himself more comfortably I had scrambled on hands and knees to Pigaitti's kitchen door—only a few feet away—and had myself safely tucked out of range around an angle in the wall; all but my eyes and the top of my head, which I risked so that I might see what went on.

Orrett was now ten or twelve feet from me, lying flat on the floor, facing Cudner, with a gun in his hand and another on the floor beside him.

Across the room, perhaps thirty feet away, Cudner was show-ing himself around his protecting corner at brief intervals to exchange shots with the man on the floor, occasionally sending one my way. We had the place to ourselves. There were four exits, and the rest of Pigatti's customers had used them all.

I had my gun out, but I was playing a waiting game. Cudner, I figured, had been tipped off to Orrett's search for him and had arrived on the scene with no mistaken idea of the other's attitude. Just what there was between them and what bearing it had on the Montgomery murders was a mystery to me, but I didn't try to solve it now. I kept away from the bullets that were flying around as best I could and waited.

They were firing in unison. Cudner would show around his corner, both men's weapons would spit, and he would duck out of sight again. Orrett was bleeding about the head now and one of his legs sprawled crookedly behind him. I couldn't determine whether Cudner had been hit or not.

Each had fired eight, or perhaps nine, shots when Cudner suddenly jumped out into full view, pumping the gun in his left hand as fast as its mechanism would go, the gun in his right hand hanging at his side. Orrett had changed guns, and was on his knees now, his fresh weapon keeping pace with his enemy's.

That couldn't last!

Cudner dropped his left-hand gun, and, as he raised the other, he sagged forward and went down on one knee. Orrett stopped firing abruptly and fell over on his back—spread out full-length. Cudner fired once more—wildly, into the ceiling—and pitched down on his face.

I sprang to Orrett's side and kicked both of his guns away. He was lying still but his eyes were open.

"Are you Cudner, or was he?"

"He."

"Good!" he said, and closed his eyes.

I crossed to where Cudner lay and turned him over on his back. His chest was literally shot to pieces.

His thick lips worked, and I put my ear down to them.

"I get him?"

"Yes," I lied, "he's already cold."

His dying face twisted into a triumphant grin.

"Sorry... three in hotel..." he gasped hoarsely. "Mistake... wrong room... got one... had to... other two... protect myself... I...."

He shuddered and died.

A WEEK LATER the hospital people let me talk to Orrett. I told him what Cudner had said before he died.

"That's the way I doped it out," Orrett said from out of the depths of the bandages in which he was swathed. "That's why I moved and changed my name the next day."

"I suppose you've got it nearly figured out by now," he said after a while.

"No," I confessed, "I haven't. I've an idea what it was all about but I could stand having a few details cleared up."

"I'm sorry I can't clear them up for you, but I've got to cover myself up. I'll tell you a story, though, and it may help you. Once upon a time there was a high-class crook—what the newspapers call a Master Mind. Came a day when he found he had accumulated enough money to give up the game and settle down as an honest man.

"But he had two lieutenants—one in New York and one in San Francisco—and they were the only men in the world who knew he was a crook. And, besides that, he was afraid of both of them. So he thought he'd rest easier if they were out of the way. And it happened that neither of these lieutenants had ever seen the other.

"So this Master Mind convinced each of them that the other was double-crossing him and would have to be bumped off for the safety of all concerned. And both of them fell for it. The New Yorker went to San Francisco to get the other, and the San Franciscan was told that the New Yorker would arrive on such-and-such a day and would stay at such-and-such a hotel.

"The Master Mind figured that there was an even chance of both men passing out when they met—and he was nearly right at that. But he was sure that one would die, and then, even if the other missed hanging, there would only be one man left for him to dispose of later."

There weren't as many details in the story as I would have liked to have, but it explained a lot.

"How do you figure out Cudner's getting into the wrong room?" I asked.

"That was funny! Maybe it happened like this: My room was 609 and the killing was done in 906. Suppose Cudner went to the hotel on the day he knew I was due and took a quick slant at the register. He wouldn't want to be seen looking at it if he could avoid it, so he didn't turn it around, but flashed a look at it as it lay—facing the desk.

"When you read numbers of three figures upside-down you have to transpose them in your head to get them straight. Like 123. You'd get that 3-2-1, and then turn them around in your head. That's what Cudner did with mine. He was keyed up, of course, thinking of the job ahead of him, and he overlooked the fact that 609 upside-down still reads 609 just the same. So he turned it around and made it 906—Develyn's room."

"That's how I doped it," I said, "and I reckon it's about right. And then he looked at the key-rack and saw that 906 wasn't there. So he thought he might just as well get his job done right then, when he could roam the hotel corridors without attracting attention. Of course, he may have gone up to the room before Ansley and Develyn came in and waited for them, but I doubt it.

"I think it more likely that he simply happened to arrive at the hotel a few minutes after they had come in. Ansley was probably alone in the room when Cudner opened the unlocked door and came in—Develyn being in the bathroom getting the glasses.

"Ansley was about your size and age, and close enough in appearance to fit a rough description of you. Cudner went for him, and then Develyn, hearing the scuffle, dropped the bottle and glasses and rushed out, and got his.

"Cudner, being the sort he was, would figure that two murders were no worse than one, and he wouldn't want to leave any witnesses around.

"And that is probably how Ingraham got into it. He was passing on his way from his room to the elevator and perhaps heard the racket and investigated. And Cudner put a gun in his face and made him stow the two bodies in the clothespress. And then he stuck his knife in Ingraham's back and slammed the door on him. That's about the—"

An indignant nurse descended on me from behind and ordered me out of the room, accusing me of getting her patient excited.

Orrett stopped me as I turned to go.

"Keep your eye on the New York dispatches," he said, "and maybe you'll get the rest of the story. It's not over yet. Nobody has anything on me out here. That shooting in Pigatti's was self-defense so far as I'm concerned. And as soon as I'm on my feet again and can get back East there's going to be a Master Mind holding a lot of lead. That's a promise!"

I believed him.

The Tenth Clue

There were enough clues in this crime to give Mr. Hammett's nameless detective a year or so of work. But solving a mystery in that length of time didn't appeal to him. He wanted faster action—and he got it in good measure. So will you if you begin this entertaining novelette.

1

"Do You Know... Emil Bonfils?"

"MR. LEOPOLD GANTVOORT is not at home," the servant who opened the door said, "but his son, Mr. Charles, is—if you wish to see him."

"No. I had an appointment with Mr. Leopold Gantvoort for nine or a little after. It's just nine now. No doubt he'll be back soon. I'll wait."

"Very well, sir."

He stepped aside for me to enter the house, took my overcoat and hat, guided me to a room on the second floor—Gantvoort's library—and left me. I picked up a magazine from the stack on the table, pulled an ash tray over beside me, and made myself comfortable.

An hour passed. I stopped reading and began to grow impatient. Another hour passed—and I was fidgeting.

A clock somewhere below had begun to strike eleven when a young man of twenty-five or -six, tall and slender, with remarkably white skin and very dark hair and eyes, came into the room.

"My father hasn't returned yet," he said. "It's too bad that you should have been kept waiting all this time. Isn't there anything I could do for you? I am Charles Gantvoort."

"No, thank you." I got up from my chair, accepting the courteous dismissal. "I'll get in touch with him tomorrow."

"I'm sorry," he murmured, and we moved toward the door together.

As we reached the hall an extension telephone in one corner of the room we were leaving buzzed softly, and I halted in the doorway while Charles Gantvoort went over to answer it.

His back was toward me as he spoke into the instrument.

"Yes. Yes. Yes!"—sharply—*"What?* Yes"—very weakly—"Yes."

He turned slowly around and faced me with a face that was gray and tortured, with wide shocked eyes and gaping mouth—the telephone still in his hand.

"Father," he gasped, "is dead—killed!"

"Where? How?"

"I don't know. That was the police. They want me to come down at once."

He straightened his shoulders with an effort, pulling himself together, put down the telephone, and his face fell into less strained lines.

"You will pardon my—"

"Mr. Gantvoort," I interrupted his apology, "I am connected with the Continental Detective Agency. Your father called up this afternoon and asked that a detective be sent to see him tonight. He said his life had been threatened. He hadn't definitely engaged us, however, so unless you—"

"Certainly! You are employed! If the police haven't already caught the murderer I want you to do everything possible to catch him."

"All right! Let's get down to headquarters."

Neither of us spoke during the ride to the Hall of Justice. Gantvoort bent over the wheel of his car, sending it through the streets at a terrific speed. There were several questions that needed answers, but all his attention was required for his driving if he was to maintain the pace at which he was driving without piling us into something. So I didn't disturb him, but hung on and kept quiet.

Half a dozen police detectives were waiting for us when we reached the detective bureau. O'Gar—a bullet-headed detective-sergeant who dresses like the village constable in a movie, wide-brimmed black hat and all, but who isn't to be put out of the reckoning on that account—was in charge of the investigation. He and I had worked on two or three jobs together before, and hit it off excellently.

He led us into one of the small offices below the assembly room. Spread out on the flat top of a desk there were a dozen or more objects.

"I want you to look these things over carefully," the detective-sergeant told Gantvoort, "and pick out the ones that belonged to your father."

"But where is he?"

"Do this first," O'Gar insisted, "and then you can see him."

I looked at the things on the table while Charles Gantvoort made his selections. An empty jewel case; a memoranda book; three letters in slit envelopes that were addressed to the dead man; some other papers; a bunch of keys; a fountain pen; two white linen handkerchiefs; two pistol cartridges; a gold watch, with a gold knife and a gold pencil attached to it by a gold-and-platinum chain; two black leather wallets, one of them very new and the other worn; some money, both paper and silver; and a small portable typewriter, bent and twisted, and matted with hair and blood. Some of the other things were smeared with blood and some were clean.

Gantvoort picked out the watch and its attachments, the

keys, the fountain pen, the memoranda book, the handker-chiefs, the letters and other papers, and the older wallet.

"These were father's," he told us. "I've never seen any of the others before. I don't know, of course, how much money he had with him tonight, so I can't say how much of this is his."

"You're sure none of the rest of this stuff was his?" O'Gar asked.

"I don't think so, but I'm not sure. Whipple could tell you." He turned to me. "He's the man who let you in tonight. He looked after father, and he'd know positively whether any of these other things belonged to him or not."

One of the police detectives went to the telephone to tell Whipple to come down immediately.

I resumed the questioning.

"Is anything that your father usually carried with him miss-ing? Anything of value?"

"Not that I know of. All of the things that he might have been expected to have with him seem to be here."

"At what time tonight did he leave the house?"

"Before seven-thirty. Possibly as early as seven."

"Know where he was going?"

"He didn't tell me, but I supposed he was going to call on Miss Dexter."

The faces of the police detectives brightened, and their eyes grew sharp. I suppose mine did, too. There are many, many murders with never a woman in them anywhere; but seldom a very conspicuous killing.

"Who's this Miss Dexter?" O'Gar took up the inquiry.

"She's well—" Charles Gantvoort hesitated. "Well, father was on very friendly terms with her and her brother. He usually called on them—on her several evenings a week. In fact, I suspected that he intended marrying her."

"Who and what is she?"

"Father became acquainted with them six or seven months ago. I've met them several times, but don't know them very well. Miss Dexter—Creda is her given name—is about twenty-three years old, I should judge, and her brother Madden is four or five years older. He is in New York now, or on his way there, to transact some business for father."

"Did your father tell you he was going to marry her?" O'Gar hammered away at the woman angle.

"No; but it was pretty obvious that he was very much—ah—infatuated. We had some words over it a few days ago—last week. Not a quarrel, you understand, but words. From the way he talked I feared that he meant to marry her."

"What do you mean 'feared'?" O'Gar snapped at that word.

Charles Gantvoort's pale face flushed a little, and he cleared his throat embarrassedly.

"I don't want to put the Dexters in a bad light to you. I don't think—I'm sure they had nothing to do with father's—with this. But I didn't care especially for them—didn't like them. I thought they were—well—fortune hunters, perhaps. Father wasn't fabulously wealthy, but he had considerable means. And, while he wasn't feeble, still he was past fifty-seven, old enough for me to feel that Creda Dexter was more interested in his money than in him."

"How about your father's will?"

"The last one of which I have any knowledge—drawn up two or three years ago—left everything to my wife and me jointly. Father's attorney, Mr. Murray Abernathy, could tell you if there was a later will, but I hardly think there was."

"Your father had retired from business, hadn't he?"

"Yes; he turned his import and export business over to me about a year ago. He had quite a few investments scattered around, but he wasn't actively engaged in the management of any concern."

O'Gar tilted his village constable hat back and scratched his bullet head reflectively for a moment. Then he looked at me.

"Anything else you want to ask?"

"Yes. Mr. Gantvoort, do you know, or did you ever hear your father or anyone else speak of an Emil Bonfils?"

"No."

"Did your father ever tell you that he had received a threatening letter? Or that he had been shot at on the street?"

"No."

"Was your father in Paris in 1902?"

"Very likely. He used to go abroad every year up until the time of his retirement from business."

2

"That's Something!"

O'GAR AND I took Gantvoort around to the morgue to see his father, then. The dead man wasn't pleasant to look at, even to O'Gar and me, who hadn't known him except by sight. I remembered him as a small wiry man, always smartly tailored, and with a brisk springiness that was far younger than his years.

He lay now with the top of his head beaten into a red and pulpy mess.

We left Gantvoort at the morgue and set out afoot for the Hall of Justice.

"What's this deep stuff you're pulling about Emil Bonfils and Paris in 1902?" the detective-sergeant asked as soon as we were out in the street.

"This: the dead man phoned the Agency this afternoon and said he had received a threatening letter from an Emil Bonfils with whom he had had trouble in Paris in 1902. He also said that Bonfils had shot at him the previous evening, in the street. He wanted somebody to come around and see him about it tonight. And he said that under no circumstances were the police to be let in on it—that he'd rather have Bonfils get him than have the trouble made public. That's all he would say over the phone; and that's how I happened to be on hand when Charles Gantvoort was notified of his father's death."

O'Gar stopped in the middle of the sidewalk and whistled softly.

"That's something!" he exclaimed. "Wait till we get back to headquarters—I'll show you something."

Whipple was waiting in the assembly room when we arrived at headquarters. His face at first glance was as smooth and mask-like as when he had admitted me to the house on Russian Hill earlier in the evening. But beneath his perfect servant's manner he was twitching and trembling.

We took him into the little office where we had questioned Charles Gantvoort.

Whipple verified all that the dead man's son had told us. He was positive that neither the typewriter, the jewel case, the two cartridges, or the newer wallet had belonged to Gantvoort.

We couldn't get him to put his opinion of the Dexters in words, but that he disapproved of them was easily seen. Miss Dexter, he said, had called up on the telephone three times this night at about eight o'clock, at nine, and at nine-thirty. She had asked for Mr. Leopold Gantvoort each time, but she had left no message. Whipple was of the opinion that she was expecting Gantvoort, and he had not arrived.

He knew nothing, he said, of Emil Bonfils or of any threatening letters. Gantvoort had been out the previous night from eight until midnight. Whipple had not seen him closely enough when he came home to say whether he seemed excited or not. Gantvoort usually carried about a hundred dollars in his pockets.

"Is there anything that you know of that Gantvoort had on his person tonight which isn't among these things on the desk?" O'Gar asked.

"No, sir. Everything seems to be here—watch and chain, money, memorandum book, wallet, keys, handkerchiefs, fountain pen—everything that I know of."

"Did Charles Gantvoort go out tonight?"

"No, sir. He and Mrs. Gantvoort were at home all evening."

"Positive?"

Whipple thought a moment.

"Yes, sir, I'm fairly certain. But I know Mrs. Gantvoort wasn't out. To tell the truth, I didn't see Mr. Charles from about eight o'clock until he came downstairs with this gentleman"—pointing to me—"at eleven. But I'm fairly certain he was home all evening. I think Mrs. Gantvoort said he was."

Then O'Gar put another question—one that puzzled me at the time.

"What kind of collar buttons did Mr. Gantvoort wear?"

"You mean Mr. Leopold?"

"Yes."

"Plain gold ones, made all in one piece. They had a London jeweler's mark on them."

"Would you know them if you saw them?"

"Yes, sir."

We let Whipple go home then.

"Don't you think," I suggested when O'Gar and I were alone with this desk-load of evidence that didn't mean anything at all to me yet, "it's time you were loosening up and telling me what's what?"

"I guess so—listen! A man named Lagerquist, a grocer, was driving through Golden Gate Park tonight, and passed a machine standing on a dark road, with its lights out. He thought there was something funny about the way the man in it was sitting at the wheel, so he told the first patrolman he met about it.

"The patrolman investigated and found Gantvoort sitting

at the wheel—dead—with his head smashed in and this dingus"—putting one hand on the bloody typewriter—"on the seat beside him. That was at a quarter of ten. The doc says Gantvoort was killed—his skull crushed—with this typewriter.

"The dead man's pockets, we found, had all been turned inside out; and all this stuff on the desk, except this new wallet, was scattered about in the car—some of it on the floor and some on the seats. This money was there too—nearly a hundred dollars of it. Among the papers was this."

He handed me a sheet of white paper upon which the following had been typewritten:

L. F. G.—

I want what is mine. 6,000 miles and 21 years are not enough to hide you from the victim of your treachery. I mean to have what you stole.

E. B.

"L.F.G. could be Leopold F. Gantvoort," I said. "And E.B. could be Emil Bonfils. Twenty-one years is the time from 1902 to 1923, and 6,000 miles is, roughly, the distance between Paris and San Francisco."

I laid the letter down and picked up the jewel case. It was a black imitation leather one, lined with white satin, and unmarked in any way.

Then I examined the cartridges. There were two of them, S.W. .45-caliber, and deep crosses had been cut in their soft noses—an old trick that makes the bullet spread out like a saucer when it hits.

"These in the car, too?"

"Yep—and this."

From a vest pocket O'Gar produced a short tuft of blond hair—hairs between an inch and two inches in length. They had been cut off, not pulled out by the roots.

"Any more?"

There seemed to be an endless stream of things.

He picked up the new wallet from the desk—the one that both Whipple and Charles Gantvoort had said did not belong to the dead man—and slid it over to me.

"That was found in the road, three or four feet from the car."

It was of a cheap quality, and had neither manufacturer's name nor owner's initials on it. In it were two ten-dollar bills, three small newspaper clippings, and a typewritten list of six names and addresses, headed by Gantvoort's.

The three clippings were apparently from the Personal columns of three different newspapers—the type wasn't the same—and they read:

GEORGE—

   Everything is fixed. Don't wait too long.

                 D.D.D.

R.H.T.—

   They do not answer.

                 FLO.

CAPPY.—

   Twelve on the dot and look sharp.

                 BINGO.

The names and addresses on the typewritten list, under Ganvoort's, were:

Quincy Heathcote, 1223 S. Jason Street, Denver; B.D. Thornton, 96 Hughes Circle, Dallas; Luther G. Randall, 615 Columbia Street, Portsmouth; J.H. Boyd Willis, 4544 Harvard Street, Boston; Hannah Hindmarsh, 218 E. 79th Street, Cleveland.

"What else?" I asked when I had studied these.

The detective-sergeant's supply hadn't been exhausted yet.

"The dead man's collar buttons—both front and back—had been taken out, though his collar and tie were still in place. And his left shoe was gone. We hunted high and low all around, but didn't find either shoe or collar buttons."

"Is that all?"

I was prepared for anything now.

"What the hell do you want?" he growled. "Ain't that enough?"

"How about fingerprints?"

"Nothing stirring! All we found belonged to the dead man."

"How about the machine he was found in?"

"A coupé belonging to a Doctor Wallace Girargo. He phoned in at six this evening that it had been stolen from near the corner of McAllister and Polk Streets. We're checking up on him—but I think he's all right."

The things that Whipple and Charles Gantvoort had identified as belonging to the dead man told us nothing. We went over them carefully, but to no advantage. The memoranda book contained many entries, but they all seemed totally foreign to the murder. The letters were quite as irrelevant.

The serial number of the typewriter with which the murder had been committed had been removed, we found—apparently filed out of the frame.

"Well, what do you think?" O'Gar asked when we had given up our examination of our clues and sat back burning tobacco.

"I think we want to find Monsieur Emil Bonfils."

"It wouldn't hurt to do that," he grunted. "I guess our best bet is to get in touch with these five people on the list with Gantvoort's name. Suppose that's a murder list? That this Bonfils is out to get all of them?"

"Maybe. We'll get hold of them anyway. Maybe we'll find that some of them have already been killed. But whether they have been killed or are to be killed or not, it's a cinch they have some connection with this affair. I'll get off a batch of telegrams to the Agency's branches, having the names on the list taken care of. I'll try to have the three clippings traced, too."

O'Gar looked at his watch and yawned.

"It's after four. What say we knock off and get some sleep? I'll leave word for the department's expert to compare the typewriter with that letter signed E.B. and with that list to see if they were written on it. I guess they were, but we'll make sure. I'll have the park searched all around where we found Gantvoort as soon as it gets light enough to see, and maybe the missing shoe and the collar buttons will be found. And I'll have a couple of the boys out calling on all the typewriter shops in the city to see if they can get a line on this one."

I stopped at the nearest telegraph office and got off a wad of messages. Then I went home to dream of nothing even remotely connected with crime or the detecting business.

3

"A Sleek Kitten That Dame!"

AT ELEVEN O'CLOCK that same morning, when, brisk and fresh with five hours' sleep under my belt, I arrived at the police detective bureau, I found O'Gar slumped down at his desk, staring dazedly at a black shoe, half a dozen collar buttons, a rusty flat key, and a rumpled newspaper—all lined up before him.

"What's all this? Souvenir of your wedding?"

"Might as well be." His voice was heavy with disgust. "Listen to this: one of the porters of the Seamen's National Bank found a package in the vestibule when he started cleaning up this morning. It was this shoe—Gantvoort's missing one—wrapped in this sheet of a five-day-old *Philadelphia Record,* and with these collar buttons and this old key in it. The heel of the shoe, you'll notice, has been pried off, and is still missing. Whipple identifies it all right, as well as two of the collar buttons, but he never saw the key before. These other four collar buttons are new, and common gold-rolled ones. The key don't look like it had had much use for a long time. What do you make of all that?"

I couldn't make anything out of it.

"How did the porter happen to turn the stuff in?"

"Oh, the whole story was in the morning papers—all about the missing shoe and collar buttons and all."

"What did you learn about the typewriter?" I asked.

"The letter and the list were written with it, right enough; but we haven't been able to find where it came from yet. We checked up the doc who owns the coupé, and he's in the clear. We accounted for all his time last night. Lagerquist, the grocer who found Gantvoort, seems to be all right, too. What did you do?"

"Haven't had any answers to the wires I sent last night. I dropped in at the Agency on my way down this morning, and got four operatives out covering the hotels and looking up all the people named Bonfils they can find—there are two or three families by that name listed in the directory. Also I sent our New York branch a wire to have the steamship records searched to see if an Emil Bonfils had arrived recently; and I put a cable through to our Paris correspondent to see what he could dig up over there."

"I guess we ought to see Gantvoort's lawyer—Abernathy—and that Dexter woman before we do anything else," the detective-sergeant said.

"I guess so," I agreed, "let's tackle the lawyer first. He's the most important one, the way things now stand."

Murray Abernathy, attorney-at-law, was a long, stringy, slow-spoken old gentleman who still clung to starched-bosom shirts. He was too full of what he thought were professional ethics to give us as much help as we had expected; but by letting him talk—letting him ramble along in his own way—we did get a little information from him. What we got amounted to this:

The dead man and Creda Dexter had intended being married the coming Wednesday. His son and her brother were both opposed to the marriage, it seemed, so Gantvoort and the woman had planned to be married secretly in Oakland, and catch a boat for the Orient that same afternoon; figuring that by the time their lengthy honeymoon was over they could return to a son and brother who had become resigned to the marriage.

A new will had been drawn up, leaving half of Gantvoort's estate to his new wife and half to his son and daughter-in-law. But the new will had not been signed yet, and Creda Dexter knew it had not been signed. She knew—and this was one of the few points upon which Abernathy would make a positive statement—that under the old will, still in force, everything went to Charles Gantvoort and his wife.

The Gantvoort estate, we estimated from Abernathy's round-about statements and allusions, amounted to about a million and a half in cash value. The attorney had never heard of Emil Bonfils, he said, and had never heard of any threats or attempts at murder directed toward the dead man. He knew nothing—or would tell us nothing—that threw any light upon the nature of the thing that the threatening letter had accused the dead man of stealing.

From Abernathy's office we went to Creda Dexter's apartment, in a new and expensively elegant building only a few minutes' walk from the Gantvoort residence.

Creda Dexter was a small woman in her early twenties. The first thing you noticed about her were her eyes. They were large and deep and the color of amber, and their pupils were never at rest. Continuously they changed size, expanded and contracted—slowly at times, suddenly at others—ranging incessantly from the size of pinheads to an extent that threatened to blot out the amber irises.

With the eyes for a guide, you discovered that she was pronouncedly feline throughout. Her every movement was the slow, smooth, sure one of a cat; and the contours of her rather pretty face, the shape of her mouth, her small nose, the set of her eyes, the swelling of her brows, were all cat-like. And the effect was heightened by the way she wore her hair, which was thick and tawny.

"Mr. Gantvoort and I," she told us after the preliminary explanations had been disposed of, "were to have been married the day after tomorrow. His son and daughter-in-law were both opposed to the marriage, as was my brother Madden. They all seemed to think that the difference between our ages was too great. So to avoid any unpleasantness, we had planned to be married quietly and then go abroad for a year or more, feeling sure that they would all have forgotten their grievances by the time we returned.

"That was why Mr. Gantvoort persuaded Madden to go to New York. He had some business there—something to do with the disposal of his interest in a steel mill—so he used it as an excuse to get Madden out of the way until we were off on our wedding trip. Madden lived here with me, and it would have been nearly impossible for me to have made any preparations for the trip without him seeing them."

"Was Mr. Gantvoort here last night?" I asked her.

"No. I expected him—we were going out. He usually walked over—it's only a few blocks. When eight o'clock came and he hadn't arrived, I telephoned his house, and Whipple told me that he had left nearly an hour before. I called up again, twice, after that. Then, this morning, I called up again before I had seen the papers, and I was told that he—"

She broke off with a catch in her voice—the only sign of sorrow she displayed throughout the interview. The impression of her we had received from Charles Gantvoort and Whipple had prepared us for a more or less elaborate display of grief on her part. But she disappointed us. There was nothing crude about her work—she didn't even turn on the tears for us.

"Was Mr. Gantvoort here night before last?"

"Yes. He came over at a little after eight and stayed until nearly twelve. We didn't go out."

"Did he walk over and back?"

"Yes, so far as I know."

"Did he ever say anything to you about his life being threatened?"

"No."

She shook her head decisively.

"Do you know Emil Bonfils?"

"No."

"Ever hear Mr. Gantvoort speak of him?"

"No."

"At what hotel is your brother staying in New York?"

The restless black pupils spread out abruptly, as if they were about to overflow into the white areas of her eyes. That was the first clear indication of fear I had seen. But, outside of those tell-tale pupils, her composure was undisturbed.

"I don't know."

"When did he leave San Francisco?"

"Thursday—four days ago."

O'Gar and I walked six or seven blocks in thoughtful silence after we left Creda Dexter's apartment, and then he spoke.

"A sleek kitten—that dame! Rub her the right way, and she'll purr pretty. Rub her the wrong way—and look out for the claws!"

"What did that flash of her eyes when I asked about her brother tell you?" I asked.

"Something—but I don't know what! It wouldn't hurt to look him up and see if he's really in New York. If he is there today it's a cinch he wasn't here last night—even the mail planes take twenty-six or twenty-eight hours for the trip."

"We'll do that," I agreed. "It looks like this Creda Dexter wasn't any too sure that her brother wasn't in on the killing. And there's nothing to show that Bonfils didn't have help. I can't figure Creda being in on the murder, though. She knew the new will hadn't been signed. There'd be no sense in her working herself out of that three-quarters of a million berries."

We sent a lengthy telegram to the Continental's New York branch, and then dropped in at the Agency to see if any replies had come to the wires I had got off the night before.

They had.

None of the people whose names appeared on the type-written list with Gantvoort's had been found; not the least trace had been found of any of them. Two of the addresses given were altogether wrong. There were no houses with those numbers on those streets—and there never had been.

4

"Maybe That Ain't So Foolish!"

WHAT WAS LEFT of the afternoon, O'Gar and I spent going over the street between Gantvoort's house on Russian Hill and the building in which the Dexters lived. We questioned everyone we could find—man, woman and child—who lived, worked, or played along any of the three routes the dead man could have taken.

We found nobody who had heard the shot that had been fired by Bonfils on the night before the murder. We found nobody who had seen anything suspicious on the night of the murder. Nobody who remembered having seen him picked up in a coupé.

Then we called at Gantvoort's house and questioned Charles Gantvoort again, his wife, and all the servants—and we learned nothing. So far as they knew, nothing belonging to the dead man was missing—nothing small enough to be concealed in the heel of a shoe.

The shoes he had worn the night he was killed were one of three pairs made in New York for him two months before. He could have removed the heel of the left one, hollowed it out sufficiently to hide a small object in it, and then nailed it on again; though Whipple insisted that he would have noticed the effects of any tampering with the shoe unless it had been done by an expert repairman.

This field exhausted, we returned to the Agency. A telegram had just come from the New York branch, saying that none of the steamship companies' records showed the arrival of an Emil Bonfils from either England, France, or Germany within the past six months.

The operatives who had been searching the city for Bonfils had all come in empty-handed. They had found and investigated eleven persons named Bonfils in San Francisco, Oakland, Berkeley, and Alameda. Their investigations had definitely cleared all eleven. None of these Bonfilses knew an Emil Bonfils. Combing the hotels had yielded nothing.

O'Gar and I went to dinner together—a quiet, grouchy sort of meal during which we didn't speak six words apiece—and then came back to the Agency to find that another wire had come in from New York.

> Madden Dexter arrived McAlpin Hotel this morning with Power of Attorney to sell Gantvoort interest in B.F. and F. Iron Corporation. Denies knowledge of Emil Bonfils or of murder. Expects to finish business and leave for San Francisco tomorrow.

I let the sheet of paper upon which I had decoded the telegram slide out of my fingers, and we sat listlessly facing each other across my desk, looking vacantly each at the other, listening to the clatter of charwomen's buckets in the corridor.

"It's a funny one," O'Gar said softly to himself at last.

I nodded. It was.

"We got nine clues," he spoke again presently, "and none of them have got us a damned thing.

"Number one: the dead man called up you people and told you that he had been threatened and shot at by an Emil Bonfils that he'd had a run-in with in Paris a long time ago.

"Number two: the typewriter he was killed with and that the letter and list were written on. We're still trying to trace it, but with no breaks so far. What the hell kind of a weapon was that, anyway? It looks like this fellow Bonfils got hot and hit Gantvoort with the first thing he put his hand on. But what was the typewriter doing in a stolen car? And why were the numbers filed off it?"

I shook my head to signify that I couldn't guess the answer, and O'Gar went on enumerating our clues.

"Number three: the threatening letter, fitting in with what Gantvoort had said over the phone that afternoon.

"Number four: those two bullets with the crosses in their snoots.

"Number five: the jewel case.

"Number six: that bunch of yellow hair.

"Number seven: the fact that the dead man's shoe and collar buttons were carried away.

"Number eight: the wallet, with two ten-dollar bills, three clippings, and the list in it, found in the road.

"Number nine: finding the shoe next day, wrapped up in a five-day-old Philadelphia paper, and with the missing collar buttons, four more, and a rusty key in it.

"That's the list. If they mean anything at all, they mean that Emil Bonfils whoever he is—was flimflammed out of something by Gantvoort in Paris in 1902, and that Bonfils came to get it back. He picked Gantvoort up last night in a stolen car, bringing his typewriter with him—for God knows what reason! Gantvoort put up an argument, so Bonfils bashed in his noodle with the typewriter, and then went through his pockets, apparently not taking anything. He decided that what he was looking for was in Gantvoort's left shoe, so he took the shoe away with him. And then—but there's no sense to the collar button trick, or the phoney list, or—"

"Yes there is!" I cut in, sitting up, wide awake now. "That's our tenth clue—the one we're going to follow from now on. That list was, except for Gantvoort's name and address, a fake. Our people would have found at least one of the five people whose names were on it if it had been on the level. But they didn't find the least trace of any of them. And two of the addresses were of street numbers that didn't exist!

"That list was faked up, put in the wallet with the clippings and twenty dollars—to make the play stronger—and planted in the road near the car to throw us off-track. And if that's so, then it's a hundred to one that the rest of the things were cooked up too.

"From now on I'm considering all those nine lovely clues as nine bum steers. And I'm going just exactly contrary to them. I'm looking for a man whose name isn't Emil Bonfils, and whose initials aren't either E or B; who isn't French, and who wasn't in Paris in 1902. A man who hasn't light hair, doesn't carry a .45-calibre pistol, and has no interest in Personal advertisements in newspapers. A man who didn't kill Gantvoort to recover anything that could have been hidden in a shoe or on a collar button. That's the sort of a guy I'm hunting for now!"

The detective-sergeant screwed up his little green eyes reflectively and scratched his head.

"Maybe that ain't so foolish!" he said. "You might be right at that. Suppose you are—what then? That Dexter kitten didn't do it—it cost her three-quarters of a million. Her brother didn't do it—he's in New York. And, besides, you don't croak a guy just because you think he's too old to marry your sister. Charles Gantvoort? He and his wife are the only ones who make any money out of the old man dying before the new will was signed. We have only their word for it that Charles was home that night. The servants didn't see him between eight and eleven. You were there, and you didn't see him until eleven. But me and you both believe him when he says he was home all that evening. And neither of us think he bumped the old man off—though of course he might. Who then?"

"This Creda Dexter," I suggested, "was marrying Gantvoort for his money, wasn't she? You don't think she was in love with him, do you?"

"No. I figure, from what I saw of her, that she was in love with the million and a half."

"All right," I went on. "Now she isn't exactly homely—not by a long shot. Do you reckon Gantvoort was the only man who ever fell for her?"

"I got you! I got you!" O'Gar exclaimed. "You mean there might have been some young fellow in the running who didn't have any million and a half behind him, and who didn't take kindly to being nosed out by a man who did. Maybe—maybe."

"Well, suppose we bury all this stuff we've been working on and try out that angle."

"Suits me," he said. "Starting in the morning, then, we spend our time hunting for Gantvoort's rival for the paw of this Dexter kitten."

5

"Meet Mr. Smith"

RIGHT OR WRONG, that's what we did. We stowed all those lovely clues away in a drawer, locked the drawer, and forgot them. Then we set out to find Creda Dexter's masculine acquaintances and sift them for the murderer.

But it wasn't as simple as it sounded.

All our digging into her past failed to bring to light one man who could be considered a suitor. She and her brother had been in San Francisco three years. We traced them back the length of that period, from apartment to apartment. We questioned everyone we could find who even knew her by sight. And nobody could tell us of a single man who had shown an interest in her besides Gantvoort. Nobody, apparently, had ever seen her with any man except Gantvoort or her brother.

All of which, while not getting us ahead, at least convinced us that we were on the right trail. There must have been, we argued, at least one man in her life in those three years besides Gantvoort. She wasn't—unless we were very much mistaken—the sort of woman who would discourage masculine attention; and she was certainly endowed by nature to attract it. And if there was another man, then the very fact that he had been kept so thoroughly under cover strengthened the probability of him having been mixed up in Gantvoort's death.

We were unsuccessful in learning where the Dexters had lived before they came to San Francisco, but we weren't so very interested in their earlier life. Of course it was possible that some old-time lover had come upon the scene again recently; but in that case it should have been easier to find the recent connection than the old one.

There was no doubt, our explorations showed, that Gantvoort's son had been correct in thinking the Dexters were fortune hunters. All their activities pointed to that, although there seemed to be nothing downright criminal in their pasts.

I went up against Creda Dexter again, spending an entire afternoon in her apartment, banging away with question after question, all directed toward her former love affairs. Who had she thrown over for Gantvoort and his million and a half? And the answer was always *nobody*—an answer that I didn't choose to believe.

We had Creda Dexter shadowed night and day—and it carried us ahead not an inch. Perhaps she suspected that she was being watched. Anyway, she seldom left her apartment, and then on only the most innocent of errands. We had her apartment watched whether she was in it or not. Nobody visited it. We tapped her telephone—and all our listening-in netted us nothing. We had her mail covered—and she didn't receive a single letter, not even an advertisement.

Meanwhile, we had learned where the three clippings found in the wallet had come from—from the Personal columns of a New York, a Chicago, and a Portland newspaper. The one in the Portland paper had appeared two days before the murder, the Chicago one four days before, and the New York one five days before. All three of those papers would have been on the San Francisco newsstands the day of the murder—ready to be purchased and cut out by anyone who was looking for material to confuse detectives with.

The Agency's Paris correspondent had found no less than six Emil Bonfilses—all bloomers so far as our job was concerned—and had a line on three more.

But O'Gar and I weren't worrying over Emil Bonfils any more—that angle was dead and buried. We were plugging away at our new task—the finding of Gantvoort's rival.

Thus the days passed, and thus the matter stood when Madden Dexter was due to arrive home from New York.

Our New York branch had kept an eye on him until he left that city, and had advised us of his departure, so I knew what train he was coming on. I wanted to put a few questions to him before his sister saw him. He could tell me what I wanted to know, and he might be willing to if I could get to him before his sister had an opportunity to shut him up.

If I had known him by sight I could have picked him up when he left his train at Oakland, but I didn't know him; and I didn't want to carry Charles Gantvoort or anyone else along with me to pick him out for me.

So I went up to Sacramento that morning, and boarded his train there. I put my card in an envelope and gave it to a messenger boy in the station. Then I followed the boy through the train, while he called out:

"Mr. Dexter! Mr. Dexter!"

In the last car—the observation-club car—a slender, dark-haired man in well-made tweeds turned from watching the station platform through a window and held out his hand to the boy.

I studied him while he nervously tore open the envelope and read my card. His chin trembled slightly just now, emphasizing the weakness of a face that couldn't have been strong at its best. Between twenty-five and thirty, I placed him; with his hair parted in the middle and slicked down; large, too-expressive brown eyes; small well-shaped nose; neat brown mustache; very red, soft lips—that type.

I dropped into the vacant chair beside him when he looked up from the card.

"You are Mr. Dexter?"

"Yes," he said. "I suppose it's about Mr. Gantvoort's death that you want to see me?"

"Uh-huh. I wanted to ask you a few questions, and since I happened to be in Sacramento, I thought that by riding back on the train with you I could ask them without taking up too much of your time."

"If there's anything I can tell you," he assured me, "I'll be only too glad to do it. But I told the New York detectives all I knew, and they didn't seem to find it of much value."

"Well, the situation has changed some since you left New York." I watched his face closely as I spoke. "What we thought of no value then may be just what we want now."

I paused while he moistened his lips and avoided my eyes. He may not know anything, I thought, but he's certainly jumpy. I let him wait a few minutes while I pretended deep thoughtfulness. If I played him right, I was confident I could turn him inside out. He didn't seem to be made of very tough material.

We were sitting with our heads close together, so that the four or five other passengers in the car wouldn't overhear our talk; and that position was in my favor. One of the things that every detective knows is that it's often easy to get information—even a confession—out of a feeble nature simply by putting your face close to his and talking in a loud tone. I couldn't talk loud here, but the closeness of our faces was by itself an advantage.

"Of the men with whom your sister was acquainted," I came out with it at last, "who, outside of Mr. Gantvoort, was the most attentive?"

He swallowed audibly, looked out of the window, fleetingly at me, and then out of the window again.

"Really, I couldn't say."

"All right. Let's get at it this way. Suppose we check off one by one all the men who were interested in her and in whom she was interested."

He continued to stare out of the window.

"Who's first?" I pressed him.

His gaze flickered around to meet mine for a second, with a sort of timid desperation in his eyes.

"I know it sounds foolish, but I, her brother, couldn't give you the name of even one man in whom Creda was interested before she met Gantvoort. She never, so far as I know, had the slightest feeling for any man before she met him. Of course it is possible that there may have been someone that I didn't know anything about, but—"

It did sound foolish, right enough! The Creda Dexter I had talked to—a sleek kitten, as O'Gar had put it—didn't impress me as being at all likely to go very long without having at least one man in tow. This pretty little guy in front of me was lying. There couldn't be any other explanation.

I went at him tooth and nail. But when he reached Oakland early that night he was still sticking to his original statement—that Gantvoort was the only one of his sister's suitors that he knew anything about. And I knew that I had blundered, had underrated Madden Dexter, had played my hand wrong in trying to shake him down too quickly—in driving too directly at the point I was interested in. He was either a lot stronger than I had figured him, or his interest in concealing Gantvoort's murderer was much greater than I had thought it would be.

But I had this much: if Dexter was lying—and there couldn't be much doubt of that—then Gantvoort *had* had a rival, and Madden Dexter believed or knew that this rival had killed Gantvoort.

When we left the train at Oakland I knew I was licked, that he wasn't going to tell me what I wanted to know—not this night, anyway. But I clung to him, stuck at his side when we boarded the ferry for San Francisco, in spite of the obviousness of his desire to get away from me. There's always a chance of something unexpected happening; so I continued to ply him with questions as our boat left the slip.

Presently a man came toward where we were sitting—a big burly man in a light overcoat, carrying a black bag.

"Hello, Madden!" he greeted my companion, striding over to him with outstretched hand. "Just got in and was trying to remember your phone number," he said, setting down his bag, as they shook hands warmly.

Madden Dexter turned to me.

"I want you to meet Mr. Smith," he told me, and then gave my name to the big man, adding, "he's with the Continental Detective Agency here."

That tag—clearly a warning for Smith's benefit—brought me to my feet, all watchfulness. But the ferry was crowded—a hundred persons were within sight of us, all around us. I relaxed, smiled pleasantly, and shook hands with Smith. Whoever Smith was, and whatever connection he might have with the murder—and if he hadn't any, why should Dexter have been in such a hurry to tip him off to my identity?—he couldn't do anything here. The crowd around us was all to my advantage.

That was my second mistake of the day.

Smith's left hand had gone into his overcoat pocket—or rather, through one of those vertical slits that certain styles of overcoats have so that inside pockets may be reached without unbuttoning the overcoat. His hand had gone through that slit, and his coat had fallen away far enough for me to see a snub-nosed automatic in his hand—shielded from everyone's sight but mine—pointing at my waist-line.

"Shall we go on deck?" Smith asked—and it was an order.

I hesitated. I didn't like to leave all these people who were so blindly standing and sitting around us. But Smith's face wasn't the face of a cautious man. He had the look of one who might easily disregard the presence of a hundred witnesses.

I turned around and walked through the crowd. His right hand lay familiarly on my shoulder as he walked behind me; his left hand held his gun, under the overcoat, against my spine.

The deck was deserted. A heavy fog, wet as rain,—the fog of San Francisco Bay's winter nights,—lay over boat and water, and had driven everyone else inside. It hung about us, thick and impenetrable; I couldn't see so far as the end of the boat, in spite of the lights glowing overhead.

I stopped.

Smith prodded me in the back.

"Farther away, where we can talk," he rumbled in my ear.

I went on until I reached the rail.

The entire back of my head burned with sudden fire... tiny points of light glittered in the blackness before me... grew larger... came rushing toward me....

6

"Those Damned Horns!"

SEMI-CONSCIOUSNESS! I FOUND myself mechanically keeping afloat somehow and trying to get out of my overcoat. The back of my head throbbed devilishly. My eyes burned. I felt heavy and logged, as if I had swallowed gallons of water.

The fog hung low and thick on the water—there was nothing else to be seen anywhere. By the time I had freed myself of the encumbering overcoat my head had cleared somewhat, but with returning consciousness came increased pain.

A light glimmered mistily off to my left, and then vanished. From out of the misty blanket, from every direction, in a dozen different keys, from near and far, fog-horns sounded. I stopped swimming and floated on my back, trying to determine my whereabouts.

After a while I picked out the moaning, evenly spaced blasts of the Alcatraz siren. But they told me nothing. They came to me out of the fog without direction—seemed to beat down upon me from straight above.

I was somewhere in San Francisco Bay, and that was all I knew, though I suspected the current was sweeping me out toward the Golden Gate.

A little while passed, and I knew that I had left the path of the Oakland ferries—no boat had passed close to me for some time. I was glad to be out of that track. In this fog a boat was a lot more likely to run me down than to pick me up.

The water was chilling me, so I turned over and began swimming, just vigorously enough to keep my blood circulating while I saved my strength until I had a definite goal to try for.

A horn began to repeat its roaring note nearer and nearer, and presently the lights of the boat upon which it was fixed came into sight. One of the Sausalito ferries, I thought.

It came quite close to me, and I halloed until I was breathless and my throat was raw. But the boat's siren, crying its warning, drowned my shouts.

The boat went on and the fog closed in behind it.

The current was stronger now, and my attempts to attract the attention of the Sausalito ferry had left me weaker. I floated, letting the water sweep me where it would, resting.

Another light appeared ahead of me suddenly—hung there for an instant—disappeared.

I began to yell, and worked my arms and legs madly, trying to drive myself through the water to where it had been.

I never saw it again.

Weariness settled upon me, and a sense of futility. The water was no longer cold. I was warm with a comfortable, soothing numbness. My head stopped throbbing; there was no feeling at all in it now. No lights, now, but the sound of fog-horns... fog-horns... fog-horns ahead of me, behind me, to either side; annoying me, irritating me.

But for the moaning horns I would have ceased all effort. They had become the only disagreeable detail of my situation—the water was pleasant, fatigue was pleasant. But the horns tormented me. I cursed them petulantly and decided to swim until I could no longer hear them, and then, in the quiet of the friendly fog, go to sleep....

Now and then I would doze, to be goaded into wakefulness by the wailing voice of a siren.

"Those damned horns! Those damned horns!" I complained aloud, again and again.

One of them, I found presently, was bearing down upon me from behind, growing louder and stronger. I turned and waited. Lights, dim and steaming, came into view.

With exaggerated caution to avoid making the least splash, I swam off to one side. When this nuisance was past I could go to sleep. I sniggered softly to myself as the lights drew abreast, feeling a foolish triumph in my cleverness in eluding the boat. Those damned horns....

Life—the hunger for life—all at once surged back into my being.

I screamed at the passing boat, and with every iota of my being struggled toward it. Between strokes I tilted up my head and screamed....

7

"You Have a Lot of Fun, Don't You?"

WHEN I RETURNED to consciousness for the second time that evening, I was lying on my back on a baggage truck, which was moving. Men and women were crowding around, walking beside the truck, staring at me with curious eyes.

I sat up.

"Where are we?" I asked.

A little red-faced man in uniform answered my question.

"Just landing in Sausalito. Lay still. We'll take you over to the hospital."

I looked around.

"How long before this boat goes back to San Francisco?"

"Leaves right away."

I slid off the truck and started back aboard the boat.

"I'm going with it," I said.

Half an hour later, shivering and shaking in my wet clothes, keeping my mouth clamped tight so that my teeth wouldn't sound like a dice-game, I climbed into a taxi at the Ferry Building and went to my flat.

There, I swallowed half a pint of whisky, rubbed myself with a coarse towel until my skin was sore, and, except for an enormous weariness and a worse headache, I felt almost human again.

I reached O'Gar by phone, asked him to come up to my flat right away, and then called up Charles Gantvoort.

"Have you seen Madden Dexter yet?" I asked him.

"No, but I talked to him over the phone. He called me up as soon as he got in. I asked him to meet me in Mr. Abernathy's office in the morning, so we could go over that business he transacted for father."

"Can you call him up now and tell him that you have been called out of town—will have to leave early in the morning—and that you'd like to run over to his apartment and see him tonight?"

"Why yes, if you wish."

"Good! Do that. I'll call for you in a little while and go over to see him with you."

"What is—"

"I'll tell you about it when I see you," I cut him off.

O'Gar arrived as I was finishing dressing.

"So he told you something?" he asked, knowing of my plan to meet Dexter on the train and question him.

"Yes," I said with sour sarcasm, "but I came near forgetting what it was. I grilled him all the way from Sacramento to Oakland, and couldn't get a whisper out of him. On the ferry coming over he introduces me to a man he calls Mr. Smith, and he tells Mr. Smith that I'm a gumshoe. This, mind you, all happens in the middle of a crowded ferry! Mr. Smith puts a gun in my belly, marches me out on deck, raps me across the back of the head, and dumps me into the bay."

"You have a lot of fun, don't you?" O'Gar grinned, and then wrinkled his forehead. "Looks like Smith would be the man we want then—the buddy who turned the Gantvoort trick. But what the hell did he want to give himself away by chucking you overboard for?"

"Too hard for me," I confessed, while trying to find which of my hats and caps would sit least heavily upon my bruised head. "Dexter knew I was hunting for one of his sister's former lovers, of course. And he must have thought I knew a whole lot more than I do, or he wouldn't have made that raw play—tipping my mitt to Smith right in front of me.

"It may be that after Dexter lost his head and made that break on the ferry, Smith figured that I'd be on to him soon, if not right away; and so he'd take a desperate chance on putting me out of the way. But we'll know all about it in a little while," I said, as we went down to the waiting taxi and set out for Gantvoort's.

"You ain't counting on Smith being in sight, are you?" the detective-sergeant asked.

"No. He'll be holed up somewhere until he sees how things are going. But Madden Dexter will have to be out in the open to protect himself. He has an alibi, so he's in the clear so far as the actual killing is concerned. And with me supposed to be dead, the more he stays in the open, the safer he is. But it's a cinch that he knows what this is all about, though he wasn't necessarily involved in it. As near as I could see, he didn't go out on deck with Smith and me tonight. Anyway he'll be home. And this time he's going to talk—he's going to tell his little story!"

Charles Gantvoort was standing on his front steps when we reached his house. He climbed into our taxi and we headed for the Dexters' apartment. We didn't have time to answer any of the questions that Gantvoort was firing at us with every turning of the wheels.

"He's home and expecting you?" I asked him.

"Yes."

Then we left the taxi and went into the apartment building.

"Mr. Gantvoort to see Mr. Dexter," he told the Philippine boy at the switchboard.

The boy spoke into the phone.

"Go right up," he told us.

At the Dexters' door I stepped past Gantvoort and pressed the button.

Creda Dexter opened the door. Her amber eyes widened and her smile faded as I stepped past her into the apartment.

I walked swiftly down the little hallway and turned into the first room through whose open door a light showed.

And came face to face with Smith!

We were both surprised, but his astonishment was a lot more profound than mine. Neither of us had expected to see the other; but I had known he was still alive, while he had every reason for thinking me at the bottom of the bay.

I took advantage of his greater bewilderment to the extent of two steps toward him before he went into action.

One of his hands swept down.

I threw my right fist at his face—threw it with every ounce of my 180 pounds behind it, re-enforced by the memory of every second I had spent in the water and every throb of my battered head.

His hand, already darting down for his pistol, came back up too late to fend off my punch.

Something clicked in my hand as it smashed into his face, and my hand went numb.

But he went down—and lay where he fell.

I jumped across his body to a door on the opposite side of the room, pulling my gun loose with my left hand.

"Dexter's somewhere around!" I called over my shoulder to O'Gar, who with Gantvoort and Creda, was coming through the door by which I had entered. "Keep your eyes open!"

I dashed through the four other rooms of the apartment, pulling closet doors open, looking everywhere—and I found nobody.

Then I returned to where Creda Dexter was trying to revive Smith, with the assistance of O'Gar and Gantvoort.

The detective-sergeant looked over his shoulder at me.

"Who do you think this joker is?" he asked.

"My friend Mr. Smith."

"Gantvoort says he's Madden Dexter."

I looked at Charles Gantvoort, who nodded his head.

"This is Madden Dexter," he said.

8

"I Hope You Swing!"

WE WORKED UPON Dexter for nearly ten minutes before he opened his eyes.

As soon as he sat up we began to shoot questions and accusations at him, hoping to get a confession out of him before he recovered from his shakiness—but he wasn't that shaky.

All we could get out of him was:

"Take me in if you want to. If I've got anything to say I'll say it to my lawyer, and to nobody else."

Creda Dexter, who had stepped back after her brother came to, and was standing a little way off, watching us, suddenly came forward and caught me by the arm.

"What have you got on him?" she demanded, imperatively.

"I wouldn't want to say," I countered, "but I don't mind telling you this much. We're going to give him a chance in a nice modern court-room to prove that he didn't kill Leopold Gantvoort."

"He was in New York!"

"He was not! He had a friend who went to New York as Madden Dexter and looked after Gantvoort's business under that name. But if this is the real Madden Dexter then the closest he got to New York was when he met his friend on the ferry to get from him the papers connected with the B.F. & F. Iron Corporation transaction; and learned that I had stumbled upon the truth about his alibi—even if I didn't know it myself at the time."

She jerked around to face her brother.

"Is that on the level?" she asked him.

He sneered at her, and went on feeling with the fingers of one hand the spot on his jaw where my fist had landed.

"I'll say all I've got to say to my lawyer," he repeated.

"You will?" she shot back at him. "Well, I'll say what I've got to say right now!"

She flung around to face me again.

"Madden is not my brother at all! My name is Ives. Madden and I met in St. Louis about four years ago, drifted around together for a year or so, and then came to Frisco. He was a con man—still is. He made Mr. Gantvoort's acquaintance six or seven months ago, and was getting him all ribbed up to unload a fake invention on him. He brought him here a couple of times, and introduced me to him as his sister. We usually posed as brother and sister.

"Then, after Mr. Gantvoort had been here a couple times, Madden decided to change his game. He thought Mr. Gantvoort liked me, and that we could get more money out of him by working a fancy sort of badger-game on him. I was to lead the old man on until I had him wrapped around my finger—until we had him tied up so tight he couldn't get away—had something on him—something good and strong. Then we were going to shake him down for plenty of money.

"Everything went along fine for a while. He fell for me—fell hard. And finally he asked me to marry him. We had never figured on that. Blackmail was our game. But when he asked me to marry him I tried to call Madden off. I admit the old man's money had something to do with it—it influenced me— but I had come to like him a little for himself. He was mighty fine in lots of ways—nicer than anybody I had ever known.

"So I told Madden all about it, and suggested that we drop the other plan, and that I marry Gantvoort. I promised to see that Madden was kept supplied with money—I knew I could get whatever I wanted from Mr. Gantvoort. And I was on the level with Madden. I liked Mr. Gantvoort, but Madden had found him and brought him around to me; and so I wasn't going to run out on Madden. I was willing to do all I could for him.

"But Madden wouldn't hear of it. He'd have got more money in the long run by doing as I suggested—but he wanted his little handful right away. And to make him more unreasonable he got one of his jealous streaks. He beat me one night!

"That settled it. I made up my mind to ditch him. I told Mr. Gantvoort that my brother was bitterly opposed to our marrying, and he could see that Madden was carrying a grouch. So he arranged to send Madden East on that steel business, to get him out of the way until we were off on our wedding trip. And we thought Madden was completely deceived—but I should have known that he would see through our scheme. We planned to be gone about a year, and by that time I thought Madden would have forgotten me—or I'd be fixed to handle him if he tried to make any trouble.

"As soon as I heard that Mr. Gantvoort had been killed I had a hunch that Madden had done it. But then it seemed like a certainty that he was in New York the next day, and I thought I had done him an injustice. And I was glad he was out of it. But now—"

She whirled around to her erstwhile confederate.

"Now I hope you swing, you big sap!"

She spun around to me again. No sleek kitten, this, but a furious, spitting cat, with claws and teeth bared.

"What kind of looking fellow was the one who went to New York for him?"

I described the man I had talked to on the train.

"Evan Felter," she said, after a moment of thought. "He used to work with Madden. You'll probably find him hiding in Los Angeles. Put the screws on him and he'll spill all he knows—he's a weak sister! The chances are he didn't know what Madden's game was until it was all over."

"How do you like that?" she spat at Madden Dexter. "How do you like that for a starter? You messed up my little party, did you? Well, I'm going to spend every minute of my time from now until they pop you off helping them pop you!"

And she did, too—with her assistance it was no trick at all to gather up the rest of the evidence we needed to hang him. And I don't believe her enjoyment of her three-quarters of a million dollars is spoiled a bit by any qualms over what she did to Madden. She's a very respectable woman *now*, and glad to be free of the con-man.

Night Shots

Mr. Hammett's nameless detective is lured into a sweet little domestic mess with an outside mystery; as usual, he walks into a lot of excitement, not all of which comes from the muzzle of a gun.

1

THE HOUSE WAS of red brick, large and square, with a green slate roof, whose wide overhang gave the building an appearance of being too squat for its two stories; and it stood on a grassy hill, well away from the county road, upon which it turned its back to look down on the Mokelumne River.

The Ford that I had hired to bring me out from Knownburg carried me into the grounds through a high steel-meshed gate, followed the circling gravel drive, and set me down within a foot of the screen porch that ran all the way around the house's first floor.

"There's Exon's son-in-law now," the driver told me as he pocketed the bill I had given him, and prepared to drive away.

I turned to see a tall, loose-jointed man of thirty or so coming across the porch toward me—a carelessly dressed man, with a mop of rumpled brown hair over a handsome sunburned face. There was a hint of cruelty in the lips that were smiling lazily just now, and more than a hint of recklessness in his narrow gray eyes.

"Mr. Gallaway?" I asked as he came down the steps.

"Yes." His voice was a drawling baritone. "You are—"

"From the Continental Detective Agency's San Francisco branch," I finished for him.

He nodded, and held the screen-door open for me.

"Just leave your bag there. I'll have it taken up to your room."

He guided me into the house and—after I had assured him that I had already eaten luncheon—gave me a soft chair and an excellent cigar. He sprawled on his spine in an armchair opposite me—all loose-jointed angles sticking out of it in every direction—and blew smoke at the ceiling for several thoughtful minutes.

"First off," he began presently, his words coming out languidly, "I may as well tell you that I don't expect very much in the way of results. I sent for you more for the soothing effect of your presence on the household than because I expect you to do anything. I don't believe there's anything to do. However, I'm not a detective. I may be wrong. You may find out all sorts of more or less important things. If you do—fine! But I don't insist upon it."

I didn't say anything, though this beginning wasn't much to my taste. He smoked in silence for a moment, and then went on:

"My father-in-law, Talbert Exon, is a man of fifty-seven, and ordinarily a tough, hard, active, and fiery old devil. But just now he's recovering from a rather serious attack of pneumonia, which has taken most of the starch out of him. He hasn't been able to leave his bed yet, and I understand that Dr. Rench hopes to keep him on his back for another week at the very least.

"The old man has a room on the second floor—the front, right-hand corner room—just over where we are sitting. His nurse, Miss Caywood, occupies the next room, and there is a connecting door between. My room is the other front one, just across the hall from the old man's; and my wife's bedroom is next to mine—across the hall from the nurse's. I'll show you around later; I just want to make the situation clear to you first.

"Last night, or rather this morning, at about half-past one, somebody shot at Exon while he was sleeping—and missed. The bullet went into the frame of the door that leads to his nurse's room, about six inches above his body as he lay in bed. The course the bullet took in the woodwork would indicate that it had been fired from one of the windows—either through it or from just inside.

"Exon woke up, of course, but he saw nobody. The rest of us—my wife, Miss Caywood, the Figgs, and myself—were also awakened by the shot. We all rushed into his room, and we saw nothing either. There's no doubt that whoever fired it left by the window. Otherwise some of us would have seen him—we came from every other direction. However, we found nobody on the grounds, and no traces of anybody. That, I think, is all."

"Who are the Figgs, and who else is there on the place besides you and your wife, Mr. Exon, and his nurse?"

"The Figgs are Adam and Emma; she is the housekeeper and he is a sort of handy-man about the place. Their room is in the extreme rear, on the second floor. Besides them, there is Gong Lim, the cook, who sleeps in a little room near the kitchen, and the three farm hands. Joe Natara and Felipe Fadelia are Italians, and have been here for possibly more than two years; Jesus Mesa, a Mexican, has been here a year or longer. The farm hands sleep in a little house near the barns. I think—if my opinion is of any value—that none of these people had anything to do with the shooting."

"Did you dig the bullet out of the doorframe?"

"Yes. Shand, the deputy sheriff at Knownburg, dug it out. He says it is a .38-caliber bullet."

"Any guns of that caliber in the house?"

"No. A .22 and my .44—which I keep in the car—are the

only pistols on the place. Then there are two shotguns and a .30-30 rifle. Shand made a thorough search, and found nothing else in the way of firearms."

"What does Mr. Exon say?"

"Not much of anything, except that if we'll put a gun in bed with him he'll manage to take care of himself without bothering any policemen or detectives. I don't know whether he knows who shot at him or not—he's a close-mouthed old devil. From what I know of him, I imagine there are quite a few men who would think themselves justified in killing him. He was, I understand, far from being a lily in his youth—or in his mature years either, for that matter."

"Anything definite you know, or are you guessing?"

Gallaway grinned at me—a mocking grin that I was to see often before I was through with this Exon affair.

"Both," he drawled. "I know that his life has been rather more than sprinkled with swindled partners and betrayed friends; and that he saved himself from prison at least once by turning state's evidence and sending his associates there. And I know that his wife died under rather peculiar circumstances while heavily insured, and that he was for some time held on suspicion of having murdered her, but was finally released because of a lack of evidence against him. Those, I understand, are fair samples of the old boy's normal behavior; so there may be any number of people gunning for him."

"Suppose you give me a list of all the names you know of enemies he's made, and I'll have them checked up, and see what we can find that way."

He raised an indolent hand in protest.

"The names I could give you would be only a few in many,

and it might take you months to check up those few. It isn't my intention to go to all that trouble and expense. As I told you, I'm not insisting upon results. My wife is very nervous, and for some peculiar reason she seems to like the old man. So, to soothe her, I agreed to employ a private detective when she asked me to. My idea is that you hang around for a couple of days, until things quiet down and she feels safe again. Meanwhile, if you should stumble upon anything—go to it! If you don't—well and good."

My face must have shown something of what I was thinking, for his eyes twinkled and he chuckled banteringly.

"Don't, please," he drawled, "get the idea that you aren't to find my father-in-law's would-be assassin if you wish to. You're to have a free hand. Go as far as you like; except that I want you to be around the place as much as possible, so my wife will see you and feel that we are being adequately protected. Beyond that, I don't care what you do. You can apprehend criminals by the carload. As you may have gathered by now, I'm not exactly in love with my wife's father; and he's no more fond of me. To be frank, if hating weren't such an effort—if it didn't require so much energy—I think I should hate the old devil. But if you want to, and can, catch the man who shot at him, I'd be glad to have you do it. But—"

"All right," I said. "I don't like this job much; but since I'm up here I'll take it on. But, remember, I'm trying all the time."

"Sincerity and earnestness," he showed his teeth in a sardonic smile as we got to our feet, "are very praiseworthy traits."

"So I hear," I growled shortly. "Now let's take a look at Mr. Exon's room."

Gallaway's wife and the nurse were with the invalid, but I examined the room before I asked the occupants any questions.

It was a large room, with three wide windows, opening over the porch; and two doors, one of which gave to the hall, and the other to the adjoining room, occupied by the nurse. This door stood open, with a green Japanese screen across it; and, I was told, was left that way at night, so that the nurse could hear readily if her patient was restless or if he wanted attention.

A man standing on the slate roof of the porch, I found, could have easily leaned across one of the window-sills (if he did not care to step over it into the room) and fired at the man in the bed. To get from the ground to the porch roof would have required but little effort; and the descent would be still easier—he could slide down the roof, let himself go feet-first over the edge, checking his speed with hands and arms spread out on the slate, and drop down to the gravel drive. No trick at all, either coming or going. The windows were unscreened.

The sick man's bed stood just beside the connecting doorway between his room and the nurse's, which, when he was lying down, placed him between the doorway and the window from which the shot had been fired. Outside, within long rifle range, there was no building, tree, or eminence of any character from which the bullet that had been dug out of the door-frame could have been fired.

I turned from the room to the occupants, questioning the invalid first. He had been a raw-boned man of considerable size in his health, but now he was wasted and stringy and dead-white. His face was thin and hollow; small beady eyes crowded together against the thin bridge of his nose; his mouth was a colorless gash above a bony projecting chin.

His statement was a marvel of petulant conciseness.

"The shot woke me. I didn't see anything. I don't know

anything. I've got a million enemies, most of whose names I can't remember. That's all I can tell you."

He jerked this out crossly, turned his face away, closed his eyes, and refused to speak again.

Mrs. Gallaway and the nurse followed me into the latter's room, where I questioned them. They were of as opposite type as you could find anywhere; and between them there was a certain coolness, an unmistakable hostility which I was able to account for later in the day.

Mrs. Gallaway was perhaps five years older than her husband; dark, strikingly beautiful in a statuesque way, with a worried look in her dark eyes that was particularly noticeable when those eyes rested on her husband. There was no doubt that she was very much in love with him, and the anxiety that showed in her eyes at times—the pains she took to please him in each slight thing during my stay at the Exon house—convinced me that she struggled always with a fear that she would not be able to hold him, that she was about to lose him.

Mrs. Gallaway could add nothing to what her husband had told me. She had been awakened by the shot, had run to her father's room, had seen nothing—knew nothing—suspected nothing.

The nurse—Barbra Caywood was her name—told the same story, in almost the same words. She had jumped out of bed when awakened by the shot, pushed the screen away from the connecting doorway, and rushed into her patient's room. She was the first one to arrive there, and she had seen nothing but the old man sitting up in bed, roaring and shaking his feeble fists at the window.

This Barbra Caywood was a girl of twenty-one or two, and

just the sort that a man would pick to help him get well. A girl of a little under the average height, with an erect figure wherein slimness and roundness got an even break under the stiff white of her uniform; with soft golden hair above a face that was certainly made to be looked at. But she was business-like and had an air of efficiency, for all her prettiness.

From the nurse's room, Gallaway led me to the kitchen, where I questioned the Chinese cook. Gong Lim was a sad-faced Oriental whose ever-present smile somehow made him look more gloomy than ever; and he bowed and smiled and yes-yes'd me from start to finish, and told me nothing.

Adam and Emma Figg—thin and stout, respectively, and both rheumatic—entertained a wide variety of suspicions, directed at the cook and the farm hands, individually and collectively, flitting momentarily from one to the other. They had nothing upon which to base these suspicions, however, except their firm belief that nearly all crimes of violence were committed by foreigners; which, while enough for them, didn't satisfy me.

The farm hands—two smiling middle-aged and heavily mustached Italians, and a soft-eyed Mexican youth—I found in one of the fields. I talked to them for nearly two hours, and I left with a reasonable amount of assurance that neither of the three had had any part in the shooting.

2

DR. RENCH HAD just come down from a visit to his patient when Gallaway and I returned from the fields. He was a little wizened old man with mild manners and eyes, and a wonderful growth of hair on head, brows, cheeks, lips, chin, and nostrils.

The excitement, he said, had retarded Exon's recovery somewhat, but he did not think the setback would be serious. The invalid's temperature had gone up a little, but he seemed to be improving now.

I followed Dr. Rench out to his machine after he left the others, for a few questions I wanted to put to him in privacy; but the questions might as well have gone unasked for all the good they did me. He could tell me nothing of any value. The nurse, Barbra Caywood, had been secured, he said, from San Francisco, through the usual channels, which made it seem unlikely that she had worked her way into the Exon house for any hidden purpose which might have some connection with the attempt upon Exon's life.

Returning from my talk with the doctor, I came upon Hilary Gallaway and the nurse in the hall, near the foot of the stairs. His arm was resting lightly across her shoulders, and he was smiling down at her. Just as I came through the door, she twisted away, so that his arm slid off, laughed elfishly up into his face, and went on up the stairs.

I did not know whether she had seen me approaching before she eluded the encircling arm or not; nor did I know how long the arm had been there; and both of those questions would make a difference in how their positions were to be construed.

Hilary Gallaway was certainly not a man to allow a girl as pretty as the nurse to lack attention, and he was just as certainly attractive enough in himself to make his advances not too unflattering. Nor did Barbra Caywood impress me as being a girl who would dislike his admiration. But, at that, it was more than likely that there was nothing very serious between them; nothing more than a playful sort of flirtation.

But, no matter what the situation might be in that quarter, it didn't have any direct bearing upon the shooting—none that I could see, any way. But I understood now the strained relations between the nurse and Gallaway's wife.

Gallaway was grinning quizzically at me while I was chasing these thoughts around in my head.

"Nobody's safe with a detective around," he complained.

I grinned back at him. That was the only sort of an answer you could give this bird.

After dinner, Gallaway drove me to Knownburg in his roadster, and set me down on the door-step of the deputy sheriff's house. He offered to drive me back to the Exon house when I had finished my investigations in town, but I did not know how long those investigations would take, so I told him I would hire a car when I was ready to return.

Shand, the deputy sheriff, was a big, slow-spoken, slow-thinking, blond man of thirty or so—just the type best fitted for a deputy sheriff job in a San Joaquin County town—and he balanced a fat blond child on each knee while he talked to me.

"I went out to Exon's as soon as Gallaway called me up," he said. "About four-thirty in the morning, I reckon it was when

I got there. I didn't find nothing. There weren't no marks on the porch roof, but that don't mean nothing. I tried climbing up and down it myself, and I didn't leave no marks neither. The ground around the house is too firm for footprints to be followed. I found a few, but they didn't lead nowhere; and everybody had run all over the place before I got there, so I couldn't tell who they belonged to.

"Far's I can learn, there ain't been no suspicious characters in the neighborhood lately. The only folks around here who have got any grudge against the old man are the Deemses—Exon beat 'em in a law suit a couple years back—but all of them—the father and both the boys—were at home when the shooting was done."

"How long has Exon been living here?"

"Four—five years, I reckon. Came in 1918 or '19."

"Nothing at all to work on, then?"

He shifted one of the kids around to keep from having an eye jabbed by a stubby finger, and shook his head.

"Nothing I know about."

"What do you know about the Exon family?" I asked.

Shand scratched his head thoughtfully and frowned.

"I reckon it's Hilary Gallaway you're meaning," he said slowly. "I thought of that. The Gallaways showed up here a couple of years after her father had bought the place, and Hilary seems to spend most of his evenings up in Ady's back room, teaching the boys how to play poker. I hear he's fitted to teach them a lot. I don't know, myself. Ady runs a quiet game, so I let 'em alone. But naturally I don't never set in, myself. I just stay away so I won't see nothing.

"Outside of being a card-hound, and drinking pretty heavy,

and making a lot of trips to the city, where he's supposed to have a girl on the string, I don't know nothing much about Hilary. But it's no secret that him and the old man don't hit it off together very well. And then Hilary's room is just across the hall from Exon's, and their windows open out on the porch roof just a little apart. But I don't know—"

Shand confirmed what Gallaway had told me about the bullet being .38-caliber; about the absence of any pistol of that caliber on the premises; and about the lack of any reason for suspecting the farm hands or servants.

I put in the next couple hours talking to whomever I could find to talk to in Knownburg; and I learned nothing worth putting down on paper. Then I got a car and driver from the garage, and was driven out to Exon's.

Gallaway had not yet returned from town. His wife and Barbra Caywood were just about to sit down to a light luncheon before retiring, so I joined them. Exon, the nurse, said, was asleep, and had spent a quiet evening. We talked for a while—until about half-past twelve—and then went to our rooms.

My room was next to the nurse's, on the same side of the hall that divided the second story in half. I sat down and wrote my report for the day, smoked a cigar, and then—the house being quiet by this time—put a gun and a flashlight in my pockets, went downstairs, and let myself out of the kitchen door.

The moon was just coming up, lighting the grounds vaguely, except for the shadows cast by house, outbuildings, and the several clumps of shrubbery. Keeping in these shadows as much as possible, I explored the grounds, finding everything as it should be.

The lack of any evidence to the contrary pointed to last night's shot having been fired—either accidentally, or in fright at some fancied move of Exon's—by a burglar, who had been entering the sick man's room through a window. If that were so, then there wasn't one chance in a thousand of anything happening tonight. But I felt restless and ill at ease, nevertheless—possibly a result of my failure to learn the least thing of importance all day.

Gallaway's roadster was not in the garage. He had not returned from Knownburg. Beneath the farm hands' window I paused until snores in three distinct keys told me that they were all safely abed.

After an hour of this snooping around, I returned to the house. The luminous dial of my watch registered 2:35 as I stopped outside the Chinese cook's door to listen to his regular breathing.

Upstairs, I paused at the door of the Figgs' room, until my ear told me that they were sleeping. At Mrs. Gallaway's door I had to wait several minutes before she sighed and turned in bed. Barbra Caywood was breathing deeply and strongly, with the regularity of a young animal whose sleep is without disturbing dreams. The invalid's breath came to me with the evenness of slumber and the rasping of the pneumonia convalescent.

This listening tour completed, I returned to my room.

Still feeling wide-awake and restless, I pulled a chair up to a window, and sat looking at the moonlight on the river—which twisted just below the house so as to be visible from this side—smoking another cigar, and turning things over in my mind—to no great advantage.

Outside there was no sound.

Suddenly down the hall came the heavy explosion of a gun being fired indoors!

I threw myself across the room, out into the hall.

A woman's voice filled the house with its shriek—high, frenzied.

Barbra Caywood's door was unlocked when I reached it. I slammed it open. By the light of the moonbeams that slanted past her window, I saw her sitting upright in the center of her bed. She wasn't beautiful now. Her face was distorted, twisted with terror. The scream was just dying in her throat.

All this I got in the flash of time that it took me to put a running foot across her sill.

Then another shot crashed out—in Exon's room.

The girl's face jerked up—so abruptly that it seemed her neck must snap—she clutched both hands to her breast—and fell face-down among the bedclothes.

I don't know whether I went through, over, or around the screen that stood in the connecting doorway. I was circling Exon's bed. He lay on the floor on his side, facing a window. I jumped over him—leaned out the window.

In the yard that was bright now under the moon, nothing moved. There was no sound of flight.

Presently, while my eyes still searched the surrounding country, the farm hands, in their underwear, came running barefooted from the direction of their quarters. I called down to them, stationing them at points of vantage.

Meanwhile, behind me, Gong Lim and Adam Figg had put Exon back in his bed, while Mrs. Gallaway and Emma Figg tried to check the blood that spurted from a hole in Barbra Caywood's side.

I sent Adam Figg to the telephone, to wake the doctor and the deputy sheriff, and then I hurried down to the grounds.

Stepping out of the door, I came face to face with Hilary Gallaway, coming from the direction of the garage. His face was flushed, and his breath was eloquent of the refreshments that had accompanied the game in Ady's back room; but his step was steady enough, and his smile was as lazy as ever. He had apparently arrived while I was sending Figg to the phone and running downstairs—otherwise I would have heard his car.

"What's the excitement?" he asked.

"Same as last night! Meet anybody on the road? Or see anybody leaving here?"

"No."

"All right. Get in that bus of yours, and burn up the road in the other direction. Stop anybody you meet going away from here or who looks wrong! Got a gun?"

He spun on his heel with nothing of indolence.

"One in my car," he called over his shoulder, as he broke into a run.

The farm hands still at their posts, I combed the grounds from east to west and from north to south. I realized that I was spoiling my chance of finding footprints when it would be light enough to see them; but I was banking on the man I wanted still being close at hand. And then Shand had told me that the ground was unfavorable for tracing prints, anyway.

On the gravel drive in front of the house I found the pistol from which the shots had been fired—a cheap .38-caliber revolver, slightly rusty, smelling freshly of burnt powder, with three empty shells and three that had not been fired in it.

Besides that I found nothing. The murderer—from what I

had seen of the hole in the girl's side, I called him that—had vanished completely.

Shand and Dr. Rench arrived together, just as I was finishing my fruitless search. A little later, Hilary Gallaway came back—empty-handed.

3

BREAKFAST THAT MORNING was a melancholy meal, except to Hilary Gallaway. He refrained from jesting openly about the night's excitement; but his eyes twinkled whenever they met mine, and I knew he thought it a tremendously good joke for the shooting to have taken place right under my nose. During his wife's presence at the table, however, he was almost grave, as if not to offend her.

Mrs. Gallaway left the table shortly, and Dr. Rench joined us. He said that both of his patients were in as good shape as could be expected, and he thought both would recover.

The bullet had barely grazed the girl's ribs and breast bone, going through the flesh and muscles of her chest, in on the right side and out again on the left. Except for the shock and the loss of blood, she was not in danger, although she was still unconscious.

Exon was sleeping, the doctor said; so Shand and I crept up into his room to examine it. The first bullet had gone into the door-frame, about four inches above the one that had been fired the night before. The second bullet had pierced the Japanese screen, and, after passing through the girl, had lodged in the plaster of the wall. We dug out both bullets—they were of .38-caliber. Both had been apparently fired from the vicinity of one of the windows—either just inside or just outside.

Shand and I grilled the Chinese cook, the farm hands, and the Figgs, unmercifully that day. Detectives are only human—or at least this one is—and I don't mind confessing that some of my humiliation and chagrin was worked off on these people. But they came through it standing up—there was nothing to fix the shooting on any of them.

And all day long that damned Hilary Gallaway followed me from pillar to post, with a mocking glint in his eyes that said plainer than words, "I'm the logical suspect. Why don't you put me through your little third degree?" But I grinned back, and asked him nothing.

Shand had to go to town that afternoon. He called me up on the telephone later, and told me that Gallaway had left Knownburg early enough that morning to have arrived home fully half an hour before the shooting, if he had driven at his usual fast pace.

The day passed—too rapidly—and I found myself dreading the coming of night. Two nights in succession Exon's life had been attempted—and now the third night was coming.

At dinner Hilary Gallaway announced that he was going to stay home this evening. Knownburg, he said, was tame in comparison; and he grinned at me.

Dr. Rench left after the meal, saying that he would return as soon as possible, but that he had two patients on the other side of town whom he must visit. Barbra Caywood had returned to consciousness, but had been extremely hysterical, and the doctor had given her an opiate. She was asleep now. Exon was resting easily except for a high temperature.

I went up to Exon's room for a few minutes after the meal, and tried him out with a gentle question or two. But he refused to answer them, and he was too sick for me to press him.

He asked how the girl was.

"The doc says she's in no particular danger. Just loss of blood and shock. If she doesn't rip her bandages off and bleed to death in one of her hysterical spells, he says, he'll have her on her feet in a couple weeks."

Mrs. Gallaway came in then, and I went downstairs again, where I was seized by Gallaway, who insisted with bantering gravity that I tell him about some of the mysteries I had solved. He was enjoying my discomfort to the limit. He kidded me for about an hour, and had me burning up inside; but I managed to grin back with a fair pretense of indifference.

When his wife joined us presently—saying that both of the invalids were sleeping—I made my escape from her torment- ing husband, saying that I had some writing to do. But I didn't go to my room.

Instead, I crept stealthily into the girl's room, crossed to a clothespress that I had noted earlier in the day, and planted myself in it. By leaving the door open the least fraction of an inch, I could see through the connecting doorway—from which the screen had been removed—across Exon's bed, and out of the window from which three bullets had already come, and the Lord only knew what else might come.

Time passed, and I was stiff from standing still. But I had expected that—had felt it before on somewhat similar occa- sions—and I knew it would pass. But whether it did or not, I meant to stay here until something happened—if it was only the rising of the sun. Nothing else was going to be pulled off in this corner of the house without my being in on it!

Twice Mrs. Gallaway came up to look at her father and the nurse. Each time I shut my closet door entirely as soon as I heard her tip-toeing steps in the hall, I was hiding from *every- body*.

She had just gone from her second visit, when, before I had time to open my door again, I heard a faint rustling, and a soft padding on the floor. Not knowing what it was or where it was, I was afraid to push the door open.

In my narrow hiding-place I stood still and waited.

The padding was recognizable now—quiet footsteps, coming nearer. They passed not far from my clothespress door.

I waited.

An almost inaudible rustling. A pause. The softest and faintest of tearing sounds.

I came out of the closet—my gun in my hand.

Standing beside the girl's bed, leaning over her unconscious form, was old Talbert Exon, his face flushed with fever, his night shirt hanging limply around his wasted legs. One of his hands still rested upon the bedclothes he had turned down from her body. The other hand held a narrow strip of adhesive tape, with which her bandages had been fixed in place, and which he had just torn off.

He snarled at me, and both his hands went toward the girl's bandages.

The crazy, feverish glare of his eyes told me that the threat of the gun in my hand meant nothing to him. I jumped to his side, plucked his hands aside, picked him up in my arms, and carried him—kicking, clawing and swearing—back to his bed.

Then I called the others.

4

HILARY GALLAWAY, SHAND—WHO had come out from town again—and I sat over coffee and cigarettes in the kitchen, while the rest of the household helped Dr. Rench battle for Exon's life. The old man had gone through enough excitement in the last three days to kill a healthy man, let alone a pneumonia convalescent.

"But why should the old devil want to kill her?" Gallaway asked me.

"Search me," I confessed, a little testily perhaps. "I don't know why he wanted to kill her, but it's a cinch that he did. The gun was found just about where he could have thrown it when he heard me coming. I was in the girl's room when she was shot, and I got to Exon's window without wasting much time, and I saw nothing. You, yourself, driving home from Knownburg, and arriving here right after the shooting, didn't see anybody leave by the road; and I'll take an oath that nobody could have left in any other direction without either one of the farm hands or me seeing them.

"And then, tonight, I told Exon that the girl would recover if she didn't tear off her bandages; which, while true enough, gave him the idea that she had been trying to tear them off. And from that he built up a plan of tearing them off himself— knowing that she had been given an opiate, perhaps—and thinking that everybody would believe she had torn them off herself. And he was putting that plan in execution—had torn off one piece of tape—when I stopped him. He shot her intentionally, and that's flat. Maybe I couldn't prove it in court without knowing why; but I know he did. But the doc says he'll hardly live to be tried; he killed himself trying to kill the girl."

"Maybe you're right," and Gallaway's mocking grin flashed at me, "but you're a hell of a detective just the same. Why didn't you suspect me?"

"I did," I grinned back, "but not enough."

"Why not? You may be making a mistake," he drawled. "You know my room is just across the hall from his, and I could have left my window, crept across the porch, fired at him, and then run back to my room, on that first night.

"And on the second night—when you were here—you ought to know that I left Knownburg in plenty of time to have come out here, parked my car down the road a bit, fired those two shots, crept around in the shadow of the house, ran back to my car, and then come driving innocently up to the garage. You should know also that my reputation isn't any too good—that I'm supposed to be a bad egg; and you do know that I don't like the old man. And for a motive, there is the fact that my wife is Exon's only heir. What more do you want? I hope," he raised his eyebrows in burlesqued pain, "that you don't think I have any moral scruples against a well-placed murder now and then."

I laughed.

"I don't."

"Well, then?"

"If Exon had been killed that first night, and I had come up here, you'd be doing your joking behind bars long before this. And if he'd been killed the second night, even, I might have grabbed you. But I don't figure you as a man who'd bungle so easy a job—not twice, anyway. You wouldn't have missed, and then run away, leaving him alive."

He reached over for my hand and shook it gravely.

"It is comforting to have one's few virtues appreciated."

Before Talbert Exon died he sent for me. He wanted to die, he said, with his curiosity appeased; and so we traded information. I told him how I had come to suspect him—just about what I had told his son-in-law—and he told me why he had tried to kill Barbra Caywood.

Fourteen years ago he had killed his wife; not for the insurance, as he had been suspected of doing, but in a fit of jealousy. However, he had so thoroughly covered up the proofs of his guilt that he had never been brought to trial; but the murder had weighed upon him, to the extent of becoming an obsession.

He knew that he would never give himself away consciously—he was too shrewd for that—and he knew that proof of his guilt could never be found. But there was always the chance that some time, in delirium, in his sleep, or when drunk, he might tell enough to bring him to the gallows.

He thought upon this angle too often, until it became a morbid fear that always hounded him. He had given up drinking—that was easy—but there was no way of guarding against the other things.

And one of them, he said, had finally happened. He had got pneumonia, and for a week he had been out of his head, and he had talked. Coming out of that week's delirium, he had questioned the nurse. She had given him vague answers, would not tell him what he had talked about, what he had said. And then, in unguarded moments, he had discovered that her eyes rested upon him with loathing—with intense repulsion.

He knew then that he had babbled of his wife's murder; and he set about laying plans for removing the nurse before she repeated what she had heard. For so long as she remained in his house, he counted himself safe. She would not tell strangers, and it might be that for a while she would not tell anyone. Professional ethics would keep her quiet, perhaps; but he could not let her leave his house with her knowledge of his secret.

Daily and in secret, he had tested his strength, until he knew himself strong enough to walk about the room a little, and to hold a revolver steady. His bed was fortunately placed for his purpose—directly in line with one of the windows, the connecting door, and the girl's bed. In an old bond-box in his closet—and nobody but he had ever seen the things in that box—was a revolver; a revolver that could not possibly be traced to him.

On the first night, he had taken this gun out, stepped back from his bed a little, and fired a bullet into the door-frame. Then he had jumped back into bed, concealing the gun under the blankets—where none thought to look for it—until he could return it to its box.

That was all the preparation he had needed. He had established an attempted murder directed against himself; and he had shown that a bullet fired at him could easily go near—and therefore through—the connecting doorway.

On the second night, he had waited until the house had seemed quiet. Then he had peeped through one of the cracks in the Japanese screen at the girl, whom he could see in the reflected light from the moon. He had found, though, that when he stepped far enough back from the screen for it to escape powder marks, he could not see the girl, not while she was lying down. So he had fired first into the door-frame—near the previous night's bullet—to awaken her.

She had sat up in bed immediately, screaming, and he had shot her. He had intended firing another shot into her body—to make sure of her death—but my approach had made that impossible, and had made concealment of the gun impossible; so, with what strength he had left, he had thrown the revolver out of the window.

He died that afternoon, and I returned to San Francisco.

But that was not quite the end of the story.

In the ordinary course of business, the agency's bookkeeping department sent Gallaway a bill for my services. With the check that he sent by return mail, he enclosed a letter to me, from which I quote a paragraph:

> I don't want to let you miss the cream of the whole affair. The lovely Caywood, when she recovered, denied that Exon had talked of murder or any other crime during his delirium. The cause of the distaste with which she might have looked at him afterward, and the reason she would not tell him what he had said, was that his entire conversation during that week of delirium had consisted of an uninterrupted stream of obscenities and blasphemies, which seem to have shocked the girl through and through.

Zigzags of Treachery

*Here is a detective story which we think will
please all comers. It is a happy combination
of deduction and swift action.*

1

"ALL I KNOW about Dr. Estep's death," I said, "is the stuff in the papers."

Vance Richmond's lean gray face took on an expression of distaste.

"The newspapers aren't always either thorough or accurate. I'll give you the salient points as I know them; though I suppose you'll want to go over the ground for yourself, and get your information first-hand."

I nodded, and the attorney went on, shaping each word precisely with his thin lips before giving it sound.

"Dr. Estep came to San Francisco in '98 or '99—a young man of twenty-five, just through qualifying for his license. He opened an office here, and, as you probably know, became in time a rather excellent surgeon. He married two or three years after he came here. There were no children. He and his wife seem to have been a bit happier together than the average.

"Of his life before coming to San Francisco, nothing is known. He told his wife briefly that he had been born and raised in Parkersburg, W. Va., but that his home life had been so unpleasant that he was trying to forget it, and that he did not like to talk—or even think—about it. Bear that in mind.

"Two weeks ago—on the third of the month—a woman came to his office, in the afternoon. His office was in his residence on Pine Street. Lucy Coe, who was Dr. Estep's nurse and assistant, showed the woman into his office, and then went back to her own desk in the reception room.

"She didn't hear anything the doctor said to the woman, but through the closed door she heard the woman's voice now and then—a high and anguished voice, apparently pleading. Most of the words were lost upon the nurse, but she heard one coherent sentence. 'Please! Please!' she heard the woman cry, 'Don't turn me away!' The woman was with Dr. Estep for about fifteen minutes, and left sobbing into a handkerchief. Dr. Estep said nothing about the caller either to his nurse or to his wife, who didn't learn of it until after his death.

"The next day, toward evening, while the nurse was putting on her hat and coat preparatory to leaving for home, Dr. Estep came out of his office, with his hat on and a letter in his hand. The nurse saw that his face was pale—'white as my uniform,' she says—and he walked with the care of one who takes pains to keep from staggering.

"She asked him if he was ill. 'Oh, it's nothing!' he told her. 'I'll be all right in a very few minutes.' Then he went on out. The nurse left the house just behind him, and saw him drop the letter he had carried into the mail box on the corner, after which he returned to the house.

"Mrs. Estep, coming downstairs ten minutes later,—it couldn't have been any later than that,—heard, just as she reached the first floor, the sound of a shot from her husband's office. She rushed into it, meeting nobody. Her husband stood by his desk, swaying, with a hole in his right temple and a smoking revolver in his hand. Just as she reached him and put her arms around him, he fell across the desk—dead."

"Anybody else—any of the servants, for instance—able to say that Mrs. Estep didn't go to the office until after the shot?" I asked.

The attorney shook his head sharply.

"No, damn it! That's where the rub comes in!"

His voice, after this one flare of feeling, resumed its level, incisive tone, and he went on with his tale.

"The next day's papers had accounts of Dr. Estep's death, and late that morning the woman who had called upon him the day before his death came to the house. She is Dr. Estep's first wife—which is to say, his legal wife! There seems to be no reason—not the slightest—for doubting it, as much as I'd like to. They were married in Philadelphia in '96. She has a certified copy of the marriage record. I had the matter investigated in Philadelphia, and it's a certain fact that Dr. Estep and this woman—Edna Fife was her maiden name—were really married.

"She says that Estep, after living with her in Philadelphia for two years, deserted her. That would have been in '98, or just before he came to San Francisco. She has sufficient proof of her identity—that she really is the Edna Fife who married him; and my agents in the East found positive proof that Estep had practiced for two years in Philadelphia.

"And here is another point. I told you that Estep had said he was born and raised in Parkersburg. I had inquiries made there, but found nothing to show that he had ever lived there, and found ample to show that he had never lived at the address he had given his wife. There is, then, nothing for us to believe except that his talk of an unhappy early life was a ruse to ward off embarrassing questions."

"Did you do anything toward finding out whether the doctor and his first wife had ever been divorced?" I asked.

"I'm having that taken care of now, but I hardly expect to

learn that they had. That would be too crude. To get on with my story: This woman—the first Mrs. Estep—said that she had just recently learned her husband's whereabouts, and had come to see him in an attempt to effect a reconciliation. When she called upon him the afternoon before his death, he asked for a little time to make up his mind what he should do. He promised to give her his decision in two days. My personal opinion, after talking to the woman several times, is that she had learned that he had accumulated some money, and that her interest was more in getting the money than in getting him. But that, of course, is neither here nor there.

"At first the authorities accepted the natural explanation of the doctor's death—suicide. But after the first wife's appearance, the second wife—my client—was arrested and charged with murder.

"The police theory is that after his first wife's visit, Dr. Estep told his second wife the whole story; and that she, brooding over the knowledge that he had deceived her, that she was not his wife at all, finally worked herself up into a rage, went to the office after his nurse had left for the day, and shot him with the revolver that she knew he always kept in his desk.

"I don't know, of course, just what evidence the prosecution has, but from the newspapers I gather that the case against her will be built upon her finger prints on the revolver with which he was killed; an upset inkwell on his desk; splashes of ink on the dress she wore; and an inky print of her hand on a torn newspaper on his desk.

"Unfortunately, but perfectly naturally, one of the first things she did was to take the revolver out of her husband's hand. That accounts for her prints on it. He fell—as I told you—just as she put her arms around him, and, though her memory isn't very clear on this point, the probabilities are that he dragged her with him when he fell across the desk. That accounts for the upset inkwell, the torn paper, and the splashes of ink. But the prosecution will try to persuade the jury that those things all happened before the shooting—that they are proofs of a struggle."

"Not so bad," I gave my opinion.

"Or pretty damned bad—depending on how you look at it. And this is the worst time imaginable for a thing like this to come up! Within the past few months there have been no less than five widely-advertised murders of men by women who were supposed to have been betrayed, or deceived, or one thing or another.

"Not one of those five women was convicted. As a result, we have the press, the public, and even the pulpit, howling for a stricter enforcement of justice. The newspapers are lined up against Mrs. Estep as strongly as their fear of libel suits will permit. The woman's clubs are lined up against her. Everybody is clamoring for an example to be made of her.

"Then, as if all that isn't enough, the Prosecuting Attorney has lost his last two big cases, and he'll be out for blood this time—election day isn't far off."

The calm, even, precise voice was gone now. In its place was a passionate eloquence.

"I don't know what you think," Richmond cried. "You're a detective. This is an old story to you. You're more or less callous, I suppose, and skeptical of innocence in general. But I know that Mrs. Estep didn't kill her husband. I don't say it because she's my client! I was Dr. Estep's attorney, and his friend, and if I thought Mrs. Estep guilty, I'd do everything in my power to help convict her. But I know as well as I know anything that she didn't kill him—couldn't have killed him.

"She's innocent. But I know too that if I go into court with no defense beyond what I now have, she'll be convicted! There has been too much leniency shown feminine criminals, public sentiment says. The pendulum will swing the other way—Mrs. Estep, if convicted, will get the limit. I'm putting it up to you! Can you save her?"

"Our best mark is the letter he mailed just before he died," I said, ignoring everything he said that didn't have to do with the facts of the case. "It's good betting that when a man writes and mails a letter and then shoots himself, that the letter isn't altogether unconnected with the suicide. Did you ask the first wife about the letter?"

"I did, and she denies having received one."

"That wasn't right. If the doctor had been driven to suicide by her appearance, then according to all the rules there are, the letter should have been addressed to her. He might have written one to his second wife, but he would hardly have mailed *it*."

"Would she have any reason for lying about it?"

"Yes," the lawyer said slowly, "I think she would. His will leaves everything to the second wife. The first wife, being the only legal wife, will have no difficulty in breaking that will, of course; but if it is shown that the second wife had no knowledge of the first one's existence—that she really believed herself to be Dr. Estep's legal wife—then I think that she will receive at least a portion of the estate. I don't think any court would, under the circumstances, take everything away from her. But if she should be found guilty of murdering Dr. Estep, then no consideration will be shown her, and the first wife will get every penny."

"Did he leave enough to make half of it, say, worth sending an innocent person to the gallows for?"

"He left about half a million, roughly; $250,000 isn't a mean inducement."

"Do you think it would be enough for the first wife—from what you have seen of her?"

"Candidly, I do. She didn't impress me as being a person of many very active scruples."

"Where does this first wife live?" I asked.

"She's staying at the Montgomery Hotel now. Her home is in Louisville, I believe. I don't think you will gain anything by talking to her, however. She has retained Somerset, Somerset, and Quill to represent her—a very reputable firm, by the way—and she'll refer you to them. They will tell you nothing. But if there's anything dishonest about her affairs—such as the concealing of Dr. Estep's letter—I'm confident that Somerset, Somerset and Quill know nothing of it."

"Can I talk to the second Mrs. Estep—your client?"

"Not at present. I'm afraid; though perhaps in a day or two. She is on the verge of collapse just now. She has always been delicate; and the shock of her husband's death, followed by her own arrest and imprisonment, has been too much for her. She's in the city jail, you know, held without bail. I've tried to have her transferred to the prisoner's ward of the City Hospital, even; but the authorities seem to think that her illness is simply a ruse. I'm worried about her. She's really in a critical condition."

His voice was losing its calmness again, so I picked up my

hat, said something about starting to work at once, and went out. I don't like eloquence: if it isn't effective enough to pierce your hide, it's tiresome; and if it is effective enough, then it muddles your thoughts.

2

I SPENT THE next couple of hours questioning the Estep servants, to no great advantage. None of them had been near the front of the house at the time of the shooting, and none had seen Mrs. Estep immediately prior to her husband's death.

After a lot of hunting, I located Lucy Coe, the nurse, in an apartment on Vallejo Street. She was a small, brisk, business-like woman of thirty or so. She repeated what Vance Richmond had told me, and could add nothing to it.

That cleaned up the Estep end of the job; and I set out for the Montgomery Hotel, satisfied that my only hope for success—barring miracles, which usually don't happen—lay in finding the letter that I believed Dr. Estep had written to his first wife.

My drag with the Montgomery Hotel management was pretty strong—strong enough to get me anything I wanted that wasn't too far outside the law. So as soon as I got there, I hunted up Stacey, one of the assistant managers.

"This Mrs. Estep who's registered here," I asked, "what do you know about her?"

"Nothing, myself, but if you'll wait a few minutes I'll see what I can learn."

The assistant manager was gone about ten minutes.

"No one seems to know much about her," he told me when he came back. "I've questioned the telephone girls, bell-boys, maids, clerks, and the house detective; but none of them could tell me much.

"She registered from Louisville, on the second of the month.

She has never stopped here before, and she seems unfamiliar with the city—asks quite a few questions about how to get around. The mail clerks don't remember handling any mail for her, nor do the girls on the switchboard have any record of phone calls for her.

"She keeps regular hours—usually goes out at ten or later in the morning, and gets in before midnight. She doesn't seem to have any callers or friends."

"Will you have her mail watched—let me know what postmarks and return addresses are on any letters she gets?"

"Certainly."

"And have the girls on the switchboard put their ears up against any talking she does over the wire?"

"Yes."

"Is she in her room now?"

"No, she went out a little while ago."

"Fine! I'd like to go up and take a look at her stuff."

Stacey looked sharply at me, and cleared his throat.

"Is it as—ah—important as all that? I want to give you all the assistance I can, but—"

"It's this important," I assured him, "that another woman's life depends on what I can learn about this one."

"All right!" he said. "I'll tell the clerk to let us know if she comes in before we are through; and we'll go right up."

The woman's room held two valises and a trunk, all unlocked, and containing not the least thing of importance—no letters—nothing. So little, in fact, that I was more than half convinced that she had expected her things to be searched.

Downstairs again, I planted myself in a comfortable chair within sight of the key rack, and waited for a view of this first Mrs. Estep.

She came in at 11:15 that night. A large woman of forty-five or fifty, well dressed, and carrying herself with an air of assurance. Her face was a little too hard as to mouth and chin, but not enough to be ugly. A capable looking woman—a woman who would get what she went after.

3

EIGHT O'CLOCK WAS striking as I went into the Montgomery lobby the next morning and picked out a chair, this time, within eye-range of the elevators.

At 10:30 Mrs. Estep left the hotel, with me in her wake. Her denial that a letter from her husband, written immediately before his death, had come to her didn't fit in with the possibilities as I saw them. And a good motto for the detective business is, "When in doubt—shadow 'em."

After eating breakfast at a restaurant on O'Farrell Street, she turned toward the shopping district; and for a long, long time—though I suppose it was a lot shorter than it seemed to me—she led me through the most densely packed portions of the most crowded department stores she could find.

She didn't buy anything, but she did a lot of thorough looking, with me muddling along behind her, trying to act like a little fat guy on an errand for his wife; while stout women bumped me and thin ones prodded me and all sorts got in my way and walked on my feet.

Finally, after I had sweated off a couple of pounds, she left the shopping district, and cut up through Union Square, walking along casually, as if out for a stroll.

Three-quarters way through, she turned abruptly, and retraced her steps, looking sharply at everyone she passed. I was on a bench, reading a stray page from a day-old newspaper, when she went by. She walked on down Post Street to Kearny, stopping every now and then to look—or to pretend to look—

in store windows; while I ambled along sometimes beside her, sometimes almost by her side, and sometimes in front.

She was trying to check up the people around her, trying to determine whether she was being followed or not. But here, in the busy part of town, that gave me no cause for worry. On a less crowded street it might have been different, though not necessarily so.

There are four rules for shadowing: Keep behind your subject as much as possible; never try to hide from him; act in a natural manner no matter what happens; and never meet his eye. Obey them, and, except in unusual circumstances, shadowing is the easiest thing that a sleuth has to do.

Assured, after a while, that no one was following her, Mrs. Estep turned back toward Powell Street, and got into a taxi-cab at the St. Francis stand. I picked out a modest touring car from the rank of hire-cars along the Geary Street side of Union Square, and set out after her.

Our route was out Post Street to Laguna, where the taxi presently swung into the curb and stopped. The woman got out, paid the driver, and went up the steps of an apartment building. With idling engine my own car had come to rest against the opposite curb in the block above.

As the taxicab disappeared around a corner, Mrs. Estep came out of the apartment building doorway, went back to the sidewalk, and started down Laguna Street.

"Pass her," I told my chauffeur, and we drew down upon her.

As we came abreast, she went up the front steps of another building, and this time she rang a bell. These steps belonged to a building apparently occupied by four flats, each with its separate door, and the button she had pressed belonged to the right-hand second-story flat.

Under cover of my car's rear curtains, I kept my eye on the doorway while my driver found a convenient place to park in the next block.

I kept my eye on the vestibule until 5:35 P.M., when she came out, walked to the Sutter Street car line, returned to the Montgomery, and went to her room.

I called up the Old Man—the Continental Detective Agency's San Francisco manager—and asked him to detail an operative to learn who and what were the occupants of the Laguna Street flat.

That night Mrs. Estep ate dinner at her hotel, and went to a show afterward, and she displayed no interest in possible shadowers. She went to her room at a little after eleven, and I knocked off for the day.

4

THE FOLLOWING MORNING I turned the woman over to Dick Foley, and went back to the agency to wait for Bob Teale, the operative who had investigated the Laguna Street flat. He came in at a little after ten.

"A guy named Jacob Ledwich lives there," Bob said. "He's a crook of some sort, but I don't know just what. He and 'Wop' Healey are friendly, so he must be a crook! 'Porky' Grout says he's an ex-bunco man who is in with a gambling ring now; but 'Porky' would tell you a bishop was a safe-ripper if he thought it would mean five bucks for himself.

"This Ledwich goes out mostly at night, and he seems to be pretty prosperous. Probably a high-class worker of some sort. He's got a Buick—license number 645-221—that he keeps in a garage around the corner from his flat. But he doesn't seem to use the car much."

"What sort of looking fellow is he?"

"A big guy—six feet or better—and he'll weigh a couple hundred easy. He's got a funny mug on him. It's broad and heavy around the cheeks and jaw, but his mouth is a little one that looks like it was made for a smaller man. He's no youngster—middle-aged."

"Suppose you tail him around for a day or two, Bob, and see what he's up to. Try to get a room or apartment in the neighborhood—a place that you can cover his front door from."

5

VANCE RICHMOND'S LEAN face lighted up as soon as I mentioned Ledwich's name to him.

"Yes!" he exclaimed. "He was a friend, or at least an acquaintance, of Dr. Estep's. I met him once—a large man with a peculiarly inadequate mouth. I dropped in to see the doctor one day, and Ledwich was in the office. Dr. Estep introduced us."

"What do you know about him?"

"Nothing."

"Don't you know whether he was intimate with the doctor, or just a casual acquaintance?"

"No. For all I know, he might have been a friend, a patient, or almost anything. The doctor never spoke of him to me, and nothing passed between them while I was there that afternoon. I simply gave the doctor some information he had asked for and left. Why?"

"Dr. Estep's first wife—after going to a lot of trouble to see that she wasn't followed—connected with Ledwich yesterday afternoon. And from what we can learn, he seems to be a crook of some sort."

"What would that indicate?"

"I'm not sure what it means, but I can do a lot of guessing. Ledwich knew both the doctor and the doctor's first wife; then it's not a bad bet that she knew where her husband was all the time. If she did, then it's another good bet that she was getting money from him right along. Can you check up his accounts and see whether he was passing out any money that can't be otherwise accounted for?"

The attorney shook his head.

"No, his accounts are in rather bad shape, carelessly kept. He must have had more than a little difficulty with his income tax statements."

"I see. To get back to my guesses: If she knew where he was all the time, and was getting money from him, then why did his first wife finally come to see her husband? Perhaps because—"

"I think I can help you there," Richmond interrupted. "A fortunate investment in lumber nearly doubled Dr. Estep's wealth two or three months ago."

"That's it, then! She learned of it through Ledwich. She demanded, either through Ledwich, or by letter, a rather large share of it—more than the doctor was willing to give. When he refused, she came to see him in person, to demand the money under threat—we'll say—of instant exposure. He thought she was in earnest. Either he couldn't raise the money she demanded, or he was tired of leading a double life. Anyway, he thought it all over, and decided to commit suicide. This is all a guess, or a series of guesses—but it sounds reasonable to me."

"To me, too," the attorney said. "What are you going to do now?"

"I'm still having both of them shadowed—there's no other way of tackling them just now. I'm having the woman looked up in Louisville. But, you understand, I might dig up a whole flock of things on them, and when I got through still be as far as ever from finding the letter Dr. Estep wrote before he died.

"There are plenty of reasons for thinking that the woman destroyed the letter—that would have been her wisest play.

But if I can get enough on her, even at that, I can squeeze her into admitting that the letter was written, and that it said something about suicide—if it did. And that will be enough to spring your client. How is she today—any better?"

His thin face lost the animation that had come to it during our discussion of Ledwich, and became bleak.

"She went completely to pieces last night, and was removed to the hospital, where she should have been taken in the first place. To tell you the truth, if she isn't liberated soon, she won't need our help. I've done my utmost to have her released on bail—pulled every wire I know—but there's little likelihood of success in that direction.

"Knowing that she is a prisoner—charged with murdering her husband—is killing her. She isn't young, and she has always been subject to nervous disorders. The bare shock of her husband's death was enough to prostrate her—but now— You've *got* to get her out—and quickly!"

He was striding up and down his office, his voice throbbing with feeling. I left quickly.

6

FROM THE ATTORNEY'S office, I returned to the agency, where I was told that Bob Teale had phoned in the address of a furnished apartment he had rented on Laguna Street. I hopped on a street car, and went up to take a look at it.

But I didn't get that far.

Walking down Laguna Street, after leaving the car, I spied Bob Teale coming toward me. Between Bob and me—also coming toward me—was a big man whom I recognized as Jacob Ledwich: a big man with a big red face around a tiny mouth.

I walked on down the street, passing both Ledwich and Bob, without paying any apparent attention to either. At the next corner I stopped to roll a cigarette, and steal a look at the pair.

And then I came to life!

Ledwich had stopped at a vestibule cigar stand up the street to make a purchase. Bob Teale, knowing his stuff, had passed him and was walking steadily up the street.

He was figuring that Ledwich had either come out for the purpose of buying cigars or cigarettes, and would return to his flat with them; or that after making his purchase the big man would proceed to the car line, where, in either event, Bob would wait.

But as Ledwich had stopped before the cigar stand, a man across the street had stepped suddenly into a doorway, and stood there, back in the shadows. This man, I now remembered, had been on the opposite side of the street from Bob and Ledwich, and walking in the same direction.

He, too, was following Ledwich.

By the time Ledwich had finished his business at the stand, Bob had reached Sutter Street, the nearest car line. Ledwich started up the street in that direction. The man in the doorway stepped out and went after him. I followed that one.

A ferry-bound car came down Sutter Street just as I reached the corner. Ledwich and I got aboard together. The mysterious stranger fumbled with a shoe-string several pavements from the corner until the car was moving again, and then he likewise made a dash for it.

He stood beside me on the rear platform, hiding behind a large man in overalls, past whose shoulder he now and then peeped at Ledwich. Bob had gone to the corner above, and was already seated when Ledwich, this amateur detective,—there was no doubting his amateur status,—and I got on the car.

I sized up the amateur while he strained his neck peeping at Ledwich. He was small, this sleuth, and scrawny and frail. His most noticeable feature was his nose—a limp organ that twitched nervously all the time. His clothes were old and shabby, and he himself was somewhere in his fifties.

After studying him for a few minutes, I decided that he hadn't tumbled to Bob Teale's part in the game. His attention had been too firmly fixed upon Ledwich, and the distance had been too short thus far for him to discover that Bob was also tailing the big man.

So when the seat beside Bob was vacated presently, I chucked my cigarette away, went into the car, and sat down, my back toward the little man with the twitching nose.

"Drop off after a couple of blocks and go back to the apartment. Don't shadow Ledwich any more until I tell you. Just watch his place. There's a bird following him, and I want to see what he's up to," I told Bob in an undertone.

He grunted that he understood, and, after a few minutes, left the car.

At Stockton Street, Ledwich got off, the man with the twitching nose behind him, and me in the rear. In that formation we paraded around town all afternoon.

The big man had business in a number of pool rooms, cigar stores, and soft drink parlors—most of which I knew for places where you can get a bet down on any horse that's running in North America, whether at Tanforan, Tijuana, or Timonium.

Just what Ledwich did in these places, I didn't learn. I was bringing up the rear of the procession, and my interest was centered upon the mysterious little stranger. He didn't enter any of the places behind Ledwich, but loitered in their neighborhoods until Ledwich reappeared.

He had a rather strenuous time of it—laboring mightily to keep out of Ledwich's sight, and only succeeding because we were downtown, where you can get away with almost any sort of shadowing. He certainly made a lot of work for himself, dodging here and there.

After a while, Ledwich shook him.

The big man came out of a cigar store with another man. They got into an automobile that was standing beside the curb, and drove away; leaving my man standing on the edge of the sidewalk twitching his nose in chagrin. There was a taxi stand just around the corner, but he either didn't know it or didn't have enough money to pay the fare.

I expected him to return to Laguna Street then, but he didn't. He led me down Kearny Street to Portsmouth Street, where he stretched himself out on the grass, face down, lit a black pipe, and lay looking dejectedly at the Stevenson monument, probably without seeing it.

I sprawled on a comfortable piece of sod some distance away—between a Chinese woman with two perfectly round children and an ancient Portuguese in a gaily checkered suit— and we let the afternoon go by.

When the sun had gone low enough for the ground to become chilly, the little man got up, shook himself, and went back up Kearny Street to a cheap lunch-room, where he ate meagerly. Then he entered a hotel a few doors away, took a key from the row of hooks, and vanished down a dark corridor.

Running through the register, I found that the key he had taken belonged to a room whose occupant was "John Boyd, St. Louis, Mo.," and that he had arrived the day before.

This hotel wasn't of the sort where it is safe to make inquiries, so I went down to the street again, and came to rest on the least conspicuous nearby corner.

Twilight came, and the street and shop lights were turned on. It got dark. The night traffic of Kearny Street went up and down past me: Filipino boys in their too-dapper clothes, bound for the inevitable black-jack game; gaudy women still heavy-eyed from their day's sleep; plain clothes men on their way to headquarters, to report before going off duty; Chinese going to or from China-town; sailors in pairs, looking for action of any sort; hungry people making for the Italian and French restaurants; worried people going into the bail bond broker's office on the corner to arrange for the release of friends and relatives whom the police had nabbed; Italians on their homeward journeys from work; odds and ends of furtive-looking citizens on various shady errands.

Midnight came, and no John Boyd, and I called it a day, and went home.

Before going to bed, I talked with Dick Foley over the wire. He said that Mrs. Estep had done nothing of any importance all day, and had received neither mail nor phone calls. I told him to stop shadowing her until I solved John Boyd's game.

I was afraid Boyd might turn his attention to the woman, and I didn't want him to discover that she was being shadowed. I had already instructed Bob Teale to simply watch Ledwich's flat—to see when he came in and went out, and with whom— and now I told Dick to do the same with the woman.

My guess on this Boyd person was that he and the woman were working together—that she had him watching Ledwich for her, so that the big man couldn't double-cross her. But that was only a guess—and I don't gamble too much on my guesses.

7

THE NEXT MORNING I dressed myself up in an army shirt and shoes, an old faded cap, and a suit that wasn't downright ragged, but was shabby enough not to stand out too noticeably beside John Boyd's old clothes.

It was a little after nine o'clock when Boyd left his hotel and had breakfast at the grease-joint where he had eaten the night before. Then he went up to Laguna Street, picked himself a corner, and waited for Jacob Ledwich.

He did a lot of waiting. He waited all day; because Ledwich didn't show until after dark. But the little man was well-stocked with patience—I'll say that for him. He fidgeted, and stood on one foot and then the other, and even tried sitting on the curb for awhile, but he stuck it out.

I took it easy, myself. The furnished apartment Bob Teale had rented to watch Ledwich's flat from was a ground floor one, across the street, and just a little above the corner where Boyd waited. So we could watch him and the flat with one eye.

Bob and I sat and smoked and talked all day, taking turns watching the fidgeting man on the corner and Ledwich's door.

Night had just definitely settled when Ledwich came out and started up toward the car line. I slid out into the street, and our parade was under way again—Ledwich leading, Boyd following him, and we following *him*.

Half a block of this, and I got an idea!

I'm not what you'd call a brilliant thinker—such results as I get are usually the fruits of patience, industry, and unimaginative plugging, helped out now and then, maybe, by a little luck—but I do have my flashes of intelligence. And this was one of them.

Ledwich was about a block ahead of me; Boyd half that distance. Speeding up, I passed Boyd, and caught up with Ledwich. Then I slackened my pace so as to walk beside him, though with no appearance from the rear of having any interest in him.

"Jake," I said, without turning my head, "there's a guy following you!"

The big man almost spoiled my little scheme by stopping dead still, but he caught himself in time, and, taking his cue from me, kept walking.

"Who the hell are you?" he growled.

"Don't get funny!" I snapped back, still looking and walking ahead. "It ain't my funeral. But I was coming up the street when you came out, and I seen this guy duck behind a pole until you was past, and then follow you up."

That got him.

"You sure?"

"Sure! All you got to do to prove it is turn the next corner and wait."

I was two or three steps ahead of him by this time, I turned the corner, and halted, with my back against the brick building front. Ledwich took up the same position at my side.

"Want any help?" I grinned at him—a reckless sort of grin, unless my acting was poor.

"No."

His little lumpy mouth was set ugly, and his blue eyes were hard as pebbles.

I flicked the tail of my coat aside to show him the butt of my gun.

"Want to borrow the rod?" I asked.

"No."

He was trying to figure me out, and small wonder.

"Don't mind if I stick around to see the fun, do you?" I asked, mockingly.

There wasn't time for him to answer that. Boyd had quickened his steps, and now he came hurrying around the corner, his nose twitching like a tracking dog's.

Ledwich stepped into the middle of the sidewalk, so suddenly that the little man thudded into him with a grunt. For a moment they stared at each other, and there was recognition between them.

Ledwich shot one big hand out and clamped the other by a shoulder.

"What are you snooping around me for, you rat? Didn't I tell you to keep away from Frisco?"

"Aw, Jake!" Boyd begged. "I didn't mean no harm. I just thought that—"

Ledwich silenced him with a shake that clicked his mouth shut, and turned to me.

"A friend of mine," he sneered.

His eyes grew suspicious and hard again, and ran up and down me from cap to shoes.

"How'd you know my name?" he demanded.

"A famous man like you?" I asked, in burlesque astonishment.

"Never mind the comedy!" He took a threatening step toward me. "How'd you know my name?"

"None of your damned business," I snapped.

My attitude seemed to reassure him. His face became less suspicious.

"Well," he said slowly, "I owe you something for this trick, and—How are you fixed?"

"I have been dirtier." Dirty is Pacific Coast argot for prosperous.

He looked speculatively from me to Boyd, and back.

"Know 'The Circle'?" he asked me.

I nodded. The underworld calls "Wop" Healey's joint "The Circle."

"If you'll meet me there tomorrow night, maybe I can put a piece of change your way."

"Nothing stirring!" I shook my head with emphasis. "I ain't circulating that prominent these days."

A fat chance I'd have of meeting him there! "Wop" Healey and half his customers knew me as a detective. So there was nothing to do but to try to get the impression over that I was a crook who had reasons for wanting to keep away from the more notorious hang-outs for a while. Apparently it got over. He thought a while, and then gave me his Laguna Street number.

"Drop in this time tomorrow and maybe I'll have a proposition to make you—if you've got the guts."

"I'll think it over," I said noncommittally, and turned as if to go down the street.

"Just a minute," he called, and I faced him again. "What's your name?"

"Wisher," I said, "Shine, if you want a front one."

"Shine Wisher," he repeated. "I don't remember ever hearing it before."

It would have surprised me if he had—I had made it up only about fifteen minutes before.

"You needn't yell it," I said sourly, "so that everybody in the burg *will* remember hearing it."

And with that I left him, not at all dissatisfied with myself. By tipping him off to Boyd, I had put him under obligations to me, and had led him to accept me, at least tentatively, as a fellow crook. And by making no apparent effort to gain his good graces, I had strengthened my hand that much more.

I had a date with him for the next day, when I was to be given a chance to earn—illegally, no doubt—"a piece of change."

There was a chance that this proposition he had in view for me had nothing to do with the Estep affair, but then again it might; and whether it did or not, I had my entering wedge at least a little way into Jake Ledwich's business.

I strolled around for about half an hour, and then went back to Bob Teale's apartment.

"Ledwich come back?"

"Yes," Bob said, "with that little guy of yours. They went in about half an hour ago."

"Good! Haven't seen a woman go in?"

"No."

I expected to see the first Mrs. Estep arrive sometime during the evening, but she didn't. Bob and I sat around and talked and watched Ledwich's doorway, and the hours passed.

At one o'clock Ledwich came out alone.

"I'm going to tail him, just for luck," Bob said, and caught up his cap.

Ledwich vanished around a corner, and then Bob passed out of sight behind him.

Five minutes later Bob was with me again.

"He's getting his machine out of the garage."

I jumped for the telephone and put in a rush order for a fast touring car.

Bob, at the window, called out, "Here he is!"

I joined Bob in time to see Ledwich going into his vestibule. His car stood in front of the house. A very few minutes, and Boyd and Ledwich came out together. Boyd was leaning heavily on Ledwich, who was supporting the little man with an arm across his back. We couldn't see their faces in the dark, but the little man was plainly either sick, drunk, or drugged!

Ledwich helped his companion into the touring car. The red tail-lights laughed back at us for a few blocks, and then disappeared. The automobile I had ordered arrived twenty minutes later, so we sent it back unused.

At a little after three that morning, Ledwich, alone and afoot, returned from the direction of his garage. He had been gone exactly two hours.

8

NEITHER BOB NOR I went home that night, but slept in the Laguna Street apartment.

Bob went down to the corner grocer's to get what we needed for breakfast in the morning, and he brought a morning paper back with him.

I cooked breakfast while he divided his attention between Ledwich's front door and the newspaper.

"Hey!" he called suddenly, "look here!"

I ran out of the kitchen with a handful of bacon.

"What is it?"

"Listen! 'Park murder mystery!'" he read. " 'Early this morning the body of an unidentified man was found near a driveway in Golden Gate Park. His neck had been broken, according to the police; who say that the absence of any considerable bruises on the body, as well as the orderly condition of the clothes and the ground nearby, show that he did not come to his death through falling, or being struck by an automobile. It is believed that he was killed and then carried to the Park in an automobile, to be left there.'"

"Boyd!" I said.

"I bet you!" Bob agreed.

And at the morgue a very little while later, we learned that we were correct. The dead man was John Boyd.

"He was dead when Ledwich brought him out of the house," Bob said.

I nodded.

"He was! He was a little man, and it wouldn't have been much of a stunt for a big bruiser like Ledwich to have dragged him along with one arm the short distance from the door to the curb, pretending to be holding him up, like you do with a drunk. Let's go over to the Hall of Justice and see what the police have got on it—if anything."

At the detective bureau we hunted up O'Gar, the detective-sergeant in charge of the Homicide Detail, and a good man to work with.

"This dead man found in the park," I asked, "know anything about him?"

O'Gar pushed back his village constable's hat—a big black hat with a floppy brim that belongs in vaudeville—scratched his bullet-head, and scowled at me as if he thought I had a joke up my sleeve.

"Not a damned thing except that he's dead!" he said at last.

"How'd you like to know who he was last seen with?"

"It wouldn't hinder me any in finding out who bumped him off, and that's a fact."

"How do you like the sound of this?" I asked. "His name was John Boyd and he was living at a hotel down in the next block. The last person he was seen with was a guy who is tied up with Dr. Estep's first wife. You know—the Dr. Estep whose second wife is the woman you people are trying to prove a murder on. Does that sound interesting?"

"It does," he said. "Where do we go first?"

"This Ledwich—he's the fellow who was last seen with Boyd—is going to be a hard bird to shake down. We better try to crack the woman first—the first Mrs. Estep. There's a chance that Boyd was a pal of hers, and in that case when she finds out that Ledwich rubbed him out, she may open up and spill the works to us.

"On the other hand, if she and Ledwich are stacked up against Boyd together, then we might as well get her safely placed before we tie into him. I don't want to pull him before night, anyway. I got a date with him, and I want to try to rope him first."

Bob Teale made for the door.

"I'm going up and keep my eye on him until you're ready for him," he called over his shoulder.

"Good," I said. "Don't let him get out of town on us. If he tries to blow have him chucked in the can."

In the lobby of the Montgomery Hotel, O'Gar and I talked to Dick Foley first. He told us that the woman was still in her room—had had her breakfast sent up. She had received neither letters, telegrams, or phone calls since we began to watch her.

I got hold of Stacey again.

"We're going up to talk to this Estep woman, and maybe we'll take her away with us. Will you send up a maid to find out whether she's up and dressed yet? We don't want to announce ourselves ahead of time, and we don't want to burst in on her while she's in bed, or only partly dressed."

He kept us waiting about fifteen minutes, and then told us that Mrs. Estep was up and dressed.

We went up to her room, taking the maid with us.

The maid rapped on the door.

"What is it?" an irritable voice demanded.

"The maid; I want to—"

The key turned on the inside, and an angry Mrs. Estep jerked the door open. O'Gar and I advanced, O'Gar flashing his "buzzer."

"From headquarters," he said. "We want to talk to you."

O'Gar's foot was where she couldn't slam the door on us, and we were both walking ahead, so there was nothing for her to do but to retreat into the room, admitting us—which she did with no pretense of graciousness.

We closed the door, and then I threw our big load at her.

"Mrs. Estep, why did Jake Ledwich kill John Boyd?"

The expressions ran over her face like this: Alarm at Ledwich's name, fear at the word "kill," but the name John Boyd brought only bewilderment.

"Why did what?" she stammered meaninglessly, to gain time.

"Exactly," I said. "Why did Jake kill him last night in his flat, and then take him in the park and leave him?"

Another set of expressions: Increased bewilderment until I had almost finished the sentence, and then the sudden understanding of something, followed by the inevitable groping for poise. These things weren't as plain as billboards, you understand, but they were there to be read by anyone who had ever played poker—either with cards or people.

What I got out of them was that Boyd hadn't been working with or for her, and that, though she knew Ledwich had killed somebody at some time, it wasn't Boyd and it wasn't last night. Who, then? And when? Dr. Estep? Hardly! There wasn't a chance in the world that—if he had been murdered—anybody except his wife had done it—his second wife. No possible reading of the evidence could bring any other answer.

Who, then, had Ledwich killed before Boyd? Was he a wholesale murderer?

These things are flitting through my head in flashes and odd scraps while Mrs. Estep is saying:

"This is absurd! The idea of your coming up here and—"

She talked for five minutes straight, the words fairly sizzling from between her hard lips; but the words themselves didn't mean anything. She was talking for time—talking while she tried to hit upon the safest attitude to assume.

And before we could head her off, she had hit upon it— silence!

We got not another word out of her; and that is the only way in the world to beat the grilling game. The average suspect tries to talk himself out of being arrested; and it doesn't matter how shrewd a man is, or how good a liar, if he'll talk to you, and you play your cards right, you can hook him—can make him help you convict him. But if he won't talk you can't do a thing with him.

And that's how it was with this woman. She refused to pay any attention to our questions—she wouldn't speak, nod, grunt, or wave an arm in reply. She gave us a fine assortment of facial expressions, true enough, but we wanted verbal information— and we got none.

We weren't easily licked, however. Three beautiful hours of it we gave her without rest. We stormed, cajoled, threatened, and at times I think we danced; but it was no go. So in the end we took her away with us. We didn't have anything on her, but we couldn't afford to have her running around loose until we nailed Ledwich.

At the Hall of Justice we didn't book her; but simply held her as a material witness, putting her in an office with a matron and one of O'Gar's men, who were to see what they could do with her while we went after Ledwich. We had had her frisked as soon as she reached the Hall, of course; and, as we expected, she hadn't a thing of importance on her.

O'Gar and I went back to the Montgomery and gave her room a thorough overhauling—and found nothing.

"Are you sure you know what you're talking about?" the detective-sergeant asked as we left the hotel. "It's going to be a pretty joke on somebody if you're mistaken."

I let that go by without an answer.

"I'll meet you at 6:30," I said, "and we'll go up against Ledwich."

He grunted an approval, and I set out for Vance Richmond's office.

9

THE ATTORNEY SPRANG up from his desk as soon as his stenographer admitted me. His face was leaner and grayer than ever; its lines had deepened, and there was a hollowness around his eyes.

"You've *got* to do something!" he cried huskily. "I have just come from the hospital. Mrs. Estep is on the point of death! A day more of this—two days at the most—and she will—"

I interrupted him, and swiftly gave him an account of the day's happenings, and what I expected, or hoped, to make out of them. But he received the news without brightening, and shook his head hopelessly.

"But don't you see," he exclaimed when I had finished, "that that won't do? I know you can find proof of her innocence in time. I'm not complaining—you've done all that could be expected, and more! But all that's no good! I've got to have—well—a miracle, perhaps.

"Suppose that you do finally get the truth out of Ledwich and the first Mrs. Estep or it comes out during their trials for Boyd's murder? Or that you even get to the bottom of the matter in three or four days? That will be too late! If I can go to Mrs. Estep and tell her she's free now, she may pull herself together, and come through. But another day of imprisonment—two days, or perhaps even two hours—and she won't need anybody to clear her. Death will have done it! I tell you, she's—"

I left Vance Richmond abruptly again. This lawyer was bound

upon getting me worked up; and I like my jobs to be simply jobs—emotions are nuisances during business hours.

10

AT A QUARTER to seven that evening, while O'Gar remained down the street, I rang Jacob Ledwich's bell. As I had stayed with Bob Teale in our apartment the previous night, I was still wearing the clothes in which I had made Ledwich's acquaintance as Shine Wisher.

Ledwich opened the door.

"Hello, Wisher!" he said without enthusiasm, and led me upstairs.

His flat consisted of four rooms, I found, running the full length and half the breadth of the building, with both front and rear exits. It was furnished with the ordinary none-too-spotless appointments of the typical moderately priced furnished flat—alike the world over.

In his front room we sat down and talked and smoked and sized one another up. He seemed a little nervous. I thought he would have been just as well satisfied if I had forgotten to show up.

"About this job you mentioned?" I asked presently.

"Sorry," he said, moistening his little lumpy mouth, "but it's all off." And then he added, obviously as an afterthought, "for the present, at least."

I guessed from that that my job was to have taken care of Boyd—but Boyd had been taken care of for good.

He brought out some whisky after a while, and we talked over it for some time, to no purpose whatever. He was trying not to appear too anxious to get rid of me, and I was cautiously feeling him out.

Piecing together things he let fall here and there, I came to the conclusion that he was a former con man who had fallen into an easier game of late years. That was in line, too, with what "Porky" Grout had told Bob Teale.

I talked about myself with the evasiveness that would have been natural to a crook in my situation; and made one or two carefully planned slips that would lead him to believe that I had been tied up with the "Jimmy the Riveter" holdup mob, most of whom were doing long hitches at Walla Walla then.

He offered to lend me enough money to tide me over until I could get on my feet again. I told him I didn't need chicken feed so much as a chance to pick up some real jack.

The evening was going along, and we were getting nowhere.

"Jake," I said casually—outwardly casual, that is, "you took a big chance putting that guy out of the way like you did last night."

I meant to stir things up, and I succeeded.

His face went crazy.

A gun came out of his coat.

Firing from my pocket, I shot it out of his hand.

"Now behave!" I ordered.

He sat rubbing his benumbed hand and staring with wide eyes at the smouldering hole in my coat.

Looks like a great stunt—this shooting a gun out of a man's hand, but it's a thing that happens now and then. A man who is a fair shot (and that is exactly what I am—no more, no less), naturally and automatically shoots pretty close to the spot upon which his eyes are focused. When a man goes for his gun in front of you, you shoot at *him*—not at any particular part of him. There isn't time for that—you shoot at him. However, you are more than likely to be looking at his gun, and in that case it isn't altogether surprising if your bullet should hit his gun—as mine had done. But it looks impressive.

I beat out the fire around the bullet-hole in my coat, crossed the room to where his revolver had been knocked, and picked it up. I started to eject the bullets from it, but, instead, I snapped it shut again and stuck it in my pocket. Then I returned to my chair, opposite him.

"A man oughtn't to act like that," I kidded him, "he's likely to hurt somebody."

His little mouth curled up at me.

"An elbow, huh?" putting all the contempt he could in his voice; and somehow any synonym for detective seems able to hold a lot of contempt.

I might have tried to talk myself back into the Wisher role. It could have been done, but I doubted that it would be worth it; so I nodded my confession.

His brain was working now, and the passion left his face, while he sat rubbing his right hand, and his little mouth and eyes began to screw themselves up calculatingly.

I kept quiet, waiting to see what the outcome of his thinking would be. I knew he was trying to figure out just what my place in this game was. Since, to his knowledge, I had come into it no later than the previous evening, then the Boyd murder hadn't brought me in. That would leave the Estep affair—unless he was tied up in a lot of other crooked stuff that I didn't know anything about.

"You're not a city dick, are you?" he asked finally; and his voice was on the verge of friendliness now: the voice of one who wants to persuade you of something, or sell you something.

The truth, I thought, wouldn't hurt.

"No," I said, "I'm with the Continental."

He hitched his chair a little closer to the muzzle of my automatic.

"What are you after, then? Where do you come in on it?"

I tried the truth again.

"The second Mrs. Estep. She didn't kill her husband."

"You're trying to dig up enough dope to spring her?"

"Yes."

I waved him back as he tried to hitch his chair still nearer.

"How do you expect to do it?" he asked, his voice going lower and more confidential with each word.

I took still another flier at the truth.

"He wrote a letter before he died."

"Well?"

But I called a halt for the time.

"Just that," I said.

He leaned back in his chair, and his eyes and mouth grew small in thought again.

"What's your interest in the man who died last night?" he asked slowly.

"It's something on you," I said, truthfully again. "It doesn't do the second Mrs. Estep any direct good, maybe; but you and the first wife are stacked up together against her. Anything, therefore, that hurts you two will help her, somehow. I admit I'm wandering around in the dark; but I'm going ahead wherever I see a point of light—and I'll come through to daylight in the end. Nailing you for Boyd's murder is one point of light."

He leaned forward suddenly, his eyes and mouth popping open as far as they would go.

"You'll come out all right," he said very softly, "if you use a little judgment."

"What's that supposed to mean?"

"Do you think," he asked, still very softly, "that you can nail me for Boyd's murder—that you can convict me of murder?"

"I do."

But I wasn't any too sure. In the first place, though we were morally certain of it, neither Bob Teale nor I could swear that the man who had got in the machine with Ledwich was John Boyd.

We knew it was, of course, but the point is that it had been too dark for us to see his face. And, again, in the dark, we had thought him alive; it wasn't until later that we knew he had been dead when he came down the steps.

Little things, those, but a private detective on the witness stand—unless he is absolutely sure of every detail—has an unpleasant and ineffectual time of it.

"I do," I repeated, thinking these things over, "and I'm satisfied to go to the bat with what I've got on you and what I can collect between now and the time you and your accomplice go to trial."

"Accomplice?" he said, not very surprised. "That would be Edna. I suppose you've already grabbed her?"

"Yes."

He laughed.

"You'll have one sweet time getting anything out of her. In the first place, she doesn't know much, and in the second—well, I suppose you've tried, and have found out what a helpful sort she is! So don't try the old gag of pretending that she has talked!"

"I'm not pretending anything."

Silence between us for a few seconds, and then—

"I'm going to make you a proposition," he said. "You can take it or leave it. The note Dr. Estep wrote before he died was to me, and it is positive proof that he committed suicide. Give me a chance to get away—just a chance—a half-hour start—and I'll give you my word of honor to send you the letter."

"I know I can trust you," I said sarcastically.

"I'll trust you, then!" he shot back at me. "I'll turn the note over to you if you'll give me your word that I'm to have half an hour's start."

"For what?" I demanded. "Why shouldn't I take both you and the note?"

"If you can get them! But do I look like the kind of sap who would leave the note where it would be found? Do you think it's here in the room maybe?"

I didn't, but neither did I think that because he had hidden it, it couldn't be found.

"I can't think of any reason why I should bargain with you," I told him. "I've got you cold, and that's enough."

"If I can show you that your only chance of freeing the second Mrs. Estep is through my voluntary assistance, will you bargain with me?"

"Maybe—I'll listen to your persuasion, anyway."

"All right," he said, "I'm going to come clean with you. But most of the things I'm going to tell you can't be proven in court without my help; and if you turn my offer down I'll have plenty of evidence to convince the jury that these things are all false, that I never said them, and that you are trying to frame me."

That part was plausible enough. I've testified before juries all the way from the City of Washington to the State of Washington, and I've never seen one yet that wasn't anxious to believe that a private detective is a double-crossing specialist who goes around with a cold deck in one pocket, a complete forger's outfit in another, and who counts that day lost in which he railroads no innocent to the hoosegow.

11

"THERE WAS ONCE a young doctor in a town a long way from here," Ledwich began. "He got mixed up in a scandal—a pretty rotten one—and escaped the pen only by the skin of his teeth. The state medical board revoked his license.

"In a large city not far away, this young doc, one night when he was drunk,—as he usually was in those days,—told his troubles to a man he had met in a dive. The friend was a resourceful sort; and he offered, for a price, to fix the doc up with a fake diploma, so he could set up in practice in some other state.

"The young doctor took him up, and the friend got the diploma for him. The doc was the man you know as Dr. Estep, and I was the friend. The real Dr. Estep was found dead in the park this morning!"

That was news—if true!

"You see," the big man went on, "when I offered to get the phoney diploma for the young doc—whose real name doesn't matter—I had in mind a forged one. Nowadays they're easy to get—there's a regular business in them,—but twenty-five years ago, while you could manage it, they were hard to get. While I was trying to get one, I ran across a woman I used to work with—Edna Fife. That's the woman you know as the first Mrs. Estep.

"Edna had married a doctor—the real Dr. Humbert Estep. He was a hell of a doctor, though; and after starving with him in Philadelphia for a couple of years, she made him close up his office, and she went back to the bunko game, taking him with her. She was good at it, I'm telling you—a real cleaner—and, keeping him under her thumb all the time, she made him a pretty good worker himself.

"It was shortly after that that I met her, and when she told me all this, I offered to buy her husband's medical diploma and other credentials. I don't know whether he wanted to sell them or not—but he did what she told him, and I got the papers.

"I turned them over to the young doc, who came to San Francisco and opened an office under the name of Humbert Estep. The real Esteps promised not to use that name any more—not much of an inconvenience for them, as they changed names every time they changed addresses.

"I kept in touch with the young doctor, of course, getting my regular rake-off from him. I had him by the neck, and I wasn't foolish enough to pass up any easy money. After a year or so, I learned that he had pulled himself together and was making good. So I jumped on a train and came to San Francisco. He was doing fine; so I camped here, where I could keep my eye on him and watch out for my own interests.

"He got married about then, and, between his practice and his investments, he began to accumulate a roll. But he tightened up on me—damn him! He wouldn't be bled. I got a regular percentage of what he made, and that was all.

"For nearly twenty-five years I got it—but not a nickel over the percentage. He knew I wouldn't kill the goose that laid the golden eggs, so no matter how much I threatened to expose him, he sat tight, and I couldn't budge him. I got my regular cut, and not a nickel more.

"That went along, as I say, for years. I was getting a living out of him, but I wan't getting any big money. A few months ago

I learned that he had cleaned up heavily in a lumber deal so I made up my mind to take him for what he had.

"During all these years I had got to know the doc pretty well. You do when you're bleeding a man—you get a pretty fair idea of what goes on in his head, and what he's most likely to do if certain things should happen. So I knew the doc pretty well.

"I knew for instance, that he had never told his wife the truth about his past; that he had stalled her with some lie about being born in West Virginia. That was fine—for me! Then I knew that he kept a gun in his desk, and I knew why. It was kept there for the purpose of killing himself if the truth ever came out about his diploma. He figured that if, at the first hint of exposure, he wiped himself out, the authorities, out of respect for the good reputation he had built up, would hush things up.

"And his wife—even if she herself learned the truth—would be spared the shame of a public scandal. I can't see myself dying just to spare some woman's feeling, but the doc was a funny guy in some ways—and he was nutty about his wife.

"That's the way I had him figured out, and that's the way things turned out.

"My plan might sound complicated, but it was simple enough. I got hold of the real Esteps—it took a lot of hunting, but I found them at last. I brought the woman to San Francisco, and told the man to stay away.

"Everything would have gone fine if he had done what I told him; but he was afraid that Edna and I were going to double-cross him, so he came here to keep an eye on us. But I didn't know that until you put the finger on him for me.

"I brought Edna here and, without telling her any more

than she had to know, drilled her until she was letter-perfect in her part.

"A couple days before she came I had gone to see the doc, and had demanded a hundred thousand cool smacks. He laughed at me, and I left, pretending to be as hot as hell.

"As soon as Edna arrived, I sent her to call on him. She asked him to perform an illegal operation on her daughter. He, of course, refused. Then she pleaded with him, loud enough for the nurse or whoever else was in the reception-room to hear. And when she raised her voice she was careful to stick to words that could be interpreted the way we wanted them to. She ran off her end to perfection, leaving in tears.

"Then I sprung my other trick! I had a fellow—a fellow who's a whiz at that kind of stuff—make me a plate: an imitation of newspaper printing. It was all worded like the real article, and said that the state authorities were investigating information that a prominent surgeon in San Francisco was practicing under a license secured by false credentials. This plate measured four and an eighth by six and three-quarter inches. If you'll look at the first inside page of the *Evening Times* any day in the week you'll see a photograph just that size.

"On the day after Edna's call, I bought a copy of the first edition of the *Times*—on the street at ten in the morning. I had this scratcher friend of mine remove the photograph with acid, and print this fake article in its place.

"That evening I substituted a 'home edition' outer sheet for the one that had come with the paper we had cooked up, and made a switch as soon as the doc's newsboy made his delivery There was nothing to that part of it. The kid just tossed the paper into the vestibule. It's simply a case of duck into the doorway, trade papers, and go on, leaving the loaded one for the doc to read."

I was trying not to look too interested, but my ears were cocked for every word. At the start, I had been prepared for a string of lies. But I knew now that he was telling me the truth! Every syllable was a boast; he was half-drunk with appreciation of his own cleverness—the cleverness with which he had planned and carried out his program of treachery and murder.

I knew that he was telling the truth, and I suspected that he was telling more of it than he had intended. He was fairly bloated with vanity—the vanity that fills the crook almost invariably after a little success, and makes him ripe for the pen.

His eyes glistened, and his little mouth smiled triumphantly around the words that continued to roll out of it.

"The doc read the paper, all right—and shot himself. But first he wrote and mailed a note—to me. I didn't figure on his wife's being accused of killing him. That was plain luck.

"I figured that the fake piece in the paper would be overlooked in the excitement. Edna would then go forward, claiming to be his first wife; and his shooting himself after her first call, with what the nurse had overheard, would make his death seem a confession that Edna was his wife.

"I was sure that she would stand up under any sort of an investigation. Nobody knew anything about the doc's real past; except what he had told them, which would be found false.

"Edna had really married a Dr. Humbert Estep in Philadelphia in '96; and the twenty-seven years that had passed since then would do a lot to hide the fact that that Dr. Humbert Estep wasn't this Dr. Humbert Estep.

"All I wanted to do was convince the doc's real wife and her lawyers that she wasn't really his wife at all. And we did that! Everybody took it for granted that Edna was the legal wife.

"The next play would have been for Edna and the real wife to have reached some sort of an agreement about the estate, whereby Edna would have got the bulk—or at least half—of it; and nothing would have been made public.

"If worst came to worst, we were prepared to go to court. We were sitting pretty! But I'd have been satisfied with half the estate. It would have come to a few hundred thousand at the least, and that would have been plenty for me—even deducting the twenty thousand I had promised Edna.

"But when the police grabbed the doc's wife and charged her with his murder, I saw my way into the whole roll. All I had to do was sit tight and wait until they convicted her. Then the court would turn the entire pile over to Edna.

"I had the only evidence that would free the doc's wife: the note he had written me. But I couldn't—even if I had wanted to—have turned it in without exposing my hand. When he read that fake piece in the paper, he tore it out, wrote his message to me across the face of it, and sent it to me. So the note is a dead give-away. However, I didn't have any intention of publishing it, anyhow.

"Up to this point everything had gone like a dream. All I had to do was wait until it was time to cash in on my brains. And that's the time that the real Humbert Estep picked out to mess up the works.

"He shaved his mustache off, put on some old clothes, and came snooping around to see that Edna and I didn't run out on him. As if he could have stopped us! After you put the finger on him for me, I brought him up here.

"I intended salving him along until I could find a place to keep him until all the cards had been played. That's what I was going to hire you for—to take care of him.

"But we got to talking, and wrangling, and I had to knock him down. He didn't get up, and I found that he was dead. His neck was broken. There was nothing to do but take him out to the park and leave him.

"I didn't tell Edna. She didn't have a lot of use for him, as far as I could see, but you can't tell how women will take things. Anyhow, she'll stick, now that it's done. She's on the up and up all the time. And if she should talk, she can't do a lot of damage. She only knows her own part of the lay.

"All this long-winded story is so you'll know just exactly what you're up against. Maybe you think you can dig up the proof of these things I have told you. You can this far. You can prove that Edna wasn't the doc's wife. You can prove that I've been blackmailing him. But you can't prove that the doc's wife didn't *believe* that Edna was his real wife! It's her word against Edna's and mine.

"We'll swear that we had convinced her of it, which will give her a motive. You can't prove that the phoney news article I told you about ever existed. It'll sound like a hop-head's dream to a jury.

"You can't tie last night's murder on me—I've got an alibi that will knock your hat off! I can prove that I left here with a friend of mine who was drunk, and that I took him to his hotel and put him to bed, with the help of a night clerk and a bellboy. And what have you got against that? The word of two private detectives. Who'll believe you?

"You can convict me of conspiracy to defraud, or something—maybe. But, regardless of that, you can't free Mrs. Estep without my help.

"Turn me loose and I'll give you the letter the doc wrote me. It's the goods, right enough! In his own handwriting, written across the face of the fake newspaper story—which ought to fit the torn place in the paper that the police are supposed to be holding—and he wrote that he was going to kill himself, in words almost that plain."

That would turn the trick—there was no doubt of it. And I believed Ledwich's story. The more I thought it over the better I liked it. It fit into the facts everywhere. But I wasn't enthusiastic about giving this big crook his liberty.

"Don't make me laugh!" I said. "I'm going to put you away and free Mrs. Estep—both."

"Go ahead and try it! You're up against it without the letter; and you don't think a man with brains enough to plan a job like this one would be foolish enough to leave the note where it could be found, do you?"

I wasn't especially impressed with the difficulty of convicting this Ledwich and freeing the dead man's widow. His scheme—that coldblooded zigzag of treachery for everybody he had dealt with, including his latest accomplice, Edna Estep—wasn't as airtight as he thought it. A week in which to run out a few lines in the East, and— But a week was just what I didn't have!

Vance Richmond's words were running through my head: "But another day of imprisonment—two days, or perhaps even two hours—and she won't need anybody to clear her. Death will have done it!"

If I was going to do Mrs. Estep any good, I had to move

quick. Law or no law, her life was in my fat hands. This man before me—his eyes bright and hopeful now and his mouth anxiously pursed—was thief, blackmailer, double-crosser, and at least twice a murderer. I hated to let him walk out. But there was the woman dying in a hospital....

12

KEEPING MY EYE on Ledwich, I went to the telephone, and got Vance Richmond on the wire at his residence.

"How is Mrs. Estep?" I asked.

"Weaker! I talked with the doctor half an hour ago, and he says—"

I cut in on him; I didn't want to listen to the details.

"Get over to the hospital, and be where I can reach you by phone. I may have news for you before the night is over."

"What—Is there a chance? Are you—"

I didn't promise him anything. I hung up the receiver and spoke to Ledwich. "I'll do this much for you. Slip me the note, and I'll give you your gun and put you out the back door. There's a bull on the corner out front, and I can't take you past him."

He was on his feet, beaming.

"Your word on it?" he demanded.

"Yes—get going!"

He went past me to the phone, gave a number (which I made a note of), and then spoke hurriedly into the instrument.

"This is Shuler. Put a boy in a taxi with that envelope I gave you to hold for me, and send him out here right away."

He gave his address, said "Yes" twice and hung up.

There was nothing surprising about his unquestioning acceptance of my word. He couldn't afford to doubt that I'd play fair with him. And, also, all successful bunko men come in time to believe that the world—except for themselves—is populated by a race of human sheep who may be trusted to conduct themselves with true sheep-like docility.

Ten minutes later the door-bell rang. We answered it together, and Ledwich took a large envelope from a messenger boy, while I memorized the number on the boy's cap. Then we went back to the front room.

Ledwich slit the envelope and passed its contents to me: a piece of rough-torn newspaper. Across the face of the fake article he had told me about was written a message in a jerky hand.

> I wouldn't have suspected you, Ledwich, of such profound stupidity. My last thought will be—this bullet that ends my life also ends your years of leisure. You'll have to go to work now.
>
> ESTEP.

The doctor had died game!

I took the envelope from the big man, put the death note in it, and put them in my pocket. Then I went to a front window, flattening a cheek against the glass until I could see O'Gar, dimly outlined in the night, patiently standing where I had left him hours before.

"The city dick is still on the corner," I told Ledwich. "Here's your gat"—holding out the gun I had shot from his fingers a little while back—"take it, and blow through the back door. Remember, that's all I'm offering you—the gun and a fair start. If you play square with me, I'll not do anything to help find you—unless I have to keep myself in the clear."

"Fair enough!"

He grabbed the gun, broke it to see that it was still loaded, and wheeled toward the rear of the flat. At the door he pulled up, hesitated, and faced me again. I kept him covered with my automatic.

"Will you do me one favor I didn't put in the bargain?" he asked.

"What is it?"

"That note of the doc's is in an envelope with my handwriting and maybe my fingerprints on it. Let me put it in a fresh envelope, will you? I don't want to leave any broader trail behind than I have to."

With my left hand—my right being busy with the gun—I fumbled for the envelope and tossed it to him. He took a plain envelope from the table, wiped it carefully with his handkerchief, put the note in it, taking care not to touch it with the balls of his fingers, and passed it back to me; and I put it in my pocket.

I had a hard time to keep from grinning in his face.

That fumbling with the handkerchief told me that the envelope in my pocket was empty, that the death-note was in Ledwich's possession—though I hadn't seen it pass there. He had worked one of his bunko tricks upon me.

"Beat it!" I snapped, to keep from laughing in his face.

He spun on his heel. His feet pounded against the floor. A door slammed in the rear.

I tore into the envelope he had given me. I needed to be sure he had double-crossed me.

The envelope was empty.

Our agreement was wiped out.

I sprang to the front window, threw it wide open, and leaned out. O'Gar saw me immediately—clearer than I could see him. I swung my arm in a wide gesture toward the rear of the house. O'Gar set out for the alley on the run. I dashed back through Ledwich's flat to the kitchen, and stuck my head out of an already open window.

I could see Ledwich against the whitewashed fence—throwing the back gate open, plunging through it into the alley.

O'Gar's squat bulk appeared under a light at the end of the alley.

Ledwich's revolver was in his hand. O'Gar's wasn't—not quite.

Ledwich's gun swung up—the hammer clicked.

O'Gar's gun coughed fire.

Ledwich fell with a slow revolving motion over against the white fence, gasped once or twice, and went down in a pile.

I walked slowly down the stairs to join O'Gar; slowly, because it isn't a nice thing to look at a man you've deliberately sent to his death. Not even if it's the surest way of saving an innocent life, and if the man who dies is a Jake Ledwich—altogether treacherous.

"Howcome?" O'Gar asked, when I came into the alley, where he stood looking down at the dead man.

"He got out on me," I said simply.

"He must've."

I stooped and searched the dead man's pockets until I found the suicide note, still crumpled in the handkerchief. O'Gar was examining the dead man's revolver.

"Lookit!" he exclaimed. "Maybe this ain't my lucky day! He snapped at me once, and his gun missed fire. No wonder! Somebody must've been using an ax on it—the firing pin's broke clean off!"

"Is that so?" I asked; just as if I hadn't discovered, when I first picked the revolver up, that the bullet which had knocked it out of Ledwich's hand had made it harmless.

One Hour

Like all of Mr. Hammett's detective stories, this tale starts with a very ordinary police case, and just as you think you have it all figured out, it takes several unexpected turns and ends up with a bang.

1

"THIS IS MR. CHROSTWAITE," Vance Richmond said.

Chrostwaite, wedged between the arms of one of the attorney's large chairs, grunted what was perhaps meant for an acknowledgment of the introduction. I grunted back at him, and found myself a chair.

He was a big balloon of a man—this Chrostwaite—in a green plaid suit that didn't make him look any smaller than he was. His tie was a gaudy thing, mostly of yellow, with a big diamond set in the center of it, and there were more stones on his pudgy hands. Spongy fat blurred his features, making it impossible for his round purplish face to ever hold any other expression than the discontented hoggishness that was habitual to it. He reeked of gin.

"Mr. Chrostwaite is the Pacific Coast agent for the Mutual Fire Extinguisher Manufacturing Company," Vance Richmond began, as soon as I had got myself seated. "His office is on Kearny Street, near California. Yesterday, at about two-forty-five in the afternoon, he went to his office, leaving his machine—a Hudson touring car—standing in front, with the engine running. Ten minutes later, he came out. The car was gone."

I looked at Chrostwaite. He was looking at his fat knees, showing not the least interest in what his attorney was saying. I looked quickly back at Vance Richmond; his clean gray face and lean figure were downright beautiful beside his bloated client.

"A man named Newhouse," the lawyer was saying, "who was the proprietor of a printing establishment on California Street, just around the corner from Mr. Chrostwaite's office, was run down and killed by Mr. Chrostwaite's car at the corner of Clay and Kearny Streets, five minutes after Mr. Chrostwaite had left the car to go into his office. The police found the car shortly afterward, only a block away from the scene of the accident—on Montgomery near Clay.

"The thing is fairly obvious. Some one stole the car immediately after Mr. Chrostwaite left it; and in driving rapidly away, ran down Newhouse; and then, in fright, abandoned the car. But here is Mr. Chrostwaite's position; three nights ago, while driving perhaps a little recklessly out—"

"Drunk," Chrostwaite said, not looking up from his plaid knees; and though his voice was hoarse, husky—it was the hoarseness of a whisky-burnt throat—there was no emotion in his voice.

"While driving perhaps a little recklessly out Van Ness Avenue," Vance Richmond went on, ignoring the interruption, "Mr. Chrostwaite knocked a pedestrian down. The man wasn't badly hurt, and he is being compensated very generously for his injuries. But we are to appear in court next Monday to face a charge of reckless driving, and I am afraid that this accident of yesterday, in which the printer was killed, may hurt us.

"No one thinks that Mr. Chrostwaite was in his car when it killed the printer—we have a world of evidence that he wasn't. But I am afraid that the printer's death may be made a weapon against us when we appear on the Van Ness Avenue charge. Being an attorney, I know just how much capital the prosecuting attorney—if he so chooses—can make out of the really insignificant fact that the same car that knocked down the man on Van Ness Avenue killed another man yesterday. And, being an attorney, I know how likely the prosecuting attorney is to so choose. And he can handle it in such a way that we will be given little or no opportunity to tell our side.

"The worst that can happen, of course, is that, instead of the usual fine, Mr. Chrostwaite will be sent to the city jail for thirty or sixty days. That is bad enough, however, and that is what we wish to—"

Chrostwaite spoke again, still regarding his knees.

"Damned nuisance!" he said.

"That is what we wish to avoid," the attorney continued. "We are willing to pay a stiff fine, and expect to, for the accident on Van Ness Avenue was clearly Mr. Chrostwaite's fault. But we—"

"Drunk as a lord!" Chrostwaite said.

"But we don't want to have this other accident, with which we had nothing to do, given a false weight in connection with the slighter accident. What we want, then, is to find the man or men who stole the car and ran down John Newhouse. If they are apprehended before we go to court, we won't be in danger of suffering for their act. Think you can find them before Monday?"

"I'll try," I promised; "though it isn't—"

The human balloon interrupted me by heaving himself to his feet, fumbling with his fat jeweled fingers for his watch.

"Three o'clock," he said. "Got a game of golf for three-thirty." He picked up his hat and gloves from the desk. "Find 'em, will you? Damned nuisance going to jail!"

And he waddled out.

2

FROM THE ATTORNEY'S office, I went down to the Hall of Justice, and, after hunting around a few minutes, found a policeman who had arrived at the corner of Clay and Kearny Streets a few seconds after Newhouse had been knocked down.

"I was just leaving the Hall when I seen a bus scoot around the corner at Clay Street," this patrolman—a big sandy-haired man named Coffee—told me. "Then I seen people gathering around, so I went up there and found this John Newhouse stretched out. He was already dead. Half a dozen people had seen him hit, and one of 'em had got the license number of the car that done it. We found the car standing empty just around the corner on Montgomery Street, pointing north. They was two fellows in the car when it hit Newhouse, but nobody saw what they looked like. Nobody was in it when we found it."

"In what direction was Newhouse walking?"

"North along Kearny Street, and he was about three-quarters across Clay when he was knocked. The car was coming north on Kearny, too, and turned east on Clay. It mightn't have been all the fault of the fellows in the car—according to them that seen the accident. Newhouse was walking across the street looking at a piece of paper in his hand. I found a piece of foreign money—paper money—in his hand, and I guess that's what he was looking at. The lieutenant tells me it was Dutch money—a hundred-florin note, he says."

"Found out anything about the men in the car?"

"Nothing! We lined up everybody we could find in the

neighborhood of California and Kearny Streets—where the car was stolen from—and around Clay and Montgomery Streets—where it was left at. But nobody remembered seeing the fellows getting in it or getting out of it. The man that owns the car wasn't driving it—it was stole all right, I guess. At first I thought maybe they was something shady about the accident. This John Newhouse had a two- or three-day-old black eye on him. But we run that out and found that he had a attack of heart trouble or something a couple days ago, and fell, fetching his eye up against a chair. He'd been home sick for three days—just left his house half an hour or so before the accident."

"Where'd he live?"

"On Sacramento Street—way out. I got his address here somewhere."

He turned over the pages of a grimy memoranda book, and I got the dead man's house number, and the names and addresses of the witnesses to the accident that Coffee had questioned.

That exhausted the policeman's information, so I left him.

3

MY NEXT PLAY was to canvass the vicinity of where the car had been stolen and where it had been deserted, and then interview the witnesses. The fact that the police had fruitlessly gone over this ground made it unlikely that I would find anything of value; but I couldn't skip these things on that account. Ninety-nine per cent of detective work is a patient collecting of details—and your details must be got as nearly first-hand as possible, regardless of who else has worked the territory before you.

Before starting on this angle, however, I decided to run around to the dead man's printing establishment—only three blocks from the Hall of Justice—and see if any of his employees had heard anything that might help me.

Newhouse's establishment occupied the ground floor of a small building on California, between Kearny and Montgomery. A small office was partitioned off in front, with a connecting doorway leading to the press-room in the rear.

The only occupant of the small office, when I came in from the street, was a short, stocky, worried-looking blond man of forty or thereabouts, who sat at the desk in his shirt-sleeves, checking off figures in a ledger, against others on a batch of papers before him.

I introduced myself, telling him that I was a Continental Detective Agency operative, interested in Newhouse's death. He told me his name was Ben Soules, and that he was Newhouse's foreman. We shook hands, and then he waved me to a chair across the desk; pushed back the papers and book upon which he had been working, and scratched his head disgustedly with the pencil in his hand.

"This is awful!" he said. "What with one thing and another, we're heels over head in work, and I got to fool with these books that I don't know anything at all about, and—"

He broke off to pick up the telephone, which had jingled.

"Yes…. This is Soules…. We're working on them now… I'll give 'em to you by Monday noon at the least…. I know we promised them for yesterday, but… I know! I know! But the boss's death set us back. Explain that to Mr. Chrostwaite. And… And I'll promise you that we'll give them to you Monday morning, sure!"

Soules slapped the receiver irritably on its hook and looked at me.

"You'd think that since it was his own car that killed the boss, he'd have decency enough not to squawk over the delay!"

"Chrostwaite?"

"Yes—that was one of his clerks. We're printing some leaflets for him—promised to have 'em ready yesterday—but between the boss's death and having a couple new hands to break in, we're behind with everything. I been here eight years, and this is the first time we ever fell down on an order—and every damned customer is yelling his head off. If we were like most printers they'd be used to waiting; but we've been too good to them. But this Chrostwaite! You'd think he'd have some decency, seeing that his car killed the boss!"

I nodded sympathetically, slid a cigar across the desk, and waited until it was burning in Soules' mouth before I asked:

"You said something about having a couple new hands to break in. How come?"

"Yes. Mr. Newhouse fired two of our printers last week—Fincher and Key. He found that they belonged to the I.W.W., so he gave them their time."

"Any trouble with them, or anything against them except that they were Wobblies?"

"No—they were pretty good workers."

"Any trouble with them after he fired them?" I asked.

"No real trouble, though they were pretty hot. They made red speeches all over the place before they left."

"Remember what day that was?"

"Wednesday of last week, I think. Yes, Wednesday, because I hired two new men on Thursday."

"How many men do you work?"

"Three, besides myself."

"Was Mr. Newhouse sick very often?"

"Not sick enough to stay away very often, though every now and then his heart would go back on him, and he'd have to stay in bed for a week or ten days. He wasn't what you could call real well at any time. He never did anything but the office work—I run the shop."

"When was he taken sick this last time?"

"Mrs. Newhouse called up Tuesday morning and said he had had another spell, and wouldn't be down for a few days. He came in yesterday—which was Thursday—for about ten minutes in the afternoon, and said he would be back on the job this morning. He was killed just after he left."

"How did he look—very sick?"

"Not so bad. He never looked well, of course, but I couldn't see much difference from usual yesterday. This last spell hadn't been as bad as most, I reckon—he was usually laid up for a week or more."

"Did he say where he was going when he left? The reason I ask is that, living out on Sacramento Street, he would naturally have taken a car at that street if he had been going home, whereas he was run down on Clay Street."

"He said he was going up to Portsmouth Square to sit in the sun for half an hour or so. He had been cooped up indoors for two or three days, he said, and he wanted some sunshine before he went back home."

"He had a piece of foreign money in his hand when he was hit. Know anything about it?"

"Yes. He got it here. One of our customers—a man named Van Pelt—came in to pay for some work we had done yesterday afternoon while the boss was here. When Van Pelt pulled out his wallet to pay his bill, this piece of Holland money—I don't know what you call it—was among the bills. I think he said it was worth something like thirty-eight dollars. Anyway, the boss took it, giving Van Pelt his change. The boss said he wanted to show the Holland money to his boys—and he could have it changed back into American money later."

"Who is this Van Pelt?"

"He's a Hollander—is planning to open a tobacco importing business here in a month or two. I don't know much about him outside of that."

"Where's his home, or office?"

"His office is on Bush Street, near Sansome."

"Did he know that Newhouse had been sick?"

"I don't think so. The boss didn't look much different from usual."

"What's this Van Pelt's full name?"

"Hendrik Van Pelt."

"What does he look like?"

Before Soules could answer, three evenly spaced buzzes sounded above the rattle and whirring of the presses in the back of the shop.

I slid the muzzle of my gun—I had been holding it in my lap for five minutes—far enough over the edge of the desk for Ben Soules to see it.

"Put both of your hands on top of the desk," I said.

He put them there.

The press-room door was directly behind him, so that, facing him across the desk, I could look over his shoulder at it. His stocky body served to screen my gun from the view of whoever came through the door, in response to Soules' signal.

I didn't have long to wait.

Three men—black with ink—came to the door, and through it into the little office. They strolled in careless and casual, laughing and joking to one another.

But one of them licked his lips as he stepped through the door. Another's eyes showed white circles all around the irises. The third was the best actor—but he held his shoulders a trifle too stiffly to fit his otherwise careless carriage.

"Stop right there!" I barked at them when the last one was inside the office—and I brought my gun up where they could see it.

They stopped as if they had all been mounted on the same pair of legs.

I kicked my chair back, and stood up.

I didn't like my position at all. The office was entirely too small for me. I had a gun, true enough, and whatever weapons may have been distributed among these other men were out of sight. But these four men were too close to me; and a gun isn't a thing of miracles. It's a mechanical contraption that is capable of just so much and no more.

If these men decided to jump me, I could down just one of them before the other three were upon me. I knew it, and they knew it.

"Put your hands up," I ordered, "and turn around!"

None of them moved to obey. One of the inked men grinned wickedly; Soules shook his head slowly; the other two stood and looked at me.

I was more or less stumped. You can't shoot a man just because he refuses to obey an order—even if he is a criminal. If they had turned around for me, I could have lined them up against the wall, and, being behind them, have held them safe while I used the telephone.

But that hadn't worked.

My next thought was to back across the office to the street door, keeping them covered, and then either stand in the door and yell for help, or take them into the street, where I could handle them. But I put that thought away as quickly as it came to me.

These four men were going to jump me—there was no doubt of that. All that was needed was a spark of any sort to explode them into action. They were standing stiff-legged and tense, waiting for some move on my part. If I took a step backward—the battle would be on.

We were close enough for any of the four to have reached out and touched me. One of them I could shoot before I was smothered—one out of four. That meant that each of them had only one chance out of four of being the victim—low enough odds for any but the most cowardly of men.

I grinned what was supposed to be a confident grin—because I was up against it hard—and reached for the telephone: I had to do something! Then I cursed myself! I had merely changed the signal for the onslaught. It would come now when I picked up the receiver.

But I couldn't back down again—that, too, would be a signal—I had to go through with it.

The perspiration trickled across my temples from under my hat as I drew the phone closer with my left hand.

The street door opened! An exclamation of surprise came from behind me.

I spoke rapidly, without taking my eyes from the four men in front of me.

"Quick! The phone! The police!"

With the arrival of this unknown person—one of Newhouse's customers, probably—I figured I had the edge again. Even if he took no active part beyond calling the police in, the enemy would have to split to take care of him—and that would give me a chance to pot at least two of them before I was knocked over. Two out of four—each of them had an even chance of being dropped—which is enough to give even a nervy man cause for thinking a bit before he jumps.

"Hurry!" I urged the newcomer.

"Yes! Yes!" he said—and in the blurred sound of the "s" there was evidence of foreign birth.

Keyed up as I was, I didn't need any more warning than that.

I threw myself sidewise—a blind tumbling away from the spot where I stood. But I wasn't quite quick enough.

The blow that came from behind didn't hit me fairly, but I got enough of it to fold up my legs as if the knees were hinged with paper—and I slammed into a heap on the floor....

Something dark crashed toward me. I caught it with both hands. It may have been a foot kicking at my face. I wrung it as a washerwoman wrings a towel.

Down my spine ran jar after jar. Perhaps somebody was beating me over the head. I don't know. My head wasn't alive. The blow that had knocked me down had numbed me all over. My eyes were no good. Shadows swam to and fro in front of them—that was all. I struck, gouged, tore at the shadows. Sometimes I found nothing. Sometimes I found things that felt like parts of bodies. Then I would hammer at them, tear at them. My gun was gone.

My hearing was no better than my sight—or not so good. There wasn't a sound in the world. I moved in a silence that was more complete than any silence I had ever known. I was a ghost fighting ghosts.

I found presently that my feet were under me again, though some squirming thing was on my back, and kept me from standing upright. A hot, damp thing like a hand was across my face.

I put my teeth into it. I snapped my head back as far as it would go. Maybe it smashed into the face it was meant for. I don't know. Anyhow the squirming thing was no longer on my back.

Dimly I realized that I was being buffeted about by blows that I was too numb to feel. Ceaselessly, with head and shoulders and elbows and fists and knees and feet, I struck at the shadows that were around me....

Suddenly I could see again—not clearly—but the shadows were taking on colors; and my ears came back a little, so that grunts and growls and curses and the impact of blows sounded in them. My straining gaze rested upon a brass cuspidor six inches or so in front of my eyes. I knew then that I was down on the floor again.

As I twisted about to hurl a foot into a soft body above me, something that was like a burn, but wasn't a burn, ran down one leg—a knife. The sting of it brought consciousness back into me with a rush.

I grabbed the brass cuspidor and used it to club a way to my feet—to club a clear space in front of me. Men were hurling themselves upon me. I swung the cuspidor high and flung it over their heads, through the frosted glass door into California Street.

Then we fought some more.

But you can't throw a brass cuspidor through a glass door into California Street between Montgomery and Kearny without attracting attention—it's too near the heart of daytime San Francisco. So presently—when I was on the floor again with six or eight hundred pounds of flesh hammering my face into the boards—we were pulled apart, and I was dug out of the bottom of the pile by a squad of policemen.

Big sandy-haired Coffee was one of them, but it took a lot of arguing to convince him that I was the Continental operative who had talked to him a little while before.

"Man! Man!" he said, when I finally convinced him. "Them lads sure—God! have worked you over! You got a face on you like a wet geranium!"

I didn't laugh. It wasn't funny.

I looked out of the one eye, which was working just now, at the five men lined up across the office—Soules, the three inky printers, and the man with the blurred "s," who had started the slaughter by tapping me on the back of the head.

He was a rather tall man of thirty or so, with a round ruddy face that wore a few bruises now. He had been, apparently, rather well-dressed in expensive black clothing, but he was torn and ragged now. I knew who he was without asking—Hendrik Van Pelt.

"Well, man, what's the answer?" Coffee was asking me.

By holding one side of my jaw firmly with one hand I found that I could talk without too much pain.

"This is the crowd that ran down Newhouse," I said, "and it wasn't an accident. I wouldn't mind having a few more of the details myself, but I was jumped before I got around to all of them. Newhouse had a hundred-florin note in his hand when he was run down, and he was walking in the direction of police headquarters—was only half a block away from the Hall of Justice.

"Soules tells me that Newhouse said he was going up to Portsmouth Square to sit in the sun. But Soules didn't seem to know that Newhouse was wearing a black eye—the one you told me you had investigated. If Soules didn't see the shiner, then it's a good bet that Soules didn't see Newhouse's face that day!

"Newhouse was walking from his printing shop toward police headquarters with a piece of foreign paper money in his hand—remember that!

"He had frequent spells of sickness, which, according to friend Soules, always before kept him at home for a week or ten days at a time. This time he was laid up for only two and a half days.

"Soules tells me that the shop is three days behind with its orders, and he says that's the first time in eight years they've ever been behind. He blames Newhouse's death—which only happened yesterday. Apparently, Newhouse's previous sick spells never delayed things—why should this last spell?

"Two printers were fired last week, and two new ones hired the very next day—pretty quick work. The car with which Newhouse was run down was taken from just around the corner, and was deserted within quick walking distance of the shop. It was left facing north, which is pretty good evidence that its occupants went south after they got out. Ordinary car thieves wouldn't have circled back in the direction from which they came.

"Here's my guess: This Van Pelt is a Dutchman, and he had some plates for phoney hundred-florin notes. He hunted around until he found a printer who would go in with him. He found Soules, the foreman of a shop whose proprietor was now and then at home for a week or more at a time with a bad heart. One of the printers under Soules was willing to go in with them. Maybe the other two turned the offer down. Maybe Soules didn't ask them at all. Anyhow, they were discharged, and two friends of Soules were given their places.

"Our friends then got everything ready, and waited for Newhouse's heart to flop again. It did—Monday night. As soon as his wife called up next morning and said he was sick, these birds started running off their counterfeits. That's why they fell behind with their regular work. But this spell of Newhouse's was lighter than usual. He was up and moving around within two days, and yesterday afternoon he came down here for a few minutes.

"He must have walked in while all of our friends were extremely busy in some far corner. He must have spotted some of the phoney money, immediately sized up the situation, grabbed one bill to show the police, and started out for police headquarters—no doubt thinking he had not been seen by our friends here.

"They must have got a glimpse of him as he was leaving, however. Two of them followed him out. They couldn't, afoot, safely knock him over within a block or two of the Hall of Justice. But, turning the corner, they found Chrostwaite's car standing there with idling engine. That solved their getaway problem. They got in the car and went on after Newhouse. I suppose the original plan was to shoot him—but he crossed Clay Street with his eyes fastened upon the phoney money in his hand. That gave them a golden chance. They piled the car into him. It was sure death, they knew—his bum heart would finish the job if the actual collision didn't kill him. Then they deserted the car and came back here.

"There are a lot of loose ends to be gathered in—but this pipe-dream I've just told you fits in with all the facts we know—and I'll bet a month's salary I'm not far off anywhere. There ought to be a three-day crop of Dutch notes cached somewhere! You people—"

I suppose I'd have gone on talking forever—in the giddy, head-swimming intoxication of utter exhaustion that filled me—if the big sandy-haired patrolman hadn't shut me off by putting a big hand across my mouth.

"Be quiet, man," he said, lifting me out of the chair, and

spreading me flat on my back on the desk. "I'll have an ambulance here in a second for you."

The office was swirling around in front of my one open eye—the yellow ceiling swung down toward me, rose again, disappeared, came back in odd shapes. I turned my head to one side to avoid it, and my glance rested upon the white dial of a spinning clock.

Presently the dial came to rest, and I read it—four o'clock.

I remembered that Chrostwaite had broken up our conference in Vance Richmond's office at three, and I had started to work.

"One full hour!" I tried to tell Coffee before I went to sleep.

THE POLICE WOUND up the job while I was lying on my back in bed. In Van Pelt's office on Bush Street they found a great bale of hundred-florin notes. Van Pelt, they learned, had considerable reputation in Europe as a high-class counterfeiter. One of the printers came through, stating that Van Pelt and Soules were the two who followed Newhouse out of the shop, and killed him.

The House in Turk Street

We wouldn't consider an issue complete without one of Mr. Hammett's stories in it, and after you've read this tale, you'll understand why.

I HAD BEEN told that the man for whom I was hunting lived in a certain Turk Street block, but my informant hadn't been able to give me his house number. Thus it came about that late one rainy afternoon I was canvassing this certain block, ringing each bell, and reciting a myth that went like this:

"I'm from the law office of Wellington and Berkeley. One of our clients—an elderly lady—was thrown from the rear platform of a street car last week and severely injured. Among those who witnessed the accident, was a young man whose name we don't know. But we have been told that he lives in this neighborhood." Then I would describe the man I wanted, and wind up: "Do you know of anyone who looks like that?"

All down one side of the block the answers were:

"No," "No," "No."

I crossed the street and started to work the other side. The first house: "No."

The second: "No."

The third. The fourth.

The fifth—

No one came to the door in answer to my first ring. After a while, I rang again. I had just decided that no one was at home, when the knob turned slowly and a little old woman opened the door. She was a very fragile little old woman, with a piece of grey knitting in one hand, and faded eyes that twinkled pleasantly behind gold-rimmed spectacles. She wore a stiffly starched apron over a black dress and there was white lace at her throat.

"Good evening," she said in a thin friendly voice. "I hope you didn't mind waiting. I always have to peep out to see who's here before I open the door—an old woman's timidity."

She laughed with a little gurgling sound in her throat.

"Sorry to disturb you," I apologized. "But—"

"Won't you come in, please?"

"No; I just want a little information. I won't take much of your time."

"I wish you would come in," she said, and then added with mock severity, "I'm sure my tea is getting cold."

She took my damp hat and coat, and I followed her down a narrow hall to a dim room, where a man got up as we entered. He was old too, and stout, with a thin white beard that fell upon a white vest that was as stiffly starched as the woman's apron.

"Thomas," the little fragile woman told him; "this is Mr.—"

"Tracy," I said, because that was the name I had given the other residents of the block; but I came as near blushing when I said it, as I have in fifteen years. These folks weren't made to be lied to.

Their name, I learned, was Quarre; and they were an affectionate old couple. She called him "Thomas" every time she spoke to him, rolling the name around in her mouth as if she liked the taste of it. He called her "my dear" just as frequently, and twice he got up to adjust a cushion more comfortably to her frail back.

I had to drink a cup of tea with them and eat some little spiced cookies before I could get them to listen to a question.

Then Mrs. Quarre made little sympathetic clicking sounds with her tongue and teeth, while I told about the elderly lady who had fallen off a street car. The old man rumbled in his beard that it was "a damn shame," and gave me a fat and oily cigar. I had to assure them that the fictitious elderly lady was being taken care of and was coming along nicely—I was afraid they were going to insist upon being taken to see her.

Finally I got away from the accident itself, and described the man I wanted. "Thomas," Mrs. Quarre said; "isn't that the young man who lives in the house with the railing—the one who always looks so worried?"

The old man stroked his snowy beard and pondered.

"But, my dear," he rumbled at last; "hasn't he got dark hair?"

She beamed upon her husband and then upon me.

"Thomas is *so* observant," she said with pride. "I had forgotten; but the young man I spoke of does have dark hair, so he couldn't be the one who saw the accident at all."

The old man then suggested that one who lived in the block below might be my man. They discussed this one at some length before they decided that he was too tall and too old. Mrs. Quarre suggested another. They discussed that one, and voted against him. Thomas offered a candidate; he was weighed and discarded. They chattered on:

"But don't you think, Thomas… Yes, my dear, but… Of course you're right, Thomas, but…."

Two old folks enjoying a chance contact with the world that they had dropped out of.

Darkness settled. The old man turned on a light in a tall lamp that threw a soft yellow circle upon us, and left the rest of the room dim. The room was a large one, and heavy with the thick hangings and bulky horse-hair furniture of a generation ago. I burned the cigar the old man had given me, and slumped comfortably down in my chair, letting them run on, putting in a word or two whenever they turned to me. I didn't expect to get any information here; but I was comfortable, and the cigar was a good one. Time enough to go out into the drizzle when I had finished my smoke.

Something cold touched the nape of my neck.

"Stand up!"

I didn't stand up: I couldn't. I was paralyzed. I sat and blinked at the Quarres.

And looking at them, I knew that something cold *couldn't* be against the back of my neck; a harsh voice *couldn't* have ordered me to stand up. It wasn't possible!

Mrs. Quarre still sat primly upright against the cushions her husband had adjusted to her back; her eyes still twinkled with friendliness behind her glasses; her hands were still motionless in her lap, crossed at the wrists over the piece of knitting. The old man still stroked his white beard, and let cigar smoke drift unhurriedly from his nostrils.

They would go on talking about the young men in the neighborhood who might be the man I wanted. Nothing had happened. I had dozed.

"Get up!"

The cold thing against my neck jabbed deep into the flesh.

I stood up.

"Frisk him," the harsh voice came from behind.

The old man carefully laid his cigar down, came to me, and ran his hands over my body. Satisfied that I was unarmed, he emptied my pockets, dropping the contents upon the chair that I had just left.

Mrs. Quarre was pouring herself some more tea.

"Thomas," she said; "you've overlooked that little watch pocket in the trousers."

He found nothing there.

"That's all," he told the man behind me, and returned to his chair and cigar.

"Turn around, you!" the harsh voice ordered.

I turned and faced a tall, gaunt, raw-boned man of about my own age, which is thirty-five. He had an ugly face—hollow-cheeked, bony, and spattered with big pale freckles. His eyes were of a watery blue, and his nose and chin stuck out abruptly.

"Know me?" he asked.

"No."

"You're a liar!"

I didn't argue the point: he was holding a level gun in one big freckled hand.

"You're going to know me pretty well before you're through with me," this big ugly man threatened. "You're going to—"

"Hook!" a voice came from a portièred doorway—the doorway through which the ugly man had no doubt crept up behind me. "Hook, come here!"

The voice was feminine—young, clear, and musical.

"What do you want?" the ugly man called over his shoulder.

"He's here."

"All right!" He turned to Thomas Quarre. "Keep this joker safe."

From somewhere among his whiskers, his coat, and his stiff white vest, the old man brought out a big black revolver, which he handled with no signs of either weakness or unfamiliarity.

The ugly man swept up the things that had been taken from my pockets, and carried them through the portières with him.

Mrs. Quarre smiled brightly up at me.

"Do sit down, Mr. Tracy," she said.

I sat.

Through the portières a new voice came from the next room; a drawling baritone voice whose accent was unmistakably British; cultured British.

"What's up, Hook?" this voice was asking.

The harsh voice of the ugly man:

"Plenty's up, I'm telling you! They're onto us! I started out a while ago; and as soon as I got to the street, I seen a man I knowed on the other side. He was pointed out to me in Philly five-six years ago. I don't know his name, but I remembered his mug—he's a Continental Detective Agency man. I came back in right away, and me and Elvira watched him out of the window. He went to every house on the other side of the street, asking questions or something. Then he came over and started to give this side a whirl, and after a while he rings the bell. I tell the old woman and her husband to get him in, stall him along, and see what he says for himself. He's got a song and dance about looking for a guy what seen an old woman bumped by a street car—but that's the bunk! He's gunning for us. There ain't nothing else to it. I went in and stuck him up just now. I meant to wait till you come, but I was scared he'd get nervous and beat it. Here's his stuff if you want to give it the once over."

The British voice:

"You shouldn't have shown yourself to him. The others could have taken care of him."

Hook:

"What's the diff? Chances is he knows us all anyway. But supposing he didn't, what diff does it make?"

The drawling British voice:

"It may make a deal of difference. It was stupid."

Hook, blustering:

"Stupid, huh? You're always bellyaching about other people being stupid. To hell with you, I say! If you don't like my style, to hell with you! Who does all the work? Who's the guy that swings all the jobs? Huh? Where—"

The young feminine voice:

"Now, Hook, for God's sake don't make that speech again. I've listened to it until I know it by heart!"

A rustle of papers, and the British voice:

"I say, Hook, you're correct about his being a detective. Here is an identification card among his things."

The Quarres were listening to the conversation in the next room with as much interest as I, but Thomas Quarre's eyes never left me, and his fat fingers never relaxed about the gun in his lap. His wife sipped tea, with her head cocked on one side in the listening attitude of a bird.

Except for the weapon in the old man's lap, there was not a thing to persuade the eye that melodrama was in the room; the Quarres were in every other detail still the pleasant old couple who had given me tea and expressed sympathy for the elderly lady who had been injured.

The feminine voice from the next room:

"Well, what's to be done? What's our play?"

Hook:

"That's easy to answer. We're going to knock this sleuth off, first thing!"

The feminine voice:

"And put our necks in the noose?"

Hook, scornfully:

"As if they ain't there if we don't! You don't think this guy ain't after us for the L.A. job, do you?"

The British voice:

"You're an ass, Hook, and a quite hopeless one. Suppose this chap is interested in the Los Angeles affair, as is probable; what then? He is a Continental operative. Is it likely that his organization doesn't know where he is? Don't you think they know he was coming up here? And don't they know as much about us—chances are—as he does? There's no use killing him. That would only make matters worse. The thing to do is to tie him up and leave him here. His associates will hardly come looking for him until tomorrow—and that will give us all night to manage our disappearance."

My gratitude went out to the British voice! Somebody was in my favor, at least to the extent of letting me live. I hadn't been feeling very cheerful these last few minutes. Somehow, the fact that I couldn't see these people who were deciding whether I was to live or die, made my plight seem all the more desperate. I felt better now, though far from gay; I had confidence in the drawling British voice; it was the voice of a man who habitually carries his point.

Hook, bellowing:

"Let me tell you something, brother: that guy's going to be knocked off! That's flat! I'm taking no chances. You can jaw all you want to about it, but I'm looking out for my own neck and it'll be a lot safer with that guy where he can't talk. That's flat. He's going to be knocked off!"

The feminine voice, disgustedly:

"Aw, Hook, be reasonable!"

The British voice, still drawling, but dead cold:

"There's no use reasoning with you, Hook, you've the instincts and the intellect of a troglodyte. There is only one sort of language that you understand; and I'm going to talk that language to you, my son. If you are tempted to do anything silly between now and the time of our departure, just say this to yourself two or three times: 'If he dies, I die. If he dies, I die.' Say it as if it were out of the Bible—because it's that true."

There followed a long space of silence, with a tenseness that made my not particularly sensitive scalp tingle. Beyond the portière, I knew, two men were matching glances in a battle of wills, which might any instant become a physical struggle, and my chances of living were tied up in that battle.

When, at last, a voice cut the silence, I jumped as if a gun had been fired; though the voice was low and smooth enough.

It was the British voice, confidently victorious, and I breathed again.

"We'll get the old people away first," the voice was saying. "You take charge of our guest, Hook. Tie him up neatly. But remember—no foolishness. Don't waste time questioning him—he'll lie. Tie him up while I get the bonds, and we'll be gone in less than half an hour."

The portières parted and Hook came into the room—a scowling Hook whose freckles had a greenish tinge against the sallowness of his face. He pointed a revolver at me, and spoke to the Quarres:

"He wants you."

They got up and went into the next room, and for a while an indistinguishable buzzing of whispers came from that room.

Hook, meanwhile, had stepped back to the doorway, still menacing me with his revolver; and pulled loose the plush ropes that were around the heavy curtains. Then he came around behind me, and tied me securely to the high-backed chair; my arms to the chair's arms, my legs to the chair's legs, my body to the chair's back and seat; and he wound up by gagging me with the corner of a cushion that was too well-stuffed for my comfort. The ugly man was unnecessarily rough throughout; but I was a lamb. He wanted an excuse for drilling me, and I wanted above all else that he should have no excuse.

As he finished lashing me into place, and stepped back to scowl at me, I heard the street door close softly, and then light footsteps ran back and forth overhead.

Hook looked in the direction of those footsteps, and his little watery blue eyes grew cunning.

"Elvira!" he called softly.

The portières bulged as if someone had touched them, and the musical feminine voice came through.

"What?"

"Come here."

"I'd better not. He wouldn't—"

"Damn him!" Hook flared up. "Come here!"

She came into the room and into the circle of light from the tall lamp; a girl in her early twenties, slender and lithe, and dressed for the street, except that she carried her hat in one hand. A white face beneath a bobbed mass of flame-colored hair. Smoke-grey eyes that were set too far apart for trustworthiness—though not for beauty—laughed at me; and her red mouth laughed at me, exposing the edges of little sharp animal-teeth. She was beautiful; as beautiful as the devil, and twice as dangerous.

She laughed at me—a fat man all trussed up with red plush rope, and with the corner of a green cushion in my mouth—and she turned to the ugly man.

"What do you want?"

He spoke in an undertone, with a furtive glance at the ceiling, above which soft steps still padded back and forth.

"What say we shake him?"

Her smoke-grey eyes lost their merriment and became hard and calculating.

"There's a hundred thousand he's holding—a third of it's mine. You don't think I'm going to take a Mickey Finn on that, do you?"

"Course not! Supposing we get the hundred-grand?"

"How?"

"Leave it to me, kid; leave it to me! If I swing it, will you go with me? You know I'll be good to you."

She smiled contemptuously, I thought—but he seemed to like it.

"You're whooping right you'll be good to me," she said. "But listen, Hook: we couldn't get away with it—not unless you *get him.* I know him! I'm not running away with anything that belongs to him unless he is fixed so that he can't come after it."

Hook moistened his lips and looked around the room at nothing. Apparently he didn't like the thought of tangling with the owner of the British drawl. But his desire for the girl was too strong for his fear of the other man.

"I'll do it!" he blurted. "I'll get him! Do you mean it, kid? If I get him, you'll go with me?"

She held out her hand.

"It's a bet," she said, and he believed her.

His ugly face grew warm and red and utterly happy, and he took a deep breath and straightened his shoulders. In his place, I might have believed her myself—all of us have fallen for that sort of thing at one time or another—but sitting tied up on the side-lines, I knew that he'd have been better off playing with a gallon of nitro than with this baby. She was dangerous! There was a rough time ahead for this Hook!

"This is the lay—" Hook began, and stopped, tongue-tied.

A step had sounded in the next room.

Immediately the British voice came through the portières, and there was an edge of exasperation to the drawl now:

"This is really too much! I can't"—he said reahly and cawnt—"leave for a moment without having things done all wrong. Now just what got into you, Elvira, that you must go in and exhibit yourself to our detective friend?"

Fear flashed into her smoke-grey eyes, and out again, and she spoke airily:

"Don't be altogether yellow," she said. "Your precious neck can get along all right without so much guarding."

The portières parted, and I twisted my head around as far as I could get it for my first look at this man who was responsible for my still being alive. I saw a short fat man, hatted and coated for the street, and carrying a tan traveling bag in one hand.

Then his face came into the yellow circle of light, and I saw that it was a Chinese face. A short fat Chinese, immaculately clothed in garments that were as British as his accent.

"It isn't a matter of color," he told the girl—and I understood now the full sting of her jibe; "it's simply a matter of ordinary wisdom."

His face was a round yellow mask, and his voice was the same emotionless drawl that I had heard before; but I knew that he was as surely under the girl's sway as the ugly man—or he wouldn't have let her taunt bring him into the room. But I doubted that she'd find this Anglicized oriental as easily handled as Hook.

"There was no particular need," the Chinese was still talking, "for this chap to have seen any of us." He looked at me now for the first time, with little opaque eyes that were like two black seeds. "It's quite possible that he didn't know any of us, even by description. This showing ourselves to him is the most arrant sort of nonsense."

"Aw, hell, Tai!" Hook blustered. "Quit your bellyaching, will you? What's the diff? I'll knock him off, and that takes care of that!"

The Chinese set down his tan bag and shook his head.

"There will be no killing," he drawled, "or there will be quite a bit of killing. You don't mistake my meaning, do you, Hook?"

Hook didn't. His Adam's apple ran up and down with the effort of his swallowing, and behind the cushion that was choking me, I thanked the yellow man again.

Then this red-haired she-devil put her spoon in the dish.

"Hook's always offering to do things that he has no intention of doing," she told the Chinese.

Hook's ugly face blazed red at this reminder of his promise to *get* the Chinese, and he swallowed again, and his eyes looked as if nothing would have suited him better than an opportunity to crawl under something. But the girl had him; her influence was stronger than his cowardice.

He suddenly stepped close to the Chinese, and from his advantage of a full head in height scowled down into the round yellow face that was as expressionless as a clock without hands.

"Tai," the ugly man snarled; "you're done. I'm sick and tired of all this dog you put on—acting like you was a king or something. I've took all the lip I'm going to take from a Chink! I'm going to—"

He faltered, and his words faded away into silence. Tai looked up at him with eyes that were as hard and black and inhuman as two pieces of coal. Hook's lips twitched and he flinched away a little.

I stopped sweating. The yellow man had won again. But I had forgotten the red-haired she-devil.

She laughed now—a mocking laugh that must have been like a knife to the ugly man.

A bellow came from deep in his chest, and he hurled one big fist into the round blank face of the yellow man.

The force of the punch carried Tai all the way across the room, and threw him on his side in one corner.

But he had twisted his body around to face the ugly man even as he went hurtling across the room—a gun was in his hand before he went down—and he was speaking before his legs had settled upon the floor—and his voice was a cultured British drawl.

"Later," he was saying; "we will settle this thing that is between us. Just now you will drop your pistol and stand very still while I get up."

Hook's revolver—only half out of his pocket when the oriental had covered him—thudded to the rug. He stood rigidly still while Tai got to his feet, and Hook's breath came out noisily, and each freckle stood ghastily out against the dirty scared white of his face.

I looked at the girl. There was contempt in the eyes with which she looked at Hook, but no disappointment.

Then I made a discovery: *something had changed in the room near her!*

I shut my eyes and tried to picture that part of the room as it had been before the two men had clashed. Opening my eyes suddenly, I had the answer.

On the table beside the girl had been a book and some magazines. They were gone now. Not two feet from the girl was the tan bag that Tai had brought into the room. Suppose the bag had held the bonds from the Los Angeles job that they had mentioned. It probably had. What then? It probably now held the book and magazines that had been on the table! The girl had stirred up the trouble between the two men to distract their attention while she made a switch. Where would the loot be, then? I didn't know, but I suspected that it was too bulky to be on the girl's slender person.

Just beyond the table was a couch, with a wide red cover that went all the way down to the floor. I looked from the couch to the girl. She was watching me, and her eyes twinkled with a flash of mirth as they met mine coming from the couch. The couch it was!

By now the Chinese had pocketed Hook's revolver, and was talking to him:

"If I hadn't a dislike for murder, and if I didn't think that you will perhaps be of some value to Elvira and me in effecting our departure, I should certainly relieve us of the handicap of your stupidity now. But I'll give you one more chance. I would suggest, however, that you think carefully before you give way to any more of your violent impulses." He turned to the girl. "Have you been putting foolish ideas in our Hook's head?"

She laughed.

"Nobody could put any kind in it."

"Perhaps you're right," he said, and then came over to test the lashings about my arms and body.

Finding them satisfactory, he picked up the tan bag, and held out the gun he had taken from the ugly man a few minutes before.

"Here's your revolver, Hook, now try to be sensible. We may as well go now. The old man and his wife will do as they were told. They are on their way to a city that we needn't mention by name in front of our friend here, to wait for us and their share of the bonds. Needless to say, they will wait a long while—they are out of it now. But between ourselves there must be no more treachery. If we're to get clear, we must help each other."

According to the best dramatic rules, these folks should have made sarcastic speeches to me before they left, but they didn't. They passed me without even a farewell look, and went out of sight into the darkness of the hall.

Suddenly the Chinese was in the room again, running tiptoe—an open knife in one hand, a gun in the other. This was the man I had been thanking for saving my life!

He bent over me.

The knife moved on my right side, and the rope that held that arm slackened its grip. I breathed again, and my heart went back to beating.

"Hook will be back," Tai whispered, and was gone.

On the carpet, three feet in front of me, lay a revolver.

The street door closed, and I was alone in the house for a while.

You may believe that I spent that while struggling with the red plush ropes that bound me. Tai had cut one length, loosening my right arm somewhat and giving my body more play, but I was far from free. And his whispered "Hook will be back" was all the spur I needed to throw my strength against my bonds.

I understood now why the Chinese had insisted so strongly upon my life being spared. I was the weapon with which Hook was to be removed. The Chinese figured that Hook would make some excuse as soon as they reached the street, slip back into the house, knock me off, and rejoin his confederates. If he didn't do it on his own initiative, I suppose the Chinese would suggest it.

So he had put a gun within reach—in case I could get loose—and had loosened my ropes as much as he could, not to have me free before he himself got away.

This thinking was a side-issue. I didn't let it slow up my efforts to get loose. The why wasn't important to me just now—the important thing was to have that revolver in my hand when the ugly man came into this room again.

Just as the front door opened, I got my right arm completely free, and plucked the strangling cushion from my mouth. The rest of my body was still held by the ropes—held loosely—but held. There was no time for more.

I threw myself, chair and all, forward, breaking the fall with my free arm. The carpet was thick. I went down on my face, with the heavy chair atop me, all doubled up any which way;

but my right arm was free of the tangle, and my right hand grasped the gun.

My left side—the wrong side—was toward the hall door. I twisted and squirmed and wrestled under the bulky piece of furniture that sat on my back.

An inch—two inches—six inches, I twisted. Another inch. Feet were at the hall door. Another inch.

The dim light hit upon a man hurrying into the room—a glint of metal in his hand.

I fired.

He caught both hands to his belly, bent double, and slid out across the carpet.

That was over. But that was far from being all. I wrenched at the plush ropes that held me, while my mind tried to sketch what lay ahead.

The girl had switched the bonds, hiding them under the couch—there was no question of that. She had intended coming back for them before I had time to get free. But Hook had come back first, and she would have to change her plan. What more likely than that she would now tell the Chinese that Hook had made the switch? What then? There was only one answer: Tai would come back for the bonds—both of them would come. Tai knew that I was armed now, but they had said that the bonds represented a hundred thousand dollars. That would be enough to bring them back!

I kicked the last rope loose and scrambled to the couch. The bonds were beneath it: four thick bundles of Liberty Bonds, done up with heavy rubber bands. I tucked them under one arm, and went over to the man who was dying near the door. His gun was under one of his legs, I pulled it out, stepped over him, and went into the dark hall.

Then I stopped to consider.

The girl and the Chinese would split to tackle me. One would come in the front door and the other in the rear. That would be the safest way for them to handle me. My play, obviously, was to wait just inside one of those doors for them. It would be foolish for me to leave the house. That's exactly what they would be expecting at first—and they would be lying in ambush.

Decidedly, my play was to lie low within sight of this front door and wait until one of them came through it—as one of them surely would, when they had tired of waiting for me to come out.

Toward the street door, the hall was lighted with the glow that filtered through the glass from the street lights. The stairway leading to the second-story threw a triangular shadow across part of the hall—a shadow that was black enough for any purpose. I crouched low in this three-cornered slice of night, and waited.

I had two guns: the one the Chinese had given me, and the one I had taken from Hook. I had fired one shot; that would leave me eleven still to use—unless one of the weapons had been used since it was loaded. I broke the gun Tai had given me, and in the dark ran my fingers across the back of the cylinder. My fingers touched *one* shell—under the hammer. Tai had taken no chances; he had given me one bullet—the bullet with which I had dropped Hook.

I put that gun down on the floor, and examined the one I had taken from Hook. It was *empty*. The Chinese had taken no chances at all! He had emptied Hook's gun before returning it to him after their quarrel.

I was in a hole! Alone, unarmed, in a strange house that would presently hold two who were hunting me—and that one of them was a woman didn't soothe me any—she was none the less deadly on that account.

For a moment I was tempted to make a dash for it; the thought of being out in the street again was pleasant; but I put the idea away. That would be foolishness, and plenty of it. Then I remembered the bonds under my arm. They would have to be my weapon; and if they were to serve me, they would have to be concealed.

I slipped out of my triangular shadow and went up the stairs. Thanks to the street lights, the upstairs rooms were not too dark for me to move around. Around and around I went through the rooms, hunting for a place to hide the Liberty Bonds.

But when suddenly a window rattled, as if from the draught created by the opening of an outside door somewhere, I still had the loot in my hands.

There was nothing to do now but to chuck them out of a window and trust to luck. I grabbed a pillow from a bed, stripped off the white case, and dumped the bonds into it. Then I leaned out of an already open window and looked down into the night, searching for a desirable dumping place: I didn't want the bonds to land on an ash-can or a pile of bottles, or anything that would make a racket.

And, looking out of the window, I found a better hiding-place. The window opened into a narrow court, on the other side of which was a house of the same sort as the one I was in. That house was of the same height as this one, with a flat tin roof that sloped down the other way. The roof wasn't far from me—not too far to chuck the pillow-case. I chucked it.

It disappeared over the edge of the roof and crackled softly on the tin.

If I had been a movie actor or something of the sort, I suppose I'd have followed the bonds; I suppose I'd have jumped from the sill, caught the edge of the roof with my fingers, swung a while, and then pulled myself up and away. But dangling in space doesn't appeal to me; I preferred to face the Chinese and the red-head.

Then I did another not at all heroic thing. I turned on all the lights in the room, lighted a cigarette (we all like to pose a little now and then), and sat down on the bed to await my capture. I might have stalked my enemies through the dark house, and possibly have nabbed them; but most likely I would simply have succeeded in getting myself shot. And I don't like to be shot.

The girl found me.

She came creeping up the hall, an automatic in each hand, hesitated for an instant outside the door, and then came in on the jump. And when she saw me sitting peacefully on the side of the bed, her eyes snapped scornfully at me, as if I had done something mean. I suppose she thought I should have given her an opportunity to put lead in me.

"I got him, Tai," she called, and the Chinese joined us.

"What did Hook do with the bonds?" he asked point blank.

I grinned into his round yellow face and led my ace.

"Why don't you ask the girl?"

His face showed nothing, but I imagined that his fat body stiffened a little within its fashionable British clothing. That encouraged me, and I went on with my little lie that was meant to stir things up.

"Haven't you rapped to it," I asked; "that they were fixing up to ditch you?"

"You dirty liar!" the girl screamed, and took a step toward me.

Tai halted her with an imperative gesture. He stared through her with his opaque black eyes, and as he stared the blood slid out of her face. She had this fat yellow man on her string, right enough, but he wasn't exactly a harmless toy.

"So that's how it is?" he said slowly, to no one in particular. "So that's how it is?" Then to me: "Where did they put the bonds?"

The girl went close to him and her words came out tumbling over each other:

"Here's the truth of it, Tai, so help me God! I switched the stuff myself. Hook wasn't in it. I was going to run out on both of you. I stuck them under the couch downstairs, but they're not there now. That's the God's truth!"

He was eager to believe her, and her words had the ring of truth to them. And I knew that—in love with her as he was— he'd more readily forgive her treachery with the bonds than he would forgive her for planning to run off with Hook; so I made haste to stir things up again. The old timer who said *"Divide to conquer,"* or something of the sort, knew what he was talking about.

"Part of that is right enough," I said. "She did stick the bonds under the couch—but Hook was in on it. They fixed it up between them while you were upstairs. He was to pick a fight with you, and during the argument she was to make the switch, and that is exactly what they did."

I had him!

As she wheeled savagely toward me, he stuck the muzzle of

an automatic in her side—a smart jab that checked the angry words she was hurling at me.

"I'll take your guns, Elvira," he said, and took them.

There was a purring deadliness in his voice that made her surrender them without a word.

"Where are the bonds now?" he asked me.

I grinned.

"I'm not with you, Tai. I'm against you."

He studied me with his little eyes that were like black seeds for a while, and I studied him; and I hoped that his studying was as fruitless as mine.

"I don't like violence," he said slowly, "and I believe you are a sensible person. Let us traffic, my friend."

"You name it," I suggested.

"Gladly! As a basis for our bargaining, we will stipulate that you have hidden the bonds where they cannot be found by anyone else; and that I have you completely in my power, as the shilling shockers used to have it."

"Reasonable enough," I said, "go on."

"The situation, then, is what gamblers call a standoff. Neither of us has the advantage. As a detective, you want us; but we have you. As thieves, we want the bonds; but you have them. I offer you the girl in exchange for the bonds, and that seems to me an equitable offer. It will give me the bonds and a chance to get away. It will give you no small degree of success in your task as a detective. Hook is dead. You will have the girl. All that will remain is to find me and the bonds again—by no means a hopeless task. You will have turned a defeat into more than half of a victory, with an excellent chance to make it a complete one."

"How do I know that you'll give me the girl?"

He shrugged.

"Naturally, there can be no guarantee. But, knowing that she planned to desert me for the swine who lies dead below, you can't imagine that my feelings for her are the most friendly. Too, if I take her with me, she will want a share in the loot."

I turned the lay-out over in my mind, and looked at it from this side and that and the other.

"This is the way it looks to me," I told him at last. "You aren't a killer. I'll come through alive no matter what happens. All right; why should I swap? You and the girl will be easier to find again than the bonds, and they are the most important part of the job anyway. I'll hold on to them, and take my chances on finding you folks again. Yes, I'm playing it safe."

And I meant it, for the time being, at least.

"No, I'm not a killer," he said, very softly; and he smiled the first smile I had seen on his face. It wasn't a pleasant smile: and there was something in it that made you want to shudder. "But I am other things, perhaps, of which you haven't thought. But this talking is to no purpose. Elvira!"

The girl, who had been standing a little to one side, watching us, came obediently forward.

"You will find sheets in one of the bureau drawers," he told her. "Tear one or two of them into strips strong enough to tie up your friend securely."

The girl went to the bureau. I wrinkled my head, trying to find a not too disagreeable answer to the question in my mind. The answer that came first wasn't nice: *torture*.

Then a faint sound brought us all into tense motionlessness.

The room we were in had two doors: one leading into the hall, the other into another bedroom. It was through the hall door that the faint sound had come—the sound of creeping feet.

Swiftly, silently, Tai moved backward to a position from which he could watch the hall door without losing sight of the girl and me—and the gun poised like a live thing in his fat hand was all the warning we needed to make no noise.

The faint sound again, just outside the door.

The gun in Tai's hand seemed to quiver with eagerness.

Through the other door—the door that gave to the next room—popped Mrs. Quarre, an enormous cocked revolver in her thin hand.

"Let go it, you nasty heathen," she screeched.

Tai dropped his pistol before he turned to face her, and he held his hands up high—all of which was very wise.

Thomas Quarre came through the hall door then; he also held a cocked revolver—the mate of his wife's—though, in front of his bulk, his didn't look so enormously large.

I looked at the old woman again, and found little of the friendly fragile one who had poured tea and chatted about the neighbors. This was a witch if there ever was one—a witch of the blackest, most malignant sort. Her little faded eyes were sharp with ferocity, her withered lips were taut in a wolfish snarl, and her thin body fairly quivered with hate.

"I knew it," she was shrilling. "I told Tom as soon as we got far enough away to think things over. I knew it was a frame-up! I knew this supposed detective was a pal of yours! I knew it was just a scheme to beat Thomas and me out of our shares! Well, I'll show you, you yellow monkey! And the rest of you too! I'll show the whole caboodle of you! Where are them bonds? Where are they?"

The Chinese had recovered his poise, if he had ever lost it.

"Our stout friend can tell you perhaps," he said. "I was about to extract the information from him when you so—ah—dramatically arrived."

"Thomas, for goodness sakes don't stand there dreaming," she snapped at her husband, who to all appearances was still the same mild old man who had given me an excellent cigar. "Tie up this Chinaman! I don't trust him an inch, and I won't feel easy until he's tied up. Tie him, up, and then we'll see what's to be done."

I got up from my seat on the side of the bed, and moved cautiously to a spot that I thought would be out of the line of fire if the thing I expected happened.

Tai had dropped the gun that had been in his hand, but he hadn't been searched. The Chinese are a thorough people; if one of them carries a gun at all, he usually carries two or three or more. (I remember picking up one in Oakland during the last tong war, who had five on him—one under each armpit, one on each hip, and one in his waistband.) One gun had been taken from Tai, and if they tried to truss him up without frisking him, there was likely to be fireworks. So I moved off to one side.

Fat Thomas Quarre went phlegmatically up to the Chinese to carry out his wife's orders—and bungled the job perfectly.

He put his bulk between Tai and the old woman's gun.

Tai's hands moved.

An automatic was in each.

Once more Tai ran true to racial form. When a Chinese shoots, he keeps on shooting until his gun is empty.

When I yanked Tai over backward by his fat throat, and

slammed him to the floor, his guns were still barking metal; and they clicked empty as I got a knee on one of his arms. I didn't take any chances. I worked on his throat until his eyes and tongue told me that he was out of things for a while.

Then I looked around.

Thomas Quarre was huddled against the bed, plainly dead, with three round holes in his starched white vest—holes that were brown from the closeness of the gun that had put them there.

Across the room, Mrs. Quarre lay on her back. Her clothes had somehow settled in place around her fragile body, and death had given her once more the gentle friendly look she had worn when I first saw her. One thin hand was on her bosom, covering, I found later, the two bullet-holes that were there.

The red-haired girl Elvira was gone.

Presently Tai stirred, and, after taking another gun from his clothes, I helped him sit up. He stroked his bruised throat with one fat hand, and looked coolly around the room.

"So this is how it came out?" he said.

"Uh-huh!"

"Where's Elvira?"

"Got away—for the time being."

He shrugged.

"Well, you can call it a decidedly successful operation. The Quarres and Hook dead; the bonds and I in your hands."

"Not so bad," I admitted, "but will you do me a favor?"

"If I may."

"Tell me what the hell this is all about!"

"All about?" he asked.

"Exactly! From what you people have let me overhear, I

gather that you pulled some sort of job in Los Angeles that netted you a hundred-thousand-dollars' worth of Liberty Bonds; but I can't remember any recent job of that size down there."

"Why, that's preposterous!" he said with what, for him, was almost wild-eyed amazement. "Preposterous! Of course you know all about it!"

"I do not! I was trying to find a young fellow named Fisher who left his Tacoma home in anger a week or two ago. His father wants him found on the quiet, so that he can come down and try to talk him into going home again. I was told that I might find Fisher in this block of Turk Street, and that's what brought me here."

He didn't believe me. He never believed me. He went to the gallows thinking me a liar.

When I got out into the street again (and Turk Street was a lovely place when I came free into it after my evening in that house!) I bought a newspaper that told me most of what I wanted to know.

A boy of twenty—a messenger in the employ of a Los Angeles stock and bond house—had disappeared two days before, while on his way to a bank with a wad of Liberty Bonds. That same night this boy and a slender girl with bobbed red hair had registered at a hotel in Fresno as *J.M. Riordan and wife*. The next morning the boy had been found in his room—murdered. The girl was gone. The bonds were gone.

That much the paper told me. During the next few days, digging up a little here and a little there, I succeeded in piecing together most of the story.

The Chinese—whose full name was Tai Choon Tau—had

been the brains of the mob. Their game had been a variation of the always-reliable badger game. Tai selected the victims, and he must have been a good judge of humans, for he seems never to have picked a bloomer. He would pick out some youth who was messenger or runner for a banker or broker—one who carried either cash or negotiable securities in large quantities around the city.

The girl Elvira would then *make* this lad, get him all fussed up over her—which shouldn't have been very hard for her—and then lead him gently around to running away with her and whatever he could grab in the way of his employer's bonds or currency.

Wherever they spent the first night of their flight, there Hook would appear—foaming at the mouth and loaded for bear. The girl would plead and tear her hair and so forth, trying to keep Hook—in his rôle of irate husband—from butchering the youth. Finally she would succeed, and in the end the youth would find himself without either girl or the fruits of his thievery.

Sometimes he had surrendered to the police. Two we found had committed suicide. The Los Angeles lad had been built of tougher stuff than the others. He had put up a fight, and Hook had had to kill him. You can measure the girl's skill in her end of the game by the fact that not one of the half dozen youths who had been trimmed had said the least thing to implicate her; and some of them had gone to great trouble to keep her out of it.

The house in Turk Street had been the mob's retreat, and, that it might be always a safe one, they had not worked their game in San Francisco. Hook and the girl were supposed by the neighbors to be the Quarres' son and daughter—and Tai was the Chinese cook. The Quarres' benign and respectable appearances had also come in handy when the mob had securities to be disposed of.

The Chinese went to the gallows. We threw out the widest and finest-meshed of drag-nets for the red-haired girl; and we turned up girls with bobbed red hair by the scores. But the girl Elvira was not among them.

I promised myself that some day....

www.ingramcontent.com/pod-product-compliance
Lightning Source LLC
Chambersburg PA
CBHW031158020726
47499CB00002B/417